HYPOCRITES' ISLE

HYPOCRITES' ISLE

Ken McClure

First published in 2008 by Polygon,
an imprint of Birlinn Ltd

West Newington House
10 Newington Road
Edinburgh
EH9 1QS

www.birlinn.co.uk
9 8 7 6 5 4 3 2 1

ISBN: 978 1 84697 087 0

British Library Cataloguing-in-Publication Data
A catalogue record for this book is available
on request from the British Library.

Typeset at Birlinn

Printed and bound in Britain

How Pantagruel gave no answer to the problems

Pantagruel then asked what sort of people dwelt in that damned island. They are, answered Xenomanes, all hypocrites, holy mountebanks, tumblers of beads, mumblers of ave-marias, spiritual comedians, sham saints, hermits, all of them poor rogues who, like the hermit of Lormont between Blaye and Bordeaux, live wholly on alms given them by passengers.

François Rabelais
Pantagruel, Book 4, Chapter LXIV

ONE

EDINBURGH
November 1998

A ripple of polite applause gave way to the sound of shuffling feet on tiered, wooden flooring as the audience moved down to the exit doors on either side of the Lister Medical Lecture Theatre. The theatre was located in the oldest part of the hospital, with portraits of medical men of note in its two-hundred-year history gazing down from the walls – included among them the eponymous Joseph Lister, who had been a surgeon at the hospital and who had gone on to pioneer the use of antisepsis. None of them smiled, as befitted a profession not noted for taking itself anything less than seriously.

There were other, more modern lecture rooms in the hospital and adjacent medical school buildings – and all equipped with the latest in audio-visual equipment – but it was traditional that visiting lecturers be invited to use the Lister, and the idea of walking in the footsteps of the great proved seductive to most.

Dr Frank Simmons, a senior lecturer at the adjoining medical school with an international reputation in cancer research, had a lot on his mind. He chose to remain seated at the back until the majority had left, only getting to his feet to join his friend and colleague, Dr Jack Martin, when he saw him near the back of the exiting throng.

'God, I'm getting old,' murmured Simmons, who was actually in his early forties.

'We all are,' replied Martin, who was much the same age. 'And mainly because that seminar went on for thirty-five years.'

'Then it wasn't my imagination?'

'I think that guy was trying to prove the earth was flat,' said Martin. 'I've never seen so many meaningless graphs outside of an election night. Fancy some lunch?'

Simmons checked his watch. 'I have to be back at the lab by two thirty – a sandwich maybe?'

The two men walked back to the medical school and took the lift up to the staff canteen where they waited in a short queue at the counter to pick up their food. They sat down at a table by a window where they could look out as ambulances came and went, visitors pursued their eternal search for parking places, and nurses and technicians moved to and fro in the choreography of hospital life.

'What's on your mind, Frank?' asked Martin. 'You look troubled.'

'Do you realise how many hours we must have wasted over the years listening to waffle like that?' said Simmons, before taking a serious bite of his baguette.

'I suppose that's one of those things in life it's better not to know,' smiled Martin.

'There was this advert on TV last night – an appeal for funds for cancer research. They wanted people to give a few pounds per month. It was slick, professional, really well thought-out . . .'

'They all are these days,' said Martin. 'They're deliberately de-signed to make people feel as guilty as sin if they don't put their hands in their pockets. Tugging at the heartstrings of the nation is big business. But don't knock it; some of it is coming our way.'

'But we both know how many thousands of people are in-volved in cancer research, how much money is tied up in it,' said Simmons. 'People live and die doing it. It's become a profession in its own right . . . *Mary's doing law and Justin's going into cancer research* . . .'

'I suppose it has to go on for as long as it takes,' shrugged Martin.

'I think it's more what they'll do with the money that's bothering me,' said Simmons. 'They'll take on more staff, buy more equipment and do more of the same.'

Martin looked puzzled. 'And your point?'

'It's not staff and equipment that's missing from the equation. It's ideas, new ideas . . . the things you can't buy.'

Martin took a sip of his coffee. 'Aren't you being a bit unfair?'

'I don't think so. It's time we faced facts. The public are being conned into thinking that the thing holding up a cure for cancer is a lack of funds. Not so. Jack Kennedy threw money at the problem back in the sixties, millions of dollars, and all they got out of it was a whole lot of institutes full of people in white coats – all of them still working today.'

'Come on, there's some good stuff going on.'

'Sure, but the amount of repetitive crap that's being carried out . . . and the Mickey Mouse science that shelters under the umbrella of cancer research – like the stuff we've just been listening to – that's another matter.'

'It's difficult . . .' said Martin.

'Yeah, it's difficult . . .' said Simmons.

'I didn't notice you leaping to your feet and telling our friend in the Lister that his work was going nowhere,' countered Martin, sensing accusation in Simmons' echo.

'You're right . . . you're right,' conceded Simmons. 'We sat there, knowing it was rubbish, but we listened to our head of department thanking him for coming along and telling us about his *exciting* work and we all clapped like a bunch of seals . . .'

'It's the academic way . . .'

'Quite.'

'Cheer up, Frank, the seminar wasn't that bad. No, I take that back; it was, but there's no reason for you to feel personally responsible for the slowness of cancer research. A journey of ten thousand miles and all that. You're doing your best; I'm doing my best . . .'

'I suppose,' conceded Simmons with a sigh. He looked at his watch and got to his feet. 'I'll have to go. I've got a meeting with my PhD students.'

'How are they doing?'

'No worries with Mary Hollis – she's been fine from the word go. She should be able to publish her latest findings soon – her third publication. Tom Baxter's fine too. He had a slow start but he's doing all right – a bit of a plodder but he gets there in the end. It's Gavin Donnelly, the new one, I'm not so sure about. He's either a genius or an idiot and I'm not sure which.'

'Could be every group leader's nightmare,' joked Martin. 'A student brighter than his supervisor. Only one way to cope with that: steal his results and run. But remember to acknowledge his contribution in your acceptance speech at the Swedish Academy.'

Simmons smiled. 'It's actually the alternative I'm worried about – that he's an idiot who slipped through the net and got an honours degree for good attendance.'

'Well, they do say everything's being dumbed down these days. Where did he do his degree?'

'Cambridge.'

'So he should be able to spell his name and do the four times table. What have you got him working on?'

'Genes affecting membrane structure.'

———

Simmons entered the small meeting room adjoining the main lab and apologised for being a few minutes late, using the seminar in the Lister as his excuse. 'Didn't see any of you folks there.'

Mary Hollis, a thoughtful-looking girl in her early twenties with ash-blonde hair tied back with a lilac ribbon, was pouring coffee. She smiled and said with a gentle accent that gave away her Dublin origins, 'Sorry, I've got an experiment running. I have to take samples every twenty minutes. Coffee?'

'Please.'

'Dentist,' explained Tom Baxter. 'Root canal treatment.' He gave a crooked smile which seemed to match just about everything else in his appearance. He was well over six foot tall, lanky, with narrow shoulders that never seemed to be quite horizontal. He wore a checked shirt and jeans – standard student wear – and sat slumped in one of the six chairs in the room with one long leg crossed over the other. A clipboard rested on his raised knee while he tapped the end of a biro pen against his teeth.

Simmons noticed – as he had many times before – that Tom's glasses tended to slope at the opposite angle to his shoulders. He turned to look at the third member of the group, Gavin Donnelly, who seemed to be avoiding his gaze. 'What about you, Gavin?'

Donnelly, a good head shorter than Tom but with a much more athletic build and a shock of long red hair, looked up and replied in a thick Liverpudlian accent, 'I went for a walk.'

Simmons gave him a moment to elaborate, but nothing was forthcoming so he said, 'You do realise that attendance at departmental seminars is expected for all first-year postgraduate students?'

'I hate seminars, Frank. Times have changed. We have the internet now.'

Simmons saw Mary and Tom exchange uncomfortable glances and felt slightly embarrassed himself, but he kept his cool. 'Indeed, Gavin, and it's a valuable tool,' he agreed. 'But reading articles on the net is no substitute for being able to question scientists about their work and listen to their response to informed criticism.'

'That's the theory but it doesn't work out like that, does it?'

'What d'you mean?'

'Universities have seminars for the sake of having seminars. Academics like the sound of their own voices. Half the speakers I listened to last year had very little to say at all – and did so at great length. Anything worthwhile had already been published.'

'Oh, come on, Gavin,' smiled Mary. 'Play the game. Go to seminars, collect your brownie points and stop being such a pain.'

'Hear, hear,' said Tom.

'I just think it shouldn't have to be that way,' insisted Gavin.

'But it is,' said Mary, leaning towards him and lecturing him kindly, as if he were a younger brother. 'Accept it and get on with your life.'

Simmons, who had seen a lot of students from poorer backgrounds come and go and was all too familiar with the rebel without a cause, smiled and held up his hands. 'Enough, guys,' he said. 'Gavin is obviously a man of principle and should be respected for that, but Mary has been kind enough to offer some sound advice.' He turned towards Gavin. 'Maybe he should at least consider it. Let's leave it at that and now you can all tell me what you've been doing for the past week.'

'You didn't say what the seminar was like,' said Mary as she handed Simmons his coffee and took up stance by the blackboard. 'Gerald Montague, wasn't it?'

Simmons thought he detected a hint of mischief in her enquiry. 'It wasn't very exciting,' he replied. 'Unusual approach but perhaps somewhat . . . flawed.'

'Hasn't stopped him publishing at least a dozen papers on that nonsense,' said Gavin. 'So much for peer review . . .'

Simmons gritted his teeth. 'Peer review isn't perfect, but it's still the best way we've got of screening new material for publication, Gavin,' he pointed out.

'On the other hand, there are so many old pals scratching each other's backs, you'd think they'd come clean and have a blazer badge and club tie made for themselves,' said Gavin.

'Oh, Gavin,' said Mary, running out of patience. 'Sometimes you behave like a kid who's lost his lollipop. No system is ever perfect, and if you go on setting impossibly high standards for all those around you, you're going to have such a disappointing life.'

'I'm just saying what's true,' said Gavin.

'What you *think* is true.'

Gavin looked at the floor and took a deep breath. 'Okay, what I *think* is true,' he conceded.

'Well, maybe it's a jaundiced view. Maybe you should just stop and consider for a moment before you say anything.'

'Kiss arse, you mean?'

'No, I do not,' said Mary. 'Just think before you speak.' She said this so calmly and pleasantly that Gavin smiled and showed no heart for continuing the exchange.

'Anyone want to hear what happened to the G45 cloning I've been doing?' asked Tom – an interruption welcomed by the others.

'We all do, Tom,' said Simmons.

Mary passed him the chalk stick she'd been weighing in her palm and glanced at her watch before getting up. 'Back in a mo. I have to take a sample.'

Tom took up a gangling stance beside the blackboard, adjusted his glasses so that they were no longer in danger of falling off his nose, and turned to face the others. 'As you know, I've been trying to put the C1 gene into a cloning vector so that I could move it into the H12 strain . . . well, no joy I'm afraid. Three attempts and absolutely zilch.'

Mary came back into the room, ducking her head and making exaggerated tiptoe movements as she returned to her seat.

'What vector did you use, Tom?' asked Simmons.

'Alpha 12.'

Simmons bit back the comment he was about to make. He wanted to see if anyone else would say something.

'Copy number,' said Gavin, without looking up from the doodle he was making in his notebook.

'I'm sorry?'

'Alpha 12 is a high copy-number vector. Hector and Jameson showed last year in *Molecular Microbiology* that C1 can't be cloned in high copy number – it's toxic to the cell when present in large quantities.'

Tom scratched his head. 'Really? I must have missed that.'

'No great harm done,' said Simmons. 'Use a low copy-number vector next time, Tom, and you'll have a different tale to tell next week.'

'Wish I'd seen that,' mumbled Tom as he returned to his seat. 'I feel a bit of an idiot now.'

Gavin continued his doodle.

Mary took Tom's place and chalked up some figures on the blackboard. 'I've been doing some control experiments to make sure the effect I spoke about last week was scientifically valid,' she said. 'And it is.' She chalked up some more data. 'An 80 per cent increase in the test culture, none at all in the controls.'

'Well done, you,' said Simmons.

'But you haven't shown any result for the Beta cell line,' said Gavin, glancing at what was on the blackboard.

'Well spotted, Gavin,' said Mary with an icy smile. 'That's what I'm doing today and so far, it's looking just as good as the others.'

'Touché,' said Gavin with an amused smile.

Simmons enjoyed the sparring between Mary and Gavin. He was pleased that Gavin had been so quick to spot the hole in Mary's data, but equally pleased that Mary had been ready to plug the gap. 'Well, that should wrap things up nicely,' he said. 'How about you, Gavin, what have you been up to?'

'I've been thinking.'

'About anything in particular?' enquired Simmons with a deliberate vagueness that made Tom and Mary smile.

'The approach we spoke about for altering membrane structure. I'm not sure we've picked the best way.'

'Why not?'

'Just a feeling.'

'Does this mean that you have come up with a better way?' asked Simmons calmly.

'Not yet.'

'Well, do let us know when you make the breakthrough.'

Mary hid another smile by putting her hand to her mouth. Tom stared intently at the floor.

It was six thirty when Simmons left the lab and said good night to the servitor on the door. 'Brass monkeys out there tonight, Doctor,' said the man, looking up from his book. Simmons found out what he meant almost as soon as he left the warmth of the building and saw his breath swirl in clouds around him as he made his way to the car park. He tugged his collar up and fumbled for his keys in his coat pocket, taking care with his footing on the icy surface of the inner quadrangle. He had a 'why did I ever leave California?' moment when his breath started to freeze on the windscreen almost as soon as he'd got into the car and his attempts to clear it by hand only made things worse.

Although Scottish by birth, Simmons had spent five years at the University of California at Los Angeles and had only returned to Scotland a year ago when he and his wife, Jenny, decided that they wanted their two children, Mark and Jill, to have a Scottish education – or, more correctly, grow up as British children rather than develop the mores and attitudes of sun-kissed Californians. They had bought a house a few miles outside Edinburgh – a converted farm steading – and Jenny, a nurse, had returned to working part-time as the practice nurse at the local GP's group surgery.

'You're very quiet this evening,' said Jenny as they cleared away the dishes. 'Something on your mind?'

'You could say,' agreed Simmons.

'Why don't you go up and tell the kids their story and then come down and tell me all about it? I'll have a whisky waiting for you.'

—

'But you can't feel personally responsible for the slowness of cancer research,' exclaimed Jenny when Simmons told her about the doubts he'd been expressing to Jack Martin at lunchtime.

'I'm part of it, though. I can't divorce myself from it and blame the lack of progress on other people.'

'But you work hard and you've been very successful. That's why they gave you the position in the first place.'

'It's academic success,' insisted Simmons. 'I've published a lot, but when it comes to the question of whether that has made the slightest difference to people actually suffering from the disease . . . that's another matter.'

'But surely the only alternative is to stop doing it and walk out. Will that help them?'

'No, but . . .'

'Look, you said yourself, you need lucky breaks in science and if you're not there at the bench when the break comes along, you'll miss it, right?'

Simmons nodded and took a sip of his whisky.

'What brought this on anyway? You're not usually so negative.'

'I suppose it was that damned seminar.'

Jenny smiled. 'What else is bugging you?'

'Gavin Donnelly.'

Jenny raised her eyes. 'The charming Gavin. What's he been up to?'

'Damn all. That's the trouble.'

'Well, he's not a child, even if he acts like one. It's his funeral if he doesn't do any work and finishes up not getting a PhD.'

'True, but he's clearly not stupid. He knows a lot. He obviously reads the journals. He saw right away why Tom's experiment last week hadn't worked: he noticed immediately what was missing from Mary's results when she chalked them up. It's just . . . that he does damn all himself and thinks he knows everything . . .'

'Which is your prerogative,' smiled Jenny.

'. . . and has the social skills of a lamp-post.'

'Quite. I'm not liable to forget his first visit here.'

'Let's not go there. How was your day?'

'Remarkably stress-free, I'm pleased to say.'

Simmons looked at her affectionately. 'I don't know what I'd do without you,' he said. 'You're always the same; so supportive, so steady. I go up and down like a yo-yo and . . .'

'Sssh. You'll be telling me next I'm your rock.'

'Anything good on the telly tonight?'

Jenny looked up the schedules in the paper. 'Nothing inspiring . . . there's a documentary on ancient Egypt on Channel 5 at ten – a quest to find the treasure of someone-hotep. But Channel 5 at ten? . . . I think we both know what they're going to find, don't you?'

'Zilch.'

TWO

Gavin Donnelly left the medical school, pausing to fasten up all the buttons on his denim jacket and wrap a scarf round the lower half of his face as he felt the cold air hit him. He stopped at the hospital gates, considering whether he should go back to the flat and have spaghetti on toast or nip round for a pie and a pint at the postgrad union. The halo round the street lights – a sure sign of a heavy frost to come – swung his decision in favour of the union and he skipped across the road, dodging in and out of the stopped and slow-moving traffic of the evening rush hour. The union was nearer and it would be warm – unlike the flat, which depended on electric heating, and whoever was in first to turn it on. He shared a third-floor tenement flat with three other people – a nurse and two office workers – about two miles away from the med school, in Dundas Street on the north side of Princes Street. This had been his choice over the alternative of staying in halls of residence when he arrived in Edinburgh some two months before.

Gavin ordered his food and picked up a pint of lager at the bar, before moving to a seat and shrugging his rucksack from his shoulder to guide it under the table with his foot. He draped his jacket over the back of the chair and smoothed his collar-length hair back before straightening the holed green sweater he favoured most days – Carla, the eldest of his four sisters, had knitted it for him when he'd first left home for Cambridge.

'Pie and beans!' the short, bald man behind the bar called out as the microwave bleeped. Gavin went over to pick up his food. He was halfway through eating it when he became aware of a figure at his shoulder. It was Mary Hollis.

'That looks good,' she said pleasantly.

'Then it looks better than it tastes.'

Mary sat down opposite, looking both amused and exasperated. 'Don't you ever lighten up, Gavin?'

Gavin looked bemused. 'What's the problem? I just . . .'

'Told the truth? Yes, I know.'

Gavin sighed and looked at her. 'Sorry,' he said. 'What should I have said?'

Mary shook her head and spread her hands, 'God, I don't know; made a joke or something. If you'd laughed before you said it looked better than it tasted it would have been fine, but you automatically slap people down. You defend yourself when no one's attacking you. People generally mean you no harm . . . honestly.'

Gavin suddenly smiled broadly and Mary capitulated. 'Sorry,' she said. 'Lecture over.'

'All right, Mary,' said Gavin. 'I'll believe you . . . despite a long list of acquired evidence to the contrary. I haven't seen you in here before.'

'I'm meeting Simon, my boyfriend; he's a houseman at the hospital. He gets off at seven. This is as good a place to meet as any and it's warm.'

'Can I get you a drink?'

Mary shook her head. 'He'll be here any minute, thanks all the same. We're going to see something at the Filmhouse. How about you? How are you going to spend your evening?'

'Medical library.'

'Is this to fuel the thinking process?'

'You got it.'

'You'll be doing experiments next.'

'Ouch. What was it you said about not slapping people down?'

'Sorry, but you haven't exactly been bursting a gut in the lab since you arrived and people have been noticing.'

'It's the easiest thing in the world to keep busy in a lab.'

'So?'

'Keeping busy is not doing research. It's window dressing.'

'Doing nothing isn't doing research either.'

'Like I said, I've been thinking.'

'I won't say you don't get a PhD for thinking when you do, but eventually you have to do something with the fruits of your thinking . . .'

'Unless you're a philosopher.'

'You probably still have to tell someone . . .'

'As Jean-Paul Sartre once said to Simone de Beauvoir, *Whatevah*.'

Mary smiled. 'You can be quite funny when you try. Oh, here comes Simon.' She got to her feet as a slim, fair-haired man entered the bar and came towards them. Mary did the introductions before turning to leave. 'See you tomorrow. Don't work too late.'

'Enjoy the film.'

'Good,' said Mary, looking back with a grin. 'Very good.'

—

Gavin drained his glass and thought about what Mary had said as he shrugged his shoulders into his jacket and picked up his belongings. She meant well enough but what did she know about his world? She was an only child and both her parents were academics. She fitted in: she had always fitted in. She couldn't possibly understand what it had been like for the son of a Liverpool labourer to arrive at Cambridge, knowing nothing of the ways of academia, or the customs of a society far removed from his own. Cambridge had seemed like a different planet, a strange place inhabited by exotic creatures with peculiar names and drawling accents, and often with a self-confidence he'd found mesmerising. He remembered desperately wanting to be part of it all – there was just so much he wanted to discuss and argue about and he really hadn't had the opportunity before – but it wasn't to be. There was a 'them and us' divide and he was definitely 'them'.

He had coped with the open hostility – even confronted it on occasion, and proved that first-fifteen rugger was no match for back-street Liverpool when push came to shove – but it was the middle-class deceit he'd had most problems with. He'd been used to taking people at face value: if folks smiled at you they liked you; as simple as that. But it wasn't. Too often the smiles and overtures of friendship had hidden another agenda. They hadn't been laughing with him, they'd been laughing at him. In the end, he had concluded that the only way to be accepted as an equal was to prove that you were better. The Liverpool paddy had worked harder and studied longer than anyone else. He had grafted while the others had partied, punted and picnicked, and when it came to having trouble telling the genuine from the fake? His philosophy had said screw the lot of them. He didn't need anyone.

Gavin showed his matriculation card to the woman at the desk and walked into the medical library. He'd always loved libraries and had spent a lot of his time in the local one as a child, avidly embracing the world it opened up for him. There was a special smell about them – leather and dust – that evoked memories of the past and the thrill of finding out things as a curious youngster. Tonight he was going to look for information about a cancer drug he'd seen referred to in passing in an article he'd found in the current issue of *Cell*. The drug had apparently failed to justify the initial optimism of its makers when it had first come on to the market some twenty years ago, but Gavin had found the reference to its mode of action interesting. He wanted to know more.

The warning that the library would close in fifteen minutes broke his concentration and made him curse under his breath. He had spent two hours in a paper chase that had led up one blind alley after another, but in the last fifteen minutes he had started to make real progress. He quickly made reference notes so that he could pull out the relevant journals next time and checked his watch before deciding that he had just enough time to photocopy one of the articles to take home with him.

Leaving all the other books and journals on the table, he took the relevant one across to the photocopier and inserted his card. 'Shit!' he murmured, when he saw that he only had enough credit left for two pages. The article was seven pages long.

'Problems?' asked a voice behind him.

Gavin turned to find a girl about his own age standing there. She was tall – almost as tall as he was at five feet ten – with ash-blonde hair, and blue eyes which suggested both intelligence and confidence as she waited for a reply.

'Card's run out,' he said.

'How many more do you need?'

'I've done two: I need another five.'

'Use mine.'

'You mean it? That's really good of you.' Gavin threw his expired card into the bin beside the copier and inserted the girl's card for the last five pages. Just as the last page rolled out, the closure of the library was announced and power to the machines was cut off. Gavin put his hand to his head and said, 'God, I'm sorry, you didn't get to make your copies.'

'Not your fault. I really didn't think I would. I've got quite a lot to do. It's no big deal. I'll pop in tomorrow.'

'I'm Gavin.'

'Caroline,' said the girl, turning to walk away.

'Maybe . . . I could buy you a beer?'

Caroline turned and looked thoughtful for a moment before saying, 'Why not?'

'Great. See you at the door.' Gavin hurried back to the table to pack up his belongings and return the books he'd been using to their shelves.

'Where's good around here?' he asked as they stepped out on to the street.

'You must be new to the university?'

'Two months. I'm a postgrad in molecular genetics. You?'

'Second-year med student. There's a pub I quite like called Doctors – just opposite the hospital in Forrest Road.'

'Then let's go there.'

As they spoke, Gavin noticed that Caroline seemed completely at ease, while he himself was nervous and felt the need to smile a lot. He learned that Caroline came from Keswick in the Lake District and was the daughter of a GP. 'It runs in the family: my granddad was a GP too. I'll probably end up doing the same.'

'I'm from Liverpool.'

Caroline smiled. 'I'd never have guessed . . .'

'Oh, right . . . my accent.'

'It's nice,' said Caroline. 'You sound like the early interviews with John Lennon. My folks were big Beatles fans.'

Gavin smiled non-committally.

'Tell me about your research.'

'What do you want to know?'

'Everything.'

'Well, cancer is really a cell division problem; it's uncontrolled cell division of the patient's –'

'Yes, thank you, Gavin, I am a med student.'

'Sorry. Then you'll know that the problem when it comes to tackling it is that the tumour is made up of the patient's own cells. It's not a foreign body. It's not different enough for drugs to be able to discriminate between the tumour and the body's healthy cells, so any kind of treatment – chemotherapy or radiotherapy – will end up destroying perfectly normal tissue as well.'

'Collateral damage.'

'Exactly. What we need is some way of making the tumour cells appear different to either drugs or the immune system so that we can target the difference and leave normal tissue alone. Kill the bad guys, let the good guys live.'

'But how can you if they're identical?'

'They're identical in every way except for the division process. That's the thing that's gone wrong. Normal cells stop growing and dividing after a while, but cancer cells go on and on until they finish up as tumours. That key difference is where the answer lies.'

'And you hope to find it. You're going to find a cure for cancer,' said Caroline.

'That's the plan,' said Gavin.

Caroline raised her eyebrows, slightly taken aback at the confident answer.

'It touches so many lives,' said Gavin. 'There's hardly a family in the land that hasn't been affected by it.'

'Yes, I know,' said Caroline sharply, with a look that stopped Gavin in his tracks. She took a sip of her drink and said, 'Don't you think you're perhaps underestimating the size of the problem?'

'There's no point in looking at the size of the problem when you can be looking for the solution,' said Gavin, his Liverpool accent coming to the fore.

'I'm sure you're right,' said Caroline, taking another sip of her drink and glancing at her watch. 'I'm assuming that cancer research involves team effort, or am I wrong?'

'I've never been a big fan of teamwork,' said Gavin.

'Gosh . . .' said Caroline slowly. 'It seems a lot to take on by yourself . . .'

'I'm going to give it my best shot,' said Gavin, with a smile that wasn't returned.

'Good for you. Well, it's getting late . . . I'd better be going.'

Gavin suddenly realised that things had gone pear-shaped, but wasn't quite sure why. He tried damage limitation. 'Look, maybe I could see you again?'

'I'm sure we'll bump into each other in the library.'

Gavin took the knock-back. 'Sure.'

Caroline turned to face him when they'd left the pub. 'Thanks for the drink.'

'Thanks for the photocopies. I'm going that way,' said Gavin, indicating north.

Caroline indicated south. 'Good night.'

—

Gavin made his way along George IV Bridge to the junction with the High Street. He was angry with himself for having blown it with Caroline and opted to walk home, even though the temperature had fallen below freezing and the pavements were icy. Physical effort and discomfort could bring distraction and this was what he sought. A two-mile, sub-zero walk was going to clear his head for some late-night study of the article he had copied.

The lights of Princes Street were spread out beneath him as he started to snake his way down the Mound – the broad, winding thoroughfare that joined the Old Town of Edinburgh, with its narrow, cobbled streets and towering tenements, to the grandeur of the Georgian New Town that lay to the north – a steep incline that had been constructed from earth excavated from the land in front of the Castle Rock. He had come to like this view a lot in the short time he'd been living here: the castle, majestic, illuminated, perched high up to his left on its rock, and the classically-columned art galleries nestling down below to his right. Tonight it all looked particularly beautiful because of the frost, which sparkled on the pavements and coated the black iron railings. There was even a full moon. Walt Disney couldn't have done it better.

'Hi, Gav,' said a man in his late twenties when Gavin got in. Tim Anderson, the oldest of the four flatmates and the lease agreement holder, worked for Scottish Widows, a large insurance company. He was nursing a mug of coffee and watching late-night sport on TV – highlights of football matches played earlier.

'Cathy was asking if you're going home for Christmas. I think she wants to invite her boyfriend to stay if you are.'

'I haven't made my mind up, but I'll definitely be here for New Year. I hear the fireworks are worth seeing.'

'They are. They're bloody brilliant. You're out late tonight. Get lucky?'

'Library,' said Gavin.

'Jesus, I thought students spent all their time drinking beer and getting laid.'

'Not in the library. How did Liverpool get on?'

'Won three-nil.'

'Happiness is . . .' said Gavin, kicking off his shoes.

'You know, I can remember when Hibs were in a European competition. I was in short trousers like, but I can remember.'

'Maybe the good times will come back.'

Tim shook his head. 'No, I saw them on Saturday.'

'Well, I've got some reading to do,' said Gavin, picking up his shoes and rucksack. 'Are the other two in?'

Tim nodded.

'I'll put the snib on the door. G'night.'

Gavin's room was at the back of the building. It was consequently quieter than the ones at the front but was much smaller – he had been the last to join the flat. There was barely room for a single bed, a small bedside table, one chair and a chest of drawers. There was a single, tall window looking out on the backs of other tenements and their communal drying greens, which were enclosed by buildings on all sides and segregated by rows of rusting iron railings. He looked down before closing his curtains and saw the green eyes of a cat on the prowl in the darkness. He turned on his electric fire and suffered the smell of burning dust as its single 750-watt element attempted to heat a room with a twelve-foot-high ceiling.

He pressed the button on the base of the table lamp and turned out the room light, immediately feeling at home when he saw the circular island of light in the darkness – the learning pool. He'd slid a lot of books into the learning pool over the years, and it was something he could create wherever he was in the world. He brought out the photocopy from his rucksack and pushed it under the light to begin reading.

Valdevan had been launched by the large international pharmaceutical company, Grumman Schalk, in 1979, amidst a blaze of publicity. The company's research laboratories had trumpeted their success in finally coming up with a product which targeted tumour cells in preference to the patient's healthy cells, killing the cancer cells in dramatic fashion in lab experiments. The drug had shown no significant toxic side-effects during volunteer trials, and licences had been granted for its use across the world. It seemed too good to be true, and so it had proved. The impressive success the drug had achieved in the laboratory had not translated into *in vivo* situations, and patients on Valdevan had fared no better than those being given other drugs. After a year of what amounted to dismal failure, the drug had been withdrawn from the market. Gavin scribbled down details of the lab methods used. The photographs of cell cultures had not come out well on the photocopy, but he thought he could see what he was looking for: a slight difference in the membrane of tumour cells undergoing treatment with Valdevan, when compared to those growing without the drug. He was, however, conscious of the danger of seeing what he wanted to see. After reading the paper in *Cell*, he had predicted in his own mind that there might be such a difference. He examined both illustrations again, turning them this way and that under the glow of the table lamp. Once again he felt that he could see a difference – a periodic pinching of the cell membrane in the presence of the drug – but the smudging on the photocopy definitely wasn't helping. He would have to go back and take another look at the originals. He would drop into the library first thing in the morning.

He switched off the fire, cleared the table and got ready for bed, tiptoeing to the bathroom across the cold vinyl of the hall in order not to wake the others. When he came back, he turned out the light, opened the curtains so that he could see the sky, and slipped between the sheets. They were icy cold. A frosty moon looked back at him.

THREE

Gavin saw Caroline come into the library as he was returning the last of his books to the shelves. She didn't notice him standing off to her right as she walked purposefully towards the photocopier on the other side of the room, her arms full of journals. He hesitated for a moment and then walked slowly over to join her. 'Hello again,' he said awkwardly.

Caroline gave him a look of cool appraisal before saying, 'Hello, cured cancer yet or has there been a setback along the way?'

Gavin looked down at his feet, adopting the look of embarrassed contrition that had served him well in the past where girls were concerned. 'I'm sorry,' he said, 'I must have come across as a right prat last night. Maybe you could give me another chance? I'd really like to see you again.'

'Gavin, we bumped into each other in the library last night. Let's not make *Brief Encounter* out of it. You're two months into a PhD and I'm two years into a medical degree: we don't have time to even think about other things.'

'I thought maybe an occasional beer . . .?'

Caroline softened her expression and shook her head. 'You're a strange mixture, mister: insufferable arrogance and . . . something else. All right, hangdog charm wins the day. An occasional drink – as long as we both understand that that's all there is to it?'

'Great . . . tonight?'

'No, maybe Friday.'

It was after eleven when Gavin appeared in the lab. Mary's smile was neutral; Tom just nodded.

'Professor Sutcliffe was looking for you earlier,' said Mary.

'Know why?'

'It's usual for postgrad students to be asked to help out with tutorials for the undergrads. It's supposed to be good for us – teaching experience and all that – something to put on the CV. I think he's pencilled you in for next Tuesday: microbial respiration.'

'Well, he can un-pencil me and teach his own students. The lecturers in this department are not exactly overburdened with teaching duties as far as I can see, and that's what they're paid for.'

'If you say so,' said Mary, giving up and turning away. Tom pretended to be hard at work at his bench.

'Is Frank in?' asked Gavin.

'He's in his office,' said Mary.

Gavin knocked on Frank Simmons' door. 'Got time to talk?' he asked.

Simmons swivelled slowly round in his chair and looked over his glasses. 'I suppose I should grab the opportunity while you're actually here, Gavin. Come in. Sit down.'

'Sounds like I'm in trouble?'

'You were until Mary mentioned that she met you last night on your way to spend the evening in the medical library. If it hadn't been for that I think I might have been coming round to the view – that everyone else seems to hold around here – that you've been doing damn all since you came through the door of my lab two months ago.'

Gavin gave an exaggerated shrug, but didn't have time to respond before Simmons continued, 'The Medical Research Council has given you a three-year postgraduate research studentship on my recommendation – and I don't have to tell you how stiff the competition was. I'd hate to suffer the embarrassment of being proved wrong . . .'

'I've been thinking,' said Gavin.

'What about?'

The tone of Simmons' voice left Gavin in no doubt that this was not a casual enquiry.

'I'm just about to tell you,' said Gavin, placing his rucksack on the floor between his legs and bringing out his bits and pieces in an untidy jumble, causing pens and pencils to cascade on to the floor. 'You wanted me to work on the genetics of membrane architecture . . . right?' he said, dropping to his knees to start retrieving things. 'You suggested trying to mutate a gene we agreed was likely to be a suitable target . . .' His voice took on a strained quality as he had to reach under a radiator to retrieve the last pen. 'Well, it occurred to me that that might be really difficult . . .'

'I don't remember suggesting that it would be easy . . .' said Simmons, watching the proceedings with a bemused look on his face. He was finding it difficult to remain angry with someone who was behaving like an untrained Labrador puppy in his office.

'Well, it turns out . . . we don't need to do that at all,' said Gavin, finally straightening and getting to his feet. 'There's another way.'

Simmons' expression was carved in stone, but he was inwardly impressed at the change that had come over Gavin. His usual sullenness had been replaced by an intense, youthful enthusiasm which was a pleasure to see.

'I don't know if you saw the Grieve and Morton paper in *Cell* last week, where they mentioned an old anti-cancer drug in passing called Valdevan?'

'The drug that failed because it only worked in the lab and not in people?'

'Yes, but that's not the point. The authors of the *Cell* paper mentioned somewhere in the discussion that the probable target for that

25

drug was the gene we spoke about – the S16 gene – the one you asked me to mutate . . .'

Simmons examined the notes that Gavin handed over, outlining the proposed chemical action of Valdevan. 'You do have a point . . .' he conceded.

'I've been down in the library, trying to find some pictures of cells treated with the drug to see if they show any obvious membrane changes, and I managed to come up with these. Look, I think it's quite clear. There's an irregular but definite pinching of the membrane like you thought might happen if we knocked out the S16 gene. See for yourself.' Gavin presented Simmons with a journal opened and folded back to display a photograph.

'Gosh, I see what you mean,' agreed Simmons, picking up a magnifying lens from his desk and examining the photograph more closely. 'It's not blindingly obvious but it's there. You know, I think you just may have wiped out some of these yellow cards you've been accumulating . . . if not all of them. This is an excellent piece of investigative work. Well done.'

Gavin, beaming with pleasure and growing in confidence, leaned towards Simmons and said, 'If we could get the drug company to give us some Valdevan, we could use that to simulate knocking out the gene and forget all about the hassle of trying to induce mutations. We'd save a whole bunch of time and it should be absolutely straightforward.'

'Brilliant.'

'Providing the company still has any after all this time,' said Gavin.

'Oh, I think they will,' said Simmons. 'I'm sure it's a long time since they made any on a production line, but they'll certainly still have stocks of it or the ability to make it in pilot quantities.' Simmons nodded thoughtfully. 'I think you've just made a cracking start to your PhD project.'

'I was hoping you'd think that,' said Gavin. 'I thought I might write to Grumman Schalk and ask for some Valdevan; tell them it's for research purposes and see what they say?'

'It might be better coming from me,' said Simmons.

'It was my idea,' said Gavin, causing an electric pause.

'No one's denying that, Gavin,' said Simmons evenly. 'And a very good one it is too.' He was taken aback at Gavin's reaction but managed to remain calm. 'I just thought that a request from me might carry more weight, that's all.'

Sensing that he had overstepped the mark, Gavin softened his tone. 'I'd like to do it if you don't mind, Frank. Pharmaceutical companies are usually keen to support any research they think might be of potential value to them. After all, today's PhD students are their future.'

'Fair enough – although I wouldn't point that out to them too strongly if I were you,' said Simmons. 'And don't forget to use department headed paper and give them details of your MRC scholarship, otherwise you'll get a well-deserved flea in your ear.'

'Okay, boss.'

'In the meantime, and while you're thinking about it, perhaps we should assume that Grumman Schalk will come up with the goods, in which case you could start preparing cell cultures so you can begin experiments as soon as it arrives?'

'Make a good impression in the lab, you mean?'

'That would be a side-effect of preparing to get a flying start when the drug arrives. Do you have a problem with that?'

'Guess not.'

'Good,' said Simmons. 'Get started.'

Simmons let out his breath in one long sigh when Gavin left the room. 'Give me strength,' he murmured. He was about to resume what he had been doing when another knock came at the door. Jack Martin had been waiting outside.

'A frank exchange with Gavin?' he asked.

Simmons nodded.

'Any further forward?'

'Yup. He's no idiot. He's still a pain in the arse . . . but no idiot.'

'Well, that's progress, I guess. Lorraine was asking if you and Jen would like to come over for dinner on Saturday?'

'I'm sure we'd love to if we can find a babysitter. Can I get back to you?'

'Sure.' Martin looked at his watch. 'Feel like a pub lunch?'

'I certainly do. Dealing with Gavin can drive a man to drink.'

The two men walked the short distance from the medical school to the Greyfriars Bobby pub at the head of Candlemaker Row. The name of the pub commemorated the legend of a little dog, Bobby, who had resolutely refused to leave his master's grave in nearby Greyfriars Kirkyard, and stood guard over it for fourteen years. There was a statue to the dog immediately across the road with the dog mounted on a plinth at exactly the right height for tourists to have their photograph taken with him. Two Japanese were doing just that as they arrived.

With two pints of Belhaven Best in front of them and an order for scampi in the pipeline, Martin asked, 'So what exactly is the problem with Gavin?'

'He takes working-class paranoia to new heights and combines it with the social skills of a turnip. He's come up with a very good idea, but his first concern seems to be that I'm going to steal it from him.'

'Why don't you get him to give a seminar about it? Then everyone will know it's his idea.'

'Gavin doesn't rate seminars. He thinks they're a waste of time and usually given by people who like the sound of their own voice but have nothing to say.'

'So he *is* bright.'

'That's another part of the problem. That's the sort of thing that *we* might say to each other, but would never say publicly. He does, and I constantly find myself having to argue a case that I have no heart for, simply because I'm his supervisor and have to give out the company line. It's pissing me off. He ends up saying exactly what he thinks and I'm forced into being mealy-mouthed about everything.'

'To see ourselves as others see us . . .' intoned Martin.

'A comfort.'

'What's his good idea?'

'I asked him to work on disturbing membrane architecture in tumour cells: I suggested he try mutating the S16 gene. My thinking was that division and membrane structure have to be linked, so if division control is altered in tumour cells, maybe there are differences in membrane structure too.'

'You're trying to get at division control through membrane limitation?'

Simmons nodded. 'We've not had too much success through the known division genes, and mutating the membrane genes was always going to be difficult, but he's just short-circuited the whole process by coming up with an alternative.' Simmons told Martin about Valdevan.

'Brilliant, providing you can still get it of course. It was a bit of a turkey as I remember?'

'A complete loser, but it's my bet the company will still have stocks.'

'Then the sooner you write the better?'

'That's where the trouble started. Gavin wants to write the letter himself; just about bit my head off when I suggested I do it.'

'Ah, senior lecturers don't carry too much weight in Gavin's world?'

'No one carries much weight in Gavin's world.'

'What kind of degree did he get at Cambridge?'

'A First. His director of studies confided that they had no option but to award him a First, but most of the staff would have preferred to have seen him under a train.'

'There are a few in our third year I wouldn't mind seeing join him,' said Martin ruefully. 'What's happened to society? Half the buggers are substituting attitude for ability. They see themselves as customers rather than students. They're paying so they expect a degree. You tell them they've failed an assignment and it's . . . *Excuse me? I don't think so . . .*'

Simmons smiled at Martin's impression. 'Well, Gavin's not like that. He has genuine ability . . . but no common sense.'

'Ah, if only you could teach that,' sighed Martin.

———

Simmons found Mary Hollis alone in the lab when he got back. He asked her if she would be able to babysit on Saturday evening.

'Of course,' she replied. 'Simon's on call and I'm not doing anything. I could do with catching up on some reading. By the way, what did you say to Gavin this morning?'

'Why do you ask?'

'He's been running round the lab like a mad thing, asking questions about setting up cell cultures and rooting around for equipment.'

'Music to my ears,' sighed Simmons. 'He's had a good idea. Why don't you ask him about it?'

'I did. He just smiled and put his finger to his lips.'

Simmons made a face. 'Well, I'll tell you. He's come up with an alternative way of knocking out the S16 gene – without the need to mutate it.'

'How is that possible?'

'He noticed that an old anti-tumour drug called Valdevan has been reported to target the S16 gene so we could use that instead of mutating the cells.'

'That should save you guys a whole lot of time.'

'Exactly. He's had a good idea which could save us a lot of time,' said Simmons. 'But there's no call for secrecy. He's not come up with a unifying theory to explain the universe. I'll get him to tell us all about it at the next group meeting.'

'I should have a first draft of my paper ready by next week. Will you have time to look at it?'

'I'll make time. I should think Jack Martin will be asking you to give an internal seminar about it quite soon.'

'Sure, and then it'll be time to start thinking about writing up my thesis.'

'No problems there. Good solid research and three publications under your belt if the latest one gets accepted. Seems like three years have just flown by. Any thoughts about a post-doc position?'

'I thought maybe Jerry Haldane's lab at UCLA?'

'Good choice,' said Simmons. 'And Californian sunshine as a bonus.'

'I thought maybe you could put in a word for me?'

'I'd be happy to.'

⎯⎯

'But what difference will membrane changes make?' asked Caroline, leaning forward to be heard above the din of the student union on a Friday evening.

'If membrane structure in tumour cells was changed in some way, it might be a difference we could exploit,' replied Gavin.

'How would you target the difference?'

'We'll have to cross that bridge when we come to it,' smiled Gavin.

'It's a good idea. Was it yours?'

Gavin shook his head. 'No, Frank Simmons', my supervisor. He's a bright guy, nice too.'

'So you don't mind having him on the team then?'

'Okay, okay . . . not all teams are bad. Mind you, that still doesn't alter the fact that the research community is full of dead wood.'

Caroline screwed up her eyes, held up her finger and looked

schoolmarmish. 'Enough!' she said, leaning forward to look into Gavin's eyes for signs of dissent. Finally, deciding that there was only amusement there, she asked, 'Can I get you another pint?'

'Sure,' said Gavin. He watched her disappear into the throng at the bar and, when she came back, holding a pint glass in either hand and making exaggerated slaloming movements to avoid exuberant groups of laughing people, he couldn't help but smile broadly at her.

'What is it?' she asked.

'I was just thinking how nice you look.'

'Let's not start all that, shall we? We agreed.'

'It's okay . . . I say that to all the girls who buy me a pint.'

'Even the ones who subsequently pour it over your head?'

'Just joking,' said Gavin quickly. 'But I meant it; you do look nice.'

Any reply was rendered nigh impossible as a wall of amplified sound came between them. The first band of the night had begun their set. 'Shall we dance?' asked Caroline.

'I don't.'

She dragged him to his feet. 'You do now.'

FOUR

'It's come!' A week had passed when Gavin burst into Frank Simmons' office holding a small, plastic vial in one hand and reading excitedly from a covering letter in the other. '"Five grams Valdevan . . . for research purposes only . . . not for therapeutic use. Please sign and return agreement." They've given it to me. Brilliant!'

'Good show,' said Simmons, who had been in the middle of a telephone conversation, but Gavin's enthusiasm had overcome his annoyance. 'The sooner you get started the better then.'

Mary and Tom exchanged smiles as Gavin, whistling loudly and tunelessly, started moving around the lab at a hundred miles an hour.

'He's like a ferret on speed,' whispered Tom.

'I think I preferred him when he was thinking,' replied Mary.

'Mary, what's the best way to sterilise a solution of Valdevan?' Gavin called across the lab.

'Is it soluble in water?'

Gavin scanned through the specification sheet that accompanied the letter, tracing each line with his fingertip. 'Yup, it says so.'

'Then use a Millipore syringe filter. You'll find one in the top drawer of the island bench. Be careful not to touch the business end with your fingers.'

'I'm not a complete idiot.'

'Sorry . . . I forgot . . . I think you may even have mentioned that . . .'

'Light blue touch paper and retire immediately,' whispered Tom under his breath, but Gavin was too busy to come back at Mary. He weighed out a little of the drug and dissolved it in distilled water before sucking up the solution into the barrel of a 10 ml syringe and expressing the solution through the filter membrane into a small, sterile bottle. 'There we go . . .' He returned to his desk in the corner of the lab, not so much to sit at it as sprawl over it, supporting his head with one hand while he made some calculations on a spiral-bound pad with the other, his fingers curled awkwardly round the pen. He occasionally broke off to use the end of the pen to punch numbers into a calculator as he worked out how much of the drug to add to the cell cultures. His plan – discussed and previously agreed with Frank Simmons – was to use several different concentrations of the drug in cultures: one of them would contain the manufacturer's recommended dose, the others higher or lower levels.

He rechecked his figures before circling the calculated amounts and bringing out a number of flat glass bottles from the incubator. These were the cell cultures to be used for the experiment. They contained lab-stock tumour cells maintained at human body temperature. The bottles had been mounted on a piece of apparatus which had been timed to tilt them at regular intervals, ensuring that the cells which had stuck to the glass as they grew would be evenly bathed in nutrients and encouraged to form a continuous monolayer.

He placed each of the bottles in turn on the stage of an inverted microscope. The unusual configuration of this instrument ensured that it was possible to examine the cells from below, rather than above as with a conventional microscope. In this way, it was possible to focus on them without having to penetrate the culture fluid as well as the glass.

Mary and Tom noticed that the whistling had stopped. Gavin was sitting quite motionless, his eyes glued to the binocular eyepiece in what now seemed to be an eerie silence as his fingers gently moved the fine-focus control to and fro.

Eventually he sat up and started rubbing his forehead in a nervous gesture.

'Problems?' asked Mary.

'There's something wrong . . .'

Mary stopped what she was doing and went over to take Gavin's place at the microscope. She smoothed back a wayward strand of her hair and examined all three cultures in turn. 'They're contaminated,' she said. 'Definite signs of bacterial contamination.'

'But how?'

'It's the easiest thing in the world for bacteria to get into cell cultures when you're setting them up. Your technique has to be really good, and even then some bug is still going to find its way into them on occasion. Who prepared these ones?'

'I did.'

'You did?' repeated Mary slowly. 'Why? We have a cell culture lab with trained staff. Why didn't you ask the technicians to do it?'

'I wanted to do it myself . . .'

Mary bit her lip. She was trying to think of something kind to say. 'That's fine if you wanted the experience . . . but did you ask for advice? Did you ask the technicians to show you how to do it properly?'

Gavin said not. 'I read up on it. It seemed straightforward enough . . .'

'You can learn to swim from a book, Gavin. Trouble is, you'll drown when you hit the water because you've no idea what it feels like. There's a big gulf between theory and practice in everything.'

'Shit. Where do I go from here?'

'I suggest you help yourself to a slice of humble pie and go ask the technicians for advice.'

Gavin turned and left the lab. Mary shrugged her shoulders and asked Tom, 'Do you think I was too hard on him?'

'Far from it. He seems determined to do everything on his own. One-man bands are all very well – and you have to admire the ingenuity that goes into them – but at the end of the day . . . they still sound shit.'

Mary picked up the phone and called the cell culture lab. 'Trish? It's Mary. Gavin Donnelly's coming down to see you – he's probably on his way as we speak. He screwed up his cell cultures and needs some help. Don't be too hard on him.'

'We offered to set them up for him in the first place but he insisted on doing it himself, as if he didn't trust us. '

'Well, that's ridiculous,' soothed Mary. 'You guys are the best. It's just the way Gavin is. He's such a loner . . .'

'Tosser more like . . .' murmured Tom.

'Okay, Mary. We won't tell him to go screw himself . . . this time.'

—

But Gavin was not on his way to the cell culture suite. He had left the building and was making his way across the Meadows, the large green area to the south of the medical school, which separated the southern fringes of the Old Town from the respectable sandstone Victorian villas and tenements of the Marchmont and Bruntsfield areas. He had to bow his head against a bitter wind and thrust his hands deep in the pockets of his jeans to stop his fingers going numb. He had no real idea of where he was going. He just had to get out of the building. He had made a fool of himself and it was eating away at him, making his face burn with anger and embarrassment. Humble pie definitely wasn't on the menu for today, but alcohol certainly was.

—

'You're late and you're drunk,' said Caroline when Gavin joined her in Doctors at ten past eight.

Gavin took one look at her face and mumbled, 'Give me a break, not you as well . . .'

Caroline continued to stare at him, her silence demanding an explanation.

'Look, I've just had a shit-awful day, right?'

'And I can see how you're dealing with it,' said Caroline with a look of utter distaste.

'Jesus,' murmured Gavin, avoiding her gaze by looking down at the table.

Caroline gave him a few moments to elaborate, but when nothing was forthcoming she said in carefully measured tones, 'Well, I've had a shit-awful day too.'

Gavin saw that her hands were shaking slightly. He interpreted this at first as anger, but when he looked at her he saw that there was something more. She looked hopelessly vulnerable.

'My father phoned me this morning . . . my mother's cancer has come back. She had breast cancer three years ago and they thought they'd caught it in time . . . but apparently not. It's come back. Want to top that with *your* shit-awful day?'

'Jesus, Carrie, I don't know what to say . . .'

'Of course not, you're drunk and in no position to say anything without making a complete arse of yourself, so please don't try. Just climb back into your trough of self-pity and leave me alone. This was always a bad idea.'

'Carrie . . .'

Caroline got up and left without looking back. Gavin tried to follow but stumbled over a chair leg and fell to the floor. A barman appeared at his elbow and hovered threateningly as he struggled to get up. 'All right . . . I'm going.'

The cold air made him wince as, in his drink-befuddled state, he set off in pursuit of Caroline to beg forgiveness. He called out her name every few yards. 'Carrie, I'm so sorry . . . please believe me . . .'

He finally came to a halt when, after a few minutes, he rounded a corner where he could see the road for more than two hundred yards ahead. Caroline was nowhere to be seen. 'Shit,' he murmured, finally conceding defeat. He turned slowly to start heading back. He had only gone a few yards when he was confronted by three youths who had emerged silently from the alley they had been standing in.

'Student tosser,' said one, flicking his cigarette butt across Gavin's path.

'Always moanin' about their grants. Never enough for the buggers. Look at him, pissed as a newt. These bastards are having a laugh.'

Gavin stepped off the pavement to pass them by, but one of them elbowed him in the side. 'Is that right, fucker? You havin' a laugh at us?'

Gavin tried to continue on his way but was tripped from behind and a foot thudded into his body as he tried to get up. 'Bastard!' he gasped.

Seizing on any excuse he sensed might afford him the moral high-ground, one of the yobs grabbed Gavin. 'What did you fuckin' call me?'

Gavin tried to focus on the hate-filled face but could make out little more than acne and gritted teeth. 'Oh, fuck off . . .'

Kick after kick rained in on Gavin, until a bad day ended in a pool of his own vomit and merciful unconsciousness. He awoke at three in the morning in A&E.

'Welcome back,' said a voice that sounded vaguely familiar.

'I know you . . .'

'Simon Young, Mary's boyfriend,' said the voice. 'You're in hospital.'

Gavin blinked against the light with his right eye. He couldn't open his left. He eventually recognised the tall, fair-haired man he had met in the postgrad union. 'How are you doing?'

Young smiled at the enquiry. 'I'm fine. I won't ask how *you*'re doing: I know. I've just spent the last half hour examining you. I'm glad *I* didn't offend the guy who did this to you. You obviously upset him big time . . .'

'There were three of them. I got pissed; I got mugged,' mumbled Gavin. 'Shit happens. What's the damage?'

'Three broken ribs and a face your girlfriend might struggle to recognise for a few days.'

'Don't have a girlfriend any more . . .'

'This wasn't over a girl, was it?'

'No, some locals decided to express their doubts about the value of higher education.'

'Student bashing? Happens a lot.'

'Good to know . . .'

'Your being pissed didn't help . . .'

'We'll have to disagree about that,' said Gavin, attempting to sit up. 'Where are my clothes?'

'You're in no fit state to go anywhere.'

Gavin let out an involuntary gasp. 'You may be right . . .' he agreed, putting his hands to his head as pain seemed to hit him from all directions.

'Just lie back down, get some sleep, old son,' soothed Young. 'Tomorrow is another day.'

Gavin appeared in the lab at three the following afternoon. To a large extent, what had happened had wiped out the fact that he had gone off in a huff after discovering that his cell cultures were contaminated. All people wanted to talk about were his injuries and what had happened.

'Ye gods,' murmured Mary when she saw him. 'Simon said you'd taken a bit of a beating . . .'

Gavin found it hard to adopt any facial expression at all, the left side of his face had swollen so much. It also kept his left eye closed.

'You should be home in bed.'

'I have to talk to the girls in the cell culture suite. Humble pie, remember? My favourite, yum yum.'

'I'd put a paper bag over my head first,' said Tom. 'You might scare them.'

'Fine . . . if you'll put a plastic one over yours.'

'Boys, boys,' soothed Mary, walking over to the incubator and bringing out three cell culture bottles. 'Actually, I asked around yesterday and the Macmillan group had some going spare. They say you can use these if you like.'

Gavin seemed speechless for a moment, then he said, 'That's great. I don't know what to say . . .'

'I think I'd go with "thank you very much" if I were you,' said Tom.

'Yeah . . . yeah . . . thanks a million, Mary. That was really kind.'

'No, Gavin,' said Mary, handing over the bottles. 'It was really normal behaviour round here. Try to get your head round that. Incidentally, I put your Valdevan solution in the fridge. You left it lying out on the bench.'

Gavin accepted the rebuke with a grimace and gave a nod of thanks. 'Thanks again . . . I guess this means I can set up the experiment right now.'

'I guess it does,' said Mary. 'If you think your aseptic technique is good enough, that is . . .'

'You don't think it is?'

'If you're depending on what you learned in undergraduate classes and from what you've read in books, probably not.'

Gavin took a deep breath and let it out slowly. 'Would you consider showing me?'

'Get your stuff together.'

They moved over to the corner of the lab where a bench was kept for 'clean manipulation'. Mary collected a variety of instruments and placed them in a glass beaker which she filled a third full with pure alcohol. She lit a Bunsen burner. 'Flame everything,' she said. 'Every time you remove a cap from a bottle, flame the neck to keep it sterile. Every time you use an instrument, take it from the beaker and pass it through the flame so that the burning alcohol sterilises it. After a while it'll become second nature.'

Mary took a pair of surgical gloves from the dispenser and put them on before picking up an automatic pipette. 'How much drug do you want to add to the first one?' she asked.

'0.5 mils.'

Gavin watched as Mary set the volume and expertly carried out the procedure. She made sure that she did it slowly enough for him to take in every step. 'Okay?'

'I think so.'

Mary did another two before asking, 'Want to try?'

'Sure,' said Gavin.

Mary gave up her seat to Gavin, who sat down and carried out the same procedure but using a different amount of the drug. He did so with a deal less fluidity than Mary, but then he had to think about everything he did.

'Great,' said Mary. 'One more and we're through.'

Gavin went through the inoculating procedure once more. This time he was a bit clumsy with the automatic pipette and touched the tip against the bench. He was about to continue when Mary said, 'Bin it.'

Gavin discarded the tip, using the ejector mechanism, and fitted a new one.

'Never take chances,' said Mary. 'Regard all surfaces as contaminated.'

Gavin finished and carried the culture bottles carefully to the incubator where he placed them on the tilt mechanism, making sure they were seated properly before clicking the door shut and feeling himself relax. He hadn't realised he'd been so tense.

'Okay?'

Gavin attempted a smile, but the pain it brought ensured it was short-lived. 'Thanks, Mary, thanks a lot.'

'You're welcome. Maybe you should go home now and rest up?'

Gavin nodded. 'I'd better just touch base with Frank first.'

Gavin knocked on Frank Simmons' door.

Simmons frowned when he saw Gavin's face. 'God, that looks painful.'

'Looks worse than it is.'

'Sit down. Tell me about it.'

'Not much to tell really. I had a bad day, drank a bit too much and got a bit of a kickin' from three locals who figured I was pissin' their hard-earned taxes against the wall.'

'You seem to be taking it very well,' said Simmons, impressed at the way Gavin was seeking to play down such a bad experience.

'It's an average night out in Liverpool,' said Gavin, making Simmons laugh out loud. 'Anyway, I thought I'd just tell you that the experiment is up and running. Mary got me some cell cultures from the Macmillan group after I screwed up big time yesterday.'

'I heard you'd had problems. It happens to the best of us. Cell culture is more of an art than a science.'

'Mary's just given me a master class in aseptic technique.'

'Good. I'm glad things are starting to move. In the meantime, why don't you go home and get some rest? There's nothing much you can do here until the cultures have run their course.'

FIVE

Despite the discomfort from his injuries, Gavin chose to walk back to the flat. He'd had more than enough comment about his appearance for one day – if not for an entire lifetime – so the prospect of people staring at him on the bus held little attraction. He wrapped his scarf round the lower part of his face, pulled on his woollen hat with the *Nike* logo on it and kept his head down as he started out on the forty-minute trek.

At a little after five he was the first one home, and the flat was so cold he could see his breath as he went around switching on the heating. He held his hand under the hot water tap in the kitchen for a few seconds before conceding that he'd have to wait a while for the water to heat up for the bath he'd been promising himself all the way home. In the meantime he filled the kettle. A hot cup of tea would help.

Although he'd kept his jacket on, he made the mistake of attempting to bear-hug himself while he waited for it to boil, and paid the price when his ribs protested. The pain, however, served to remind him that he would need to remove the strapping before getting into a bath – something he postponed for a further twenty minutes before doing so in his room, shivering in front of the electric fire as a pile of ribbon bandage built up around his feet.

'Bloody hell,' he murmured, seeing the colouring of his torso in the mirror. Five more minutes and he decided that he couldn't wait any longer for the water heater to do its business. He compromised and settled for a not much hotter than lukewarm bath, although the cold air in the bathroom condensed the steam so quickly that it looked as if the water was hotter than it actually was. He kept changing his position in the tub – an old-style cast-iron job on claw feet that had survived the years to become fashionable again, although the chips in the enamel said that this was an untouched original – to ensure that as much of him was as totally immersed as possible at any one time; a strategy doomed to failure, as there always seemed to be one part of him sticking above the surface getting cold. On top of that there was a price to be paid in pain for each move he made. The best compromise proved to be lying flat on his back with the water lapping round his chin. His knees were exposed, but he kept them warm by filling and discharging the sponge on each in turn. He kept this up until the falling temperature of the water induced a shiver in his body.

Back in his room, his patience was tested to breaking point when it came to reapplying the strapping to his ribs. Restrictions to his arm movements ensured that he kept dropping the free end of the bandage, forcing him to start all over again.

The doorbell rang and provoked an outburst of bad language. 'If you're selling anything . . .' he muttered as, holding one end of the ribbon and wearing nothing but his jeans, he padded across the cold vinyl floor in the hall and wrenched the front door open. Caroline stood there.

'I heard what happened,' she said, trying to work out what strange bondage ritual Gavin was engaged in, but finding it difficult to reach any conclusion in the dim glow from the hall light. 'I thought I'd come and see how you were.'

Gavin's anger and frustration disappeared as if by magic. 'Thanks, that's really nice of you. Come on in.'

'I've obviously caught you at a bad time . . .'

'No, I've just had a bath and I've been trying to get this damned bandage back on but I'm one hand short of the three you seem to need. I've been at it ten minutes already.'

'Let me help.'

Caroline followed the direction of Gavin's outstretched arm back to his room and took her jacket off to lay it on the bed before taking charge of the bandaging operation. 'Maybe you should just stand still and I'll walk round you.'

Gavin stood in the middle of the floor with his arms stretched out like a shivering *Angel of the North*.

'Gosh, they didn't half make a mess of you,' said Caroline. She had just seen the damage properly for the first time as he turned to face the light. 'You look as if you got hit by a train.'

'Thanks.'

Caroline smiled and continued applying the strapping to his ribs – joking that it felt like some pagan custom involving dancing round a maypole.

'Don't go near the castle, young lady, I beg of you,' mimicked Gavin in Hammer Horror style.

'At least you look the part,' said Caroline.

'You'll make a great doctor one day,' said Gavin as she finished. 'You have a confident touch.'

'That doesn't make you great . . . just confident.'

'Making people believe you know what you're doing is half the battle. Look, about last night . . .'

'I was upset . . .'

'You were right to be. I'm so sorry about your mother too. I had no idea. Do you feel like talking about it?'

Caroline sighed and shook her head in resignation. 'She had breast cancer three years ago and finished up with radical surgery. She's been clear ever since but now it's come back, and this time it's in her liver.'

Gavin tried to keep his facial expression neutral before finally saying, 'I'm searching for something positive to say here but I don't think it's going to happen. We both know different.'

Caroline nodded. 'Yep, it's just a matter of time. God, she's only forty-seven. It's not fair.'

She started looking for tissues in her bag as the tears welled up, and sat down on the bed to dab angrily at her eyes as if embarrassed at the involuntary display of emotion.

'Shit, this must be such a bummer for you,' said Gavin. 'I'm really sorry. How's she taking it?'

'Better than my dad, he's falling to pieces. He's seen it often enough. He knows exactly what's going to happen to her. Mum doesn't.'

'She's not a medic then?'

Caroline shook her head. 'She was a geography teacher. That makes her Joe Public as far as cancer's concerned. Putting up a brave fight will win the day . . . at least, that's what she thought last time.'

'Do you think she'll jump through all the hoops again?'

Caroline looked at him.

'Radiation, chemotherapy, surgery . . . general destruction of the patient in the name of medical science. I think they have the nerve to call it treatment.'

'Where did that come from?' asked Caroline, looking shocked.

'My dad,' said Gavin. 'The Big C got him when I was fourteen. At least I think it was the Big C, but it was a close-run thing between that and the medics. He was a big, strong man, but he was five stone wringing wet when they'd finished with him, screaming like a baby when anyone touched him. Sorry, that's not what you wanted to hear.'

'You have a point,' conceded Caroline. 'Maybe not the one I wanted to hear but . . . I spoke to Dad about trying to arrange hospice care when things get really bad.'

'Hospices do a great job,' Gavin agreed. 'They help folk keep their dignity right to the end. God, that's so important. I wish more of them would understand that.'

'Them?'

'The medics who think they're doing a great job when all they're doing is prolonging agony in order to make their survival charts look better – not to mention the pharmaceutical companies with their latest wonder drugs that give you eight months to live with terminal hell, instead of six, at the cost of a small family car.'

'Well, this is jolly,' said Caroline.

'Sorry.'

'You always look on the black side . . .'

'I call it reality.'

'Let's agree to differ,' said Caroline.

'Okay,' said Gavin.

'You never did get round to telling me what your bad day was all about.'

Gavin held up his hands and shook his head. 'God! Please, it pales into insignificance.'

'Let me be the judge.'

Gavin told her about the contaminated cell cultures and his embarrassment at being the cause of the problem.

'How big a setback will that be?'

'Practically none as it turns out.' He told her of Mary Hollis' efforts on his behalf.

'Then the world isn't all bad?'

'Mary's okay. She gives me a bit of a hard time but . . . she's okay.'

'Coming from you, that almost amounts to beatification!'

'Have you eaten?' asked Gavin. 'I could send out for some Chinese? Indian? Pizza? I don't think I want to play the Elephant Man in a restaurant.'

'No, I have to go. I've got an exam tomorrow and I've done so little over the past few days. I just thought I'd come by and see how you were.'

'I'm really glad you did. Does this mean I can see you again?'

'If you want to, but with things the way they are at home I'm not going to be much company for the foreseeable future . . .'

Gavin moved towards her and started to raise his arms, then

stopped in frustration. 'God, I'd cuddle you if I could, but I bloody can't!'

Caroline smiled. 'That's probably God punishing you for your *realism*.'

'Don't bring him into it. When can I see you?'

'I'll go home this weekend and see what I can do to help. How about Monday when I get back?'

'Great.'

'I'll call you when I get in.'

Back at the university, Frank Simmons was hurrying along to the common room for a 6 p.m. meeting of academic staff. He'd been considering coming up with some excuse to give it a miss because he felt sure that Gavin's refusal to play a part in the undergraduate teaching programme was going to feature, but he had a John Wayne moment and accepted that a man had to do what a man had to do. As it was, he was last to arrive and had to apologise, easing himself down on the nearest available seat. Head of Department Professor Graham Sutcliffe noted his arrival with a nod and said, 'I was just saying, Frank, we seem to have a rebellion on our hands and it's all down to your student, Gavin Donnelly.'

Simmons adopted an air of surprised innocence as he enquired, 'What's all this about?'

'Postgraduate teaching involvement. I understand Donnelly flatly refuses to participate.'

'Really? Well, I suppose it is voluntary, Graham . . .'

Sutcliffe, a large, portly man with a patrician air about him, shot him a black look. 'I think you're missing the point, Frank. The system only works when *all* the postgrad students participate. It's valuable teaching experience for them and does them no harm at all to have it on their CVs. But if one drops out it encourages others to do the same and before we know where we are . . .'

'We'll be doing it ourselves like we're paid to do,' said Simmons.

'I hope you're not suggesting that postgrad teaching involvement is in any way a case of us avoiding our responsibilities?' said Sutcliffe, positively bristling with indignation.

'I'm sure we all have the interests of the postgrads at heart, Graham,' soothed Simmons. 'But if one of them doesn't want to take part then I really think we have to accept that.'

Sutcliffe took a deep breath. 'It strikes me that the Department of Human Cell Science has to "accept" quite a lot from this young man,' he said. 'I understand he was involved in some drunken brawl the other night? Not exactly the sort of thing to burnish our image bright up at Old College, eh?'

'Gavin was attacked as he walked home,' said Simmons. 'There was no element of a brawl about it.'

Sutcliffe pursed his lips in distaste. 'Nevertheless. Moving on, I have to tell you that BBC Television has expressed an interest in visiting the department and interviewing members of our staff for a programme they're planning to do on cancer research. I'd be grateful if you would let Liz know by next Monday if you would be interested in taking part. I have already agreed to give an overview of our work and I understand Gerald Montague will also be appearing, as will distinguished colleagues from Cambridge and Mill Hill and representatives from the pharmaceutical industry. The object is to inform the public about the current state of knowledge and progress being made with regard to cancer and its treatment.'

Simmons looked at Jack Martin and exchanged a meaningful glance before quickly looking away.

'Next.' Sutcliffe paused to peer over his glasses at his notes. 'Ah, yes, Malcolm Maclean's postgrad student, Peter Morton-Brown, has suggested instigating a new weekly journal club and has volunteered to set it up and get it running. The idea is that each of the postgrad students will take it in turn to choose a paper from a current journal and present its findings to the others before discussing it in open forum. Personally, I think this is an excellent initiative from Peter and deserves our full support.'

There were no dissenting voices.

'Finally, as you know, the university has a number of artworks which it circulates among the departments. We have first choice of one from the three you will find in Liz's office for the next few days. Liz has kindly prepared a comments sheet for you if she's not there when you pop in. Now, lastly, I think Jack wants to say a few words.'

Jack Martin got to his feet and made a plea for volunteers to speak at the weekly internal seminar slots for the Spring term. 'Otherwise I'll be sending around a couple of heavies from the rugby club.'

The meeting ended in laughter after Martin managed to fill the first four Mondays with a great deal of good-humoured cajoling. As the staff filed out, he came across to Simmons, who had been one of the four volunteers, and said, 'Well, are you up for TV stardom, Frank?'

'I think I'll pass on that,' said Simmons. 'I haven't made any significant progress lately – certainly none that warrants the nation's attention.'

'As if that ever stopped anyone,' smiled Martin. 'The smell of the greasepaint, the prospect of renewed research grants . . .'

'Come on,' said Simmons. 'Let's take a look at these paintings.'

The two men walked along the corridor to Liz Manning's office and Martin popped his head round the door. 'Are we too late, Liz?' he asked, seeing that she was putting on her coat and her handbag was sitting on the desk.

'No, come in, feast your eyes and make your choice,' said Liz, who was Graham Sutcliffe's secretary.

Simmons and Martin looked at the three paintings propped up against the wall. 'Tough choice,' said Simmons.

'Modern art is always . . . challenging,' said Martin, stroking his chin.

'Or maybe it's someone having a laugh,' muttered Simmons. 'This one looks like a cat's litter tray.'

'I think that's Graham's favourite,' whispered Liz.

'Then it's mine too,' announced Simmons.

'Yep, I'll go with that,' agreed Martin. 'Mark that down as two more for the cat's litter tray, Liz.'

'It's called *Serenity*,' said Liz in a stage whisper, wide-eyed and pointing with her finger to the adjoining office door to warn them that Graham Sutcliffe hadn't yet left.

At that moment the door opened and Sutcliffe appeared with his overcoat on, briefcase in hand. 'Hello, you two. Still here?'

'We were trying to decide on a painting, Graham,' said Simmons. 'We've both gone for *Serenity*.'

'Good, that was my feeling too . . . it has a certain something . . . a haunting quality, I thought.' Sutcliffe took a long, admiring look at the painting before smiling enigmatically and sweeping out.

Martin took up stance in front of the painting, put a hand on one hip and a forefinger to his lips before saying, 'You know . . . I think he's hit the nail on the head . . . a haunting quality.'

'Out of here, you two,' said Liz.

Martin and Simmons left the building together after deciding on a beer, and walked slowly up to the Greyfriars Bobby pub, where they found the bar in the lull between after-work drinkers leaving and evening crowds arriving. Martin plumped himself down at a table while Simmons ordered beer and brought it over.

Martin took a slurp and grunted appreciatively. 'Seems like Graham's got it in for your Gavin.'

'Gavin and the establishment are natural enemies, and you don't get any more establishment than Graham.'

'Or more "anti" than Gavin by all accounts.'

'He doesn't do much forelock-touching,' agreed Simmons, who was developing a growing liking for Gavin. 'But he's more than just your average rebel without a cause.'

'So what was the mugging incident all about? Or were you just protecting him from Graham?'

'No, he really didn't start the fight. He screwed up his cell cultures the other day and responded in typical Gavin style. He threw all the toys out the pram and went off on an all-day bender. He ended up getting mugged.'

'Was he badly hurt?'

'Three broken ribs and a face like he headbutted the Forth Bridge, but he still came into the lab to set up an experiment.'

'Good for him.'

'I was impressed too. I think that's really why I stuck up for him when Graham started having a go.'

'Oh what a tangled web we weave . . .'

Simmons smiled. 'Don't we just. What do you think of the new journal club proposal?'

Martin took a sip of his beer. 'There aren't many arses in the department that Peter Morton-Brown hasn't kissed in the last two years. This is just his latest ploy to get himself noticed. He's sure as shit not going to do it through scientific brilliance. I was on his first-year assessment panel. As an investigator he couldn't find his dick in his trousers.'

'Destined for high office then.'

'It can only be a matter of time before he appears on telly, assuring the great British public that there is absolutely nothing to be alarmed about.'

'Mmm,' said Simmons. 'The trouble is we'll now be aiding and abetting him, recommending that our own students attend and saying what a good idea it all is.'

'Gavin might provide an interesting take on that . . .'

'Please! I don't even want to think about it . . .' said Simmons.

'Really? . . . I thought you might find it strangely haunting . . .'

SIX

'You're late,' said Jenny Simmons, standing at the sink as her husband came into the kitchen and wrapped his arms round her waist from behind. She moved her neck slightly away from his embrace as if to underline her annoyance.

'Sorry. There was a staff meeting and then I had a beer with Jack.'

'You two are a bad influence on each other.'

'Staff meetings are a bad influence on both of us. I think they must be sponsored by the brewing industry. Sutcliffe was having a real go at Gavin and it really pissed me off.'

'If you ask me, it's about time someone had a go at Gavin. Worrying about that boy seems to take up so much of your time these days. Is he really worth the hassle?'

'There have been times when I did wonder myself but yes, I think he is. I'm beginning to think . . . he's got it.'

'Got what? A chip on his shoulder the size of Ben Nevis?'

Simmons shushed her. 'I know you two got off on the wrong foot but –'

'The wrong foot!' exclaimed Jenny. 'The first time he came here he got hopelessly drunk and was sick all over the cat!'

'Like I say, the wrong foot, and I'm not pretending that he doesn't have shortcomings. He has. Lots. But just lately I think I see a glimpse of . . . that special something in him.'

'What special something?'

'The something that makes you a researcher. The thing that makes you more than just someone who can remember a lot of facts and figures and pass exams. You either have it or you don't, and so many people who end up in research don't.'

'That's a bit of a sweeping condemnation.'

'Maybe, but it's true. Don't worry: they don't know they don't have it. They don't even know it exists, and what you never had you never miss. You can have degrees coming out your ears, but if you don't have that extra something that enables you to think in a certain way, you're never going to do anything more than dot other people's *is* and cross other people's *ts*, however much you dress it up – and many do become quite adept at dressing it up.'

'I take it you have this something?' asked Jenny, turning to look at her husband.

Simmons let her go. 'I thought I did, but these days I'm not so sure. I seem to spend most of my time on administrative chores, form filling and writing reviews. I bitch about it but maybe I'm using it as an excuse because I've run out of ideas . . .'

'Oh, come on. You're a top man in your field. You have the respect of your peers. You have a list of publications as long as your arm, and in journals that many of them would kill to get their work into, so stop talking nonsense. You've always been too modest for your own good. However well you did, it was never good enough for *you*. That's one of the reasons I married you. I knew you were never going to end up stalking the corridors of power in a smart suit, checking the New Year Honours list to see if you were on it, but you were clever, funny, imaginative, honest – perhaps too honest for the environment you're in – and you genuinely cared about sick people and what might make things better for them. That makes you an ace person in my book – unless of course, you don't get your arse up the stairs in the next thirty seconds and read our children a story, in which case, I just might divorce you and bring in a man in a suit.'

Simmons smiled and nodded. 'On my way.'

Later, as they sat having dinner, Jenny asked, 'Have you heard about the extent of Gavin's injuries yet?'

'I talked to him this afternoon. He came in to set up some cultures.'

'Gosh, that was keen. You seemed to have enough trouble getting him to come in to the lab when he was perfectly healthy. What's brought about the change?'

'I don't think there's actually been a change, although he was hugely embarrassed about having screwed up the cultures the first time round. It's true I expected him to be just like all the others, bright-eyed and bushy-tailed when he started back in October – you know the sort of thing, in first in the morning, making himself busy about the lab, generally creating a good impression as new students usually do – but Gavin doesn't think that way. He doesn't *do* good impressions. I thought he was skiving but he wasn't; he was thinking about the project and how best to approach it. He simply didn't do anything in the lab until he came up with something worth doing.'

'And now he has?'

Simmons nodded. 'And I suspect he'll be prepared to work night and day if necessary to see it through – without any prompting from me.'

'So why was Graham having a go at him?'

'We ask the postgrad students to participate in the undergrad teaching programme – it's supposed to give them teaching experience. Graham asked Gavin to take a first-year class and he refused. Now Graham's afraid some of the others might follow suit.'

'That sounds so like Gavin,' said Jenny. 'Setting out to make an enemy of the head of department . . . and you maintain he's bright?'

'The teaching is voluntary . . .'

'But surely he can see –'

'That he should play the game?' interrupted Simmons. 'Oh yes, he can see that. He just refuses to play it.'

Jenny shook her head. 'On his own head be it . . . but surely the meeting wasn't all about Gavin?'

Simmons told her about the BBC planning to visit the department.

'Great. Does this mean you're going to be on *Horizon*, holding up a test tube and gazing into the middle distance, while a soothing voice explains just how you made the breakthrough?'

'No, I've nothing to tell them.'

'How did I know you were going to say that?' smiled Jenny. 'What about Mary's stuff? You were singing her praises the other day. She's writing it up for publication, isn't she?'

Simmons nodded. 'Sure, and it's a very nice piece of work, but it's technical progress. It's only relevant to scientists in the field. It has no bearing on anything that would matter to the general public.'

'Couldn't you sex it up to make it seem that way? You know, Edinburgh scientists in cancer breakthrough . . . hopefully in three to five years' time this will lead to significant new treatments . . .'

'I could but I'm not going to,' said Simmons flatly. 'You know how I feel about that rubbish.'

Jenny looked at him and smiled. 'God, you rise to the bait so easily. I can never resist . . .'

Gavin left the flat at just after nine the next morning and set out to walk to the lab. He was sore, but the pain was offset to some extent by the fact that it was such a pretty morning, with the sun shining on the castle ramparts as he crossed Princes Street at the junction with Hanover Street and started up the Mound. The Norway Spruce Christmas tree – a traditional present to the city from the

Norwegian government – was already in place near the top await-
ing the night, coming soon, when its lights would be ceremoni-
ously switched on by some local celebrity.

He couldn't help but think that the decorations he could see on
the lamp-posts in Princes Street paled into insignificance against the
natural beauty of the frost on the grass in Princes Street Gardens.
Their presence, however, reminded Gavin that he had still not decided whether to go home for Christmas or stay here in Edinburgh.

He knew he'd been putting it off because he'd been hoping that
Caroline might invite him home with her to the Lake District
– but that, of course, was now out of the question. Whether it had
ever been a real possibility was open to conjecture, and he was well
aware that falling heavily for someone, as he had done for Caroline,
could lead to a sense of the unreal intruding on his grasp of things.
He'd been finding it all too easy to fantasise about walking through
snow-covered woods in Cumbria with his arm round her as they
sought out holly berries and sprigs of mistletoe to bring home and
decorate a room where a log fire burned bright, filling the air with
its scent. He saw them sipping mulled wine and cuddling up on the
couch while Caroline's parents – who had taken to him instantly
– smiled benevolently and exchanged knowing glances of approval
about a possible future son-in-law.

That fantasy had been destroyed. Caroline would be going home
for Christmas, but she would be travelling alone to a house where
overwhelming sadness would preside like a blanket of fog, where
people would find it difficult to say anything and long silences would
prevail, despite forced attempts to avoid them. Cancer would be
spending Christmas with Caroline and her family, not him.

'You shouldn't be here. I told you I would check your cultures,'
said Mary Hollis when she saw Gavin come in to the lab.

'I just had to see for myself,' said Gavin. 'But don't think I'm
not grateful.'

'How are you feeling?'

'A lot better, thanks . . . and don't say I don't look it,' Gavin warned Tom who looked as if he were about to say something.

Tom shrugged and returned to what he was doing.

Gavin brought out his cell cultures one at a time and examined them under the inverted microscope. Mary watched him out of the corner of her eye, trying to gauge his reaction. Tom, with his back to the others, stopped in the middle of a calculation he was scribbling and said out loud, 'You're not going to believe this but I've forgotten the molecular weight of sodium . . .'

'Twenty-three,' said Gavin, without taking his eyes from the 'scope.

'Cheers.'

'How are they looking?' asked Mary.

'Well, at least they're not contaminated this time,' replied Gavin. 'On the other hand, there's not much sign of anything happening.'

'It's only been a day, Gavin. Give them time.'

Gavin returned the last of the culture bottles to the incubator. He had just closed the door when Peter Morton-Brown came in, full of smiles and bonhomie. 'Hi, guys. Have you heard about my new journal club?'

'Frank mentioned something about it,' said Mary, keeping her tone neutral.

'Well, what d'you think? Are you going to come along and boost the numbers?'

'I suppose . . .' said Mary.

'Sure,' said Tom with his usual lopsided shrug.

Gavin had busied himself with something at his desk.

'How about you, Gavin, are you going to join?'

'No.'

'Not interested in current research progress, huh?'

Gavin turned round and looked daggers at Morton-Brown. 'On the contrary, I am very interested. In fact, I'm *currently* engaged in it. It's your journal club I'm not interested in.'

'Don't you think it would be the perfect way to keep up to date with what's going on in science?'

'No, it would involve sitting through a lot of talks about stuff I'm not at all interested in.'

'Please yourself. I just thought it would be a help to everyone . . .'

'No, you didn't. You thought it would look good on your CV.'

'Now wait a minute . . .'

'Gentlemen, please,' interrupted Mary. 'Just let us know when you plan to have the first one, Peter,' she said, giving Morton-Brown his cue to leave. When he did, she turned to Gavin and said, 'You really are the limit.'

'He's a bullshitter.'

'You have to get along with bullshitters.'

'Why?'

'You just do!'

'You know,' said Tom thoughtfully, 'there's only one thing worse than a bullshitter . . .'

'What's that?'

'A bullshitter with a journal club to promote.'

All three of them burst out laughing. It was a good moment, a bonding moment that none of them had seen coming.

———

Over the next few days, Gavin came in early each morning to check on his cultures before going off to the library to read up on everything surrounding his project. On Monday morning his customary response to Mary's enquiry changed from 'Nothing yet' to 'Wowee! Now we're cooking.'

Mary came over to take a look at the cells. 'Not much doubt about that,' she said. 'Quite a dramatic effect. What concentration is this?'

'Manufacturer's recommended.'

'Gosh, it's hard to see how a drug that can attack tumour cells like this in the lab had absolutely no effect at all in patients.'

'Just what I was thinking,' said Gavin. 'I thought when I first read up on Valdevan that the company might be exaggerating the facts in order to make their drug seem better than it actually was, and that they had selected exceptional cells to photograph and make their point, but I was wrong. All the cells in the monolayer are behaving the same way. This drug is absolutely wonderful.'

'Except that it doesn't work in people,' said Tom.

'Maybe something inactivates it in the body?' suggested Mary.

'I guess.'

'Stomach acid maybe,' said Tom.

'I think Grumman Schalk would have checked that out,' said Gavin. 'You don't spend multi-million dollars developing a drug and then throw it away because you can't take it by mouth. You inject it.'

'I suppose.'

'Gavin's right: they must have checked every possibility under the sun before giving up on it,' said Mary. 'Why not ask them . . . or ask Frank to find out just what they did?'

'Ask Frank to do what?' said Frank Simmons, coming out of his office and hearing his name mentioned.

'I've reproduced the Valdevan effect on tumour cells,' said Gavin. 'It's much more dramatic than I expected. I can see why the company must have been excited by it at the time. We were just wondering how it could possibly have had no effect *in vivo*. Mary was saying that the company must have investigated this fully and we were wondering if you think it might be worthwhile asking them what they came up with?'

Mary positively beamed at Gavin's diplomacy. Tom looked as if he were witnessing an unnatural act.

'Worth a try,' agreed Simmons. 'But you mustn't get bogged down in investigating why an old drug didn't work. Keep sight of the original aim of the project, which is to investigate the action of the S16 gene. There's a danger of going up a blind alley here and ending up repeating everything the people at Grumman Schalk did years ago, with exactly the same result.'

'Okay, boss,' said Gavin.

'How are the cell membranes looking?'

'There are big changes,' replied Gavin. 'Definite pinching of the lipid bilayer at intervals.'

'At the lower concentration too?'

'I haven't looked yet.'

'Let's take a peek now, shall we?'

Mary and Tom returned to what they had been doing while Simmons sat down at the inverted microscope and Gavin brought out the low drug concentration culture from the incubator.

'They look quite normal,' murmured Simmons. 'Take a look.' He got up from the chair to let Gavin take his place.

'You're right – I can't see any pinching of the membrane.'

'And no cell death at that concentration?'

'Agreed,' said Gavin.

Simmons looked thoughtful. 'I think you should set up another series of cell cultures – maybe ten different concentrations of Val-devan this time. See if you can find a level that gives us membrane change but no killing. If not, we'll have to conclude that knocking out the S16 gene is a lethal event. But if you can, we're in business, and we can create stable cell populations with an altered membrane structure.'

'Okay, will do.'

'And congratulations. You've done very well. Things are really beginning to happen.'

'Thanks. You won't forget to contact the drug company?'

'I'll give them a ring now.'

Simmons returned to his office and looked out the covering letter that Grumman Schalk had sent with the drug. He saw from the letterhead that the head of development was one Professor Max Ehrman. He asked the switchboard to make the call to Denmark and waited while he was transferred three times within the company.

'Ehrman,' said a younger voice than Simmons had expected.

'Hello, Professor, this is Dr Frank Simmons at the University of Edinburgh. Your people kindly sent some Valdevan for one of my postgraduate students to use in his research.'

'It's company policy to help where we can, Doctor. Do you need more?'

'No, well, not yet anyway. I wanted to ask you something about the history of the drug.'

'The *sad* history of the drug,' said Ehrman ruefully. 'It's a bit of a taboo subject. We lost millions on it.'

'So I understand. We were just wondering in the lab if you ever found out what the problem was, and why it didn't work in patients?'

'We spent almost as much again trying to find that out,' said Ehrman. 'We had a whole research section – ten PhDs with full technical support – assigned to the problem, but in the end we drew a blank. We simply don't know.'

'And that's the way it was left?'

'We had to move on, turn our attention to new drugs, make up for lost time and money. Valdevan was consigned to the dustbin of history, as you people say.'

'But you survived,' said Simmons.

'We survived,' agreed Ehrman. 'I'll look out the final report on the drug and send you a copy if you like. Can I ask what your student is using it for?'

Simmons told him.

'Ah,' said Ehrman. 'I noticed some people suggesting recently that Valdevan probably affected the S16 gene. It's a clever approach. I'd be interested to hear how it works out.'

'I'll keep you posted – and yes, it would be interesting to see that final report you mentioned.'

'On its way. And if there's anything else we can help you with, just let us know.'

SEVEN

Gavin spent most of the afternoon two floors below in the cell culture suite where Trish Jamieson, the senior technician, had agreed to show him how to set up cell cultures from scratch. 'We are quite happy to set them up for you,' she had maintained, but Gavin insisted that his project would call for a great many over the course of the next few months and it would be as well for him to know how to do it, so that he wouldn't have to impose too much on Trish and her staff. This was, in fact, the diplomatic line that Mary had advised him to take, and he had to admit that it had gone down rather well. The initial restrained animosity – so obvious when he'd first entered the room – had since disappeared and the ambience had become much more relaxed. 'Going home for Christmas?' asked Trish as she put the cap on the final culture of the twelve she had set up, with Gavin having done the penultimate four under her supervision.

'Still not decided,' confessed Gavin. 'You?'

'You bet. Two weeks of my mum's cooking and seeing all my old mates. Hold me back!'

'Sounds okay,' agreed Gavin. 'Where do you come from?'

'Inverness. You?'

'Liverpool.'

'So what's stopping you?'

'I think I might work . . . well, at least some of the time.'

'At Christmas?'

'Well, maybe not Christmas Day, but I'd like to keep things

moving along – another good reason for learning to do this. I really appreciate it.'

'No problem, but you'd better look out some warm clothing. They turn the heating off in the university over the Christmas break.'

'Thanks for the warning.'

'Is there anything else you need to know?'

'Cell culture fluid. Am I right in thinking you always use the same one?'

'There are a number of recipes, but generally we use the richest one possible. It makes the cells grow faster, and people are always in a hurry to get results from their experiments. The others tend not to be so rich, but I can certainly leave some alternative recipes for you, if you think you might need to use another one for any reason.'

'That might be handy – just in case I run out.'

'Actually, that's a good point. It's usually impossible to get supplies of fresh serum over the break so you may have to improvise – maybe use an amino acids solution.'

—

When Gavin got back to the lab, Mary told him that Caroline had phoned and asked that he phone her back on her mobile, but not until after her afternoon lecture finished at four. He called at ten past. It sounded as if she was in a crowded corridor and having difficulty hearing him. Reducing the conversation to the bare minimum, they agreed to meet in the student union at five.

It was raining heavily when Gavin left the building and ran round to the union, pausing just inside the door to shake the water from his hair before he noticed Caroline arrive just behind him. She turned to collapse her umbrella and shake it out on the steps. He gave her a one-armed hug.

'Well, the swelling's gone down a lot,' said Caroline, examining

Gavin's face as he drew away. 'You look almost normal. How are the ribs?'

'Knitting together as we speak.' Gavin steered her through to the bar where they ordered coffee and found a table.

'How was it?' asked Gavin as he took off his denim jacket and draped it over the back of his chair.

'Much as you'd expect – pretty awful. My mother has changed almost beyond recognition.'

Gavin raised his eyes.

'I don't mean physically; it's more a personality thing. She's become so bitter. She thought that she'd taken on cancer last time and won. She says she only agreed to the removal of her breast because the doctors convinced her it would stop the chances of the cancer coming back, so now that it has . . .'

'She feels cheated.'

Caroline nodded. 'It's as if an invisible barrier has come down between us and it's not possible to get through to her, however much I try. She's there but she's not there if you know what I mean. Mum and I have always been close, but now when I talk to her it feels like I'm speaking to a stranger. There's something missing . . . the bonds between us have gone . . . she's drifting away . . .'

Gavin nodded and put his hand on Caroline's, but she didn't respond. She seemed far away.

'And your dad?'

'Oh, he's coming to terms with it. He realises that he'll have to be strong for her again and it's going to be a lot more difficult this time, particularly as she no longer has such blind faith in the medical profession.'

'Not that that would help much in this case,' said Gavin. 'Liver cancer . . .'

'Thank you . . . I'm well aware of the prognosis.'

'Do you think there's a chance she'll decline treatment and just go for pain management and hospice care?'

'You have to be very strong to do that,' said Caroline. 'I think she's going to do what most of us would in the circumstances: grab at any straw that's offered. Hearing my dad trying to convince her that treatment was improving all the time made me want to run off into the hills and scream my head off until I had no voice left.'

'And now you've got Christmas coming up . . .'

Caroline closed her eyes. 'Jesus Christ, Christmas,' she murmured. 'Deck the halls. Still, I'm sure there's probably a store out there on the net that does presents for the dying woman.'

'Ssh,' said Gavin. 'That's not you.'

Caroline looked at him and then patted the back of his hand. 'Thanks,' she said. 'But it is.' She straightened her back and placed both forearms on the table. 'So, what are *you* doing for Christmas?'

'I might stay here.'

'But why? You've got a big family.'

'Eating, drinking and watching telly with my sisters and their kids, and their husbands who think that any bloke who goes to university is of questionable sexual orientation? Maybe not. The attraction of doing nothing will wear off after one day and I'd just be sitting there thinking about the experiments I could be doing if I was here. Anyway, I want to see the New Year fireworks.'

'I think I'll come back for that too . . . if I don't feel guilty about coming away.'

Gavin lowered his head so that he could make eye contact as Caroline cast her eyes downwards. 'How can I cheer you up?'

'Tell me you've discovered a cure for cancer.'

Although Grumman Schalk had promised Frank that they would send their report on why Valdevan had failed, Gavin decided that there would be no harm in giving the matter some thought on his own. There had to be a reason why the drug didn't work in the human body when it worked so spectacularly well in the lab

– something he'd now seen for himself. It was this that kept him in the library until closing time that evening, and on just about every other when he wasn't seeing Caroline.

By the second week in December, Gavin had the results of his experiments on lowering the concentration of Valdevan. They were disappointing, and he went in to Frank Simmons' office to tell him.

'No intermediate effect, boss, but it's nice and clear: it's either death or no effect at all. I couldn't find a concentration that gave us membrane change without the killing.'

'A pity,' said Simmons, accepting the notes from Gavin. 'But if the S16 gene is essential for cell growth and division there's not a lot we can do about it – unless you feel like checking some intermediate concentrations . . . just to be absolutely sure?'

'Sure.'

'But whatever happens, this has been a first-class piece of work, and completed in a matter of weeks. I thought getting this far would certainly take up the first year of your project.'

'Coming across the paper was a big plus,' said Gavin.

'But you were the one who came across it . . . you saw the relevance. Chance favours the prepared mind and all that.'

Gavin shuffled his feet, uncomfortable with praise.

'Look, I'm well aware of your misgivings about seminars, but I really think you should consider giving one to the department about this.'

'I'll think about it.'

'Mmm,' said Simmons, looking doubtful. 'In the meantime . . .' He picked up an A4-size padded envelope. 'This arrived this morning from Grumman Schalk. It's their internal report on investigations into why Valdevan didn't work.'

Gavin extracted the plastic-covered file with the Grumman Schalk logo on it and weighed it in his hand. 'Feels like they did a pretty thorough job.'

'With twenty million dollars riding on it at the time, I think it fair to assume that they would,' smiled Simmons.

'I'm looking forward to reading this.'

'Stay focused, Gavin. It's all too easy to get diverted and start going up side-streets in the middle of a project. You should be thinking about moving on to one of the other membrane genes. Tom has a strain that is partially altered in the S23 gene. It was constructed by one of your predecessors, and I've been meaning to have someone look at its biochemistry to see if we can find a potential target for drug development.'

'Okay,' said Gavin, holding up the file. 'But maybe I'll take this home with me if you don't mind?'

'Of course . . . but give that seminar some thought.'

When the door closed, Simmons went back to reading the letter that had come with the report. It included a glossy blurb about a new research grants scheme being sponsored by Grumman Schalk, and a suggestion from Max Ehrman that he should consider applying for one. Such grants were an entirely new initiative from the company, and would be available to established researchers who held a recognised university position and were working in the broad areas of cancer diagnosis and treatment. Each grant would provide support for one or more postdoctoral workers and technical support for a period of up to three years. Larger grants would be available in exceptional circumstances.

Simmons frowned as he thought about it. In the past he had steered clear of applying to commercial companies for money because they usually had strings attached. He preferred funding from the Medical Research Council or the Wellcome Trust, although he had on one occasion been successful in attracting support from the EEC. The problem with accepting funding from drug companies was that they tended to place restrictions on what could and could not be submitted for publication. They often insisted on having the final say and this could lead to conflict.

Getting work published in peer-reviewed journals was essential to young scientists hoping to pursue a career in research, and equally so to established workers trying to attract continued funding for their work, but the criteria for publication became more complicated when commercial concerns played a part in the process. Scientists had traditionally shared their findings with one another for the common good, but drug companies had little enthusiasm for disseminating information they thought might prove useful to a competitor, and could be equally reticent about publicising the failure of a product they'd hoped might be commercially viable. Share price was all important.

Frank put the letter to one side for the moment and opened an internal mail envelope from Graham Sutcliffe. There would be a meeting with people from the BBC on 9 January to discuss the planned programme on cancer. It had been decided to hold the meeting in Edinburgh because Professors Gerald Montague, Neil Carron and Linda Surrey, who had already agreed to take part in the programme, would be in the city to attend an international scientific meeting at Heriot Watt University on genetic influences in cancer susceptibility. Senior members of staff – which included Frank – were invited to dinner with these three after the meeting. The meal would be at The Witchery by the castle.

Frank told Jenny about this when he got home.

'Don't suppose wives are invited,' she said. 'I like The Witchery.'

'Some chance if the university's paying. They make Ebenezer Scrooge look like Andrew Carnegie.'

'Thought that might be the case. How come they never have any money? They seem to pull in grants and bequests from all over the place, but they're always pleading poverty.'

'Universities are a bit like the National Health Service,' said Simmons. 'No matter how much money you pour in, it will disappear without trace into an ever-expanding system. I seem to spend half my time dealing with administrators' unending demands for facts and figures, while they plunder my grants in order to keep their own arses on seats, thinking up new forms to send out.'

'Do I sense I've touched on a sore spot?'

Simmons smiled. 'I refuse to be drawn on administrators today. Gavin got a clear result this morning. It wasn't what we wanted but it stopped us wasting our time for twelve months or more. He's doing well.'

'Good, I'm glad . . . for your sake. You went out on a limb for that boy.'

'I just did what was necessary, but we're not out of the woods yet. I'm currently trying to persuade him to give a seminar to the department about his work. If he agrees to that it really will feel like I've made progress.'

'If you say so.'

'How do you feel about asking him to Christmas dinner?'

Jenny's mouth fell open. 'I'm hoping that's a joke,' she spluttered.

'He's not going home for Christmas: Mary told me he's planning to work over the break.'

'Oh, come on, Frank, this could ruin Christmas for all of us – especially the cat.'

'Of course, if you feel that way about it let's just forget it. It was just a thought.'

Jenny looked suspiciously at her husband. 'You've just cast me in the role of pantomime villain, haven't you?'

'Don't know what you mean.'

'Oh yes you do.'

'You have every right not to have him here after last time. He may have matured considerably, but we still shouldn't take the risk . . .'

'God damn it, I can feel you playing me like a fish on the end of a line, but I can't seem to do anything about it,' complained Jenny.

'I really don't know what you're talking about, I'm sure . . .'

71

'All right, I give in. He can come, but make sure our insurance is up to date, hide all sharp objects and check we have enough fire extinguishers – and cat shampoo.'

'Can you really get cat shampoo?'

'Call it poetic licence.'

⸺

When Gavin left Frank's office he went out to a local shop to pick up a Coke and a sandwich for lunch. He planned to eat it at his desk while he skimmed through the Grumman Schalk report. When he got back, the lab was empty – a bit like the *Mary Celeste,* he thought – lights on, books open on desks, Bunsens burning and incubator lights blinking on and off at the whim of their thermostats. After a moment, he remembered that it was the day of the first meeting of Peter Morton-Brown's new journal club. He checked his watch and noted that he'd have another thirty minutes to himself.

The Grumman Schalk investigation seemed to be just as comprehensive as he'd imagined it would be. Their scientists had left no stone unturned in their attempts to discover why Valdevan had not worked in the human body, but in the end, they had failed. The bottom line was that it remained a mystery.

One thing that did catch his attention, however, was the good quality of the photographs in the report, and a much wider range of them than he had managed to find in the published papers about the drug. He was examining them with an eye lens when Mary and Tom returned to the lab. Frank was shortly behind them.

Gavin waited until Frank had gone into his office before asking, 'Did I miss much?'

'No,' said Mary. 'Peter was speaking about Gerald Montague's new paper in *UK Cell Science.*'

'Jesus,' murmured Gavin.

'I think he plans on asking Gerald Montague to be his external examiner when he's finished writing up,' said Tom.

'A match made in heaven,' said Gavin without looking up.

'You know . . .' announced Mary, 'for once, I agree. That Montague paper was rubbish. How the hell does he go on getting that nonsense published?'

This was so unexpected, coming from Mary, that both Tom and Gavin looked at her in surprise, not sure what to say.

'He's one of the managing editors of the journal,' said Gavin.

'Oh, God,' said Mary, sitting down as if she felt too weak to stand. 'Are things really that awful in science these days?'

Tom and Gavin looked at each other, equally alarmed at what they were hearing from someone who was usually so positive.

'Hey, come on, Mary, of course they're not,' said Tom.

'They're no worse in science than they are in anything else,' said Gavin, as if it were the best he could manage.

Mary got up and left the lab.

'Time of the month,' said Gavin.

Tom looked at him. 'You can probably go to jail for saying things like that.'

EIGHT

Mary returned to the lab shortly afterwards, outwardly calm and composed, and got on with her work as if nothing had happened. Tom gave a slight shrug of his shoulders and a glance in Gavin's direction, which was returned with a slight widening of the eyes. Tom started to hum tunelessly as he pipetted diluting fluid into a series of test tubes, while Gavin went back to examining photographs with his eye lens. He was still doing this an hour later when Frank Simmons came out of his office and dumped a pile of scientific papers on his desk.

'From my biochemistry reprint collection,' he said. 'I thought you might find them useful.'

'That was kind,' said Gavin with a jaundiced look that brought a smile to Simmons' lips.

'Not at all. What are you up to?' he asked, seeing what was lying open on Gavin's desk.

'I thought I'd have a quick look through the GS report while you guys were at the journal club.'

Simmons nodded but felt suspicious. 'And what has your quick look told you?' he asked.

'I think you were right. They seem to have done a pretty thorough job, but, at the end of the day, they didn't get anywhere. They've no idea why the drug didn't work on patients.'

Simmons had the distinct impression that Gavin was telling him what he wanted to hear. 'Then maybe we should just leave it at that, shall we?'

'Yes, boss,' said Gavin. 'No point in going up blind alleys.'

Simmons returned to his office and sighed as he slumped down into his chair. The fact that Gavin had quoted his own advice back at him was making him doubly suspicious about what Gavin was thinking. He knew it was all too easy for research students to go off at a tangent when they weren't fully committed to their designated project, and that certainly would apply to Gavin, whose imagination had clearly been fired by seeing how well Valdevan worked *in vitro*. If Gavin's heart was in something, he could be left alone to get on with it. If it wasn't . . . he'd have to keep a close eye on him.

Simmons' suspicions were well-founded, because Gavin had just discovered something that was occupying his full attention. He waited until Frank had returned to his office before picking up his eye lens and resuming what he had been doing. He had seen something in the report photographs that put a whole new slant on the Valdevan story and his pulse was racing. The more convinced he became of what he was seeing, the more excited he became, until he found it impossible to sit still any longer. Without saying anything to anyone, he got up, grabbed his jacket and left the lab.

Gavin started out across the Meadows. The blustery, wet weather of the past few days, with its accompanying strong westerly winds, had given way to clear skies and a slight but bitterly cold wind coming in from the east, but he welcomed the icy breaths he took as he headed for nowhere in particular at a brisk pace.

Because the drug had failed to kill tumour cells in patients suffering from cancer, the Grumman Schalk team had understandably assumed that either it had been inactivated in the body or had been prevented in some way from reaching the site of the tumour. They had put all their time and effort into determining what the problem was, but in the end had drawn a blank. Gavin now knew that they had been wasting their time. It was quite clear from the photographs he had been examining for the past hour that the drug *had* reached the tumour cells and *had* been active when it got there.

Close examination of the photographs of cells taken from patients showed what he now recognised as the typical membrane pinching caused by Valdevan, despite no mention of this by the company in their report – but of course, they had not been looking for slight membrane defects; they had been looking for cell death.

Gavin's discovery had left him with a puzzle. The fact that you could have membrane damage without resultant cell death implied that the S16 was *not* an essential gene. If the drug could knock it out and the cells could continue to grow and divide, this was the very opposite of what he'd found in his lab experiments, where membrane pinching was always followed by cell death.

Forty minutes of walking round in circles deep in thought brought some measure of calm to his mind, which was important because he had decisions to make. Frank didn't want him investigating the failure of Valdevan because he felt that Grumman Schalk had already taken it as far as it could go. But what he'd seen in the photographs was making him reluctant to stop and switch to studying something else, when so much remained unanswered.

Apart from anything else, biochemistry was not Gavin's favourite branch of science. It could be long, tedious and boring, with constant, fidgety adjustments to experimental times and conditions being necessary before things started to work – if they ever did. What was certain was that he couldn't start work on a biochemical study of the new strain and continue to investigate the failure of Valdevan. There weren't enough hours in the day.

He supposed he could come clean with Frank: tell him what he had seen in the photographs and hope that he might change his mind, but on the other hand, he might not. He took a kick at a discarded Coke can lying in the grass beside the path and swore under his breath. He couldn't leave things the way they were, he decided. One way or another he had to follow it up.

It dawned on him that he could work on Valdevan over the Christmas break. No one would be around at that time for nearly two weeks and, even if Frank should find out what he was up to, he could hardly insist that he work on something else in what was officially a holiday period. He felt more relaxed. All he had to do now was work out exactly what he was going to do . . .

—

'I'm sorry, I don't understand the significance,' said Caroline when the pair met in Doctors at eight and Gavin, full of enthusiasm, told her what he had discovered.

'Don't you see? The company thought that Valdevan wasn't reaching the tumours in cancer patients – either that or it was being inactivated in the body in some way – but it wasn't either of these things. The drug *did* reach the tumours and it *was* still active when it did.'

'But it still didn't work,' said Caroline.

Gavin brushed the objection aside as if it were trivial. 'I know, but the research angle changes, don't you see? Frank's been insisting that the company had probably investigated every angle that could be investigated, but that's not true. They were asking the wrong questions about the wrong problem. They spent hundreds of man hours altering drug composition and changing the ways of administering it in order to ensure that Valdevan got to the cancer when it was getting there all along!'

'Maybe the concentration was too low when it got there?'

'They monitored drug levels in the patients. It was well above what killed the cells in the lab experiments.'

'But it still didn't work,' said Caroline, leaning across the table to make her point. 'Surely that has to be the bottom line, doesn't it?'

'But that's exactly what I want to investigate,' said Gavin.

'But you'll be right back at the beginning, and now you'll have an even bigger problem to investigate than the company thought *they* had. *You* don't even have a working hypothesis about why it didn't work.'

'It's still worth doing,' said Gavin stubbornly.

Caroline looked doubtful. 'What's Frank saying to all this?' she asked.

There was a pause which allowed disbelief to grow in her eyes. 'You're going to say you haven't told him?'

'There's a conflict of interest,' said Gavin.

Caroline had to prompt him. 'I'm waiting.'

'Frank doesn't want me spending any more time on Valdevan. He wants me to move on and try a biochemical approach, using a strain deficient in another gene.'

'I'm with Frank,' said Caroline. 'If Valdevan didn't work before, it's not going to now. If one of the biggest pharmaceutical companies in the world had to give up on it after shelling out millions of dollars, what are you going to come up with that's so different?'

'If they got the basis of the report all wrong, God knows what else they might have missed.'

'Mmm,' said Caroline.

Gavin took a sip of his beer and sighed deeply. 'Okay, maybe I am getting a bit carried away here,' he conceded. 'But the company's efforts to find out what the problem was were misdirected. They don't count. It would be like starting over.'

'But that's exactly my point,' agreed Caroline. 'It would; and that means having an enormous mountain to climb with little chance of reaching the top.'

'But it's an exciting mountain, don't you think?' said Gavin, with what he hoped might be an argument-winning smile.

Caroline gave a small shake of the head. 'Is it one you'd want to gamble your entire future on?'

Gavin made a face and started to examine his beer.

'What Frank says is scientifically sound and sensible.'

Gavin continued examining his beer.

'Don't tell me I'm actually getting through to you?' asked Caroline with an amused smile.

78

'Look, I agree there's a lot in what you say . . .'

'Good. That's a start.'

'Okay, look, I'll make a start on the biochemistry, but I'm not giving up on Valdevan and I'm definitely going to work on it over the Christmas break.'

'As long as you make a start on the biochemistry . . .' said Caroline, deciding to be satisfied with one concession. 'Right,' she announced. 'No more beer. Let's go see the Christmas lights.'

Although Gavin would have preferred to continue sitting in the warm, drinking lager and munching his favourite bacon-flavoured crisps, he agreed without argument, and seeing the look on Caroline's face as they walked down the Mound and along Princes Street made it worthwhile.

'You're like a kid,' he laughed as he watched her try to keep walking straight while looking up at the lights, occasionally pirouetting to enhance the effect.

'I love Christmas and everything about it . . . people change for the better . . . it's like the way it should be all the time . . . I want it to snow . . . I want to build a snowman . . . I want to drink mulled wine and sing "Hark the Herald Angels" . . . I want to go to see a school nativity play where Joseph forgets his lines and Mary drops the baby Jesus . . . I want to waken at three in the morning and smell a Christmas tree in the house . . . I love all these things . . . At least I used to . . .' she added, suddenly coming down to earth. 'But God, it's going to be so different this time . . .'

'Just take it one day at a time,' said Gavin. 'Christ! I sound like a Country and Western singer. Are any of the rest of your family coming?'

'My aunt and uncle usually come up from Manchester, but they've decided it would be *inappropriate* this year. What a prissy little word. Makes me think of town hall officials.' Caroline stopped walking and looked to the other side of Princes Street where the shops were. 'I'm hungry.'

'What d'you fancy?'

'Something bad for me . . . a burger with heaps of chips and lashings of relish and fizzy Coke with lots of sugar and caffeine . . .'

Gavin grabbed her hand and they ran laughing across the broad street to McDonald's on the corner of Castle Street.

They found a table by the window where they could look out and up at the floodlit castle while they ate.

'Now I'm filled with remorse,' said Caroline, putting both hands on her stomach and pushing her empty tray away.

'Sin followed by remorse, the unending circle of life,' said Gavin.

'I am absolutely stuffed.'

'C'mon, let's walk it off.'

'I'd have to walk to Birmingham.'

They dumped the detritus of their feast in the waste bin and left the warmth of the restaurant to hit the cold air again.

'Frank's asked me to Christmas dinner at his place,' said Gavin.

'That's nice. Will you go?'

'I made a right arse of myself the first time I went there. I think his wife, Jenny, hates me.' Gavin told her about the episode with the cat. Caroline closed her eyes as it unfolded.

'I'd never drunk malt whisky before . . .'

'I'm surprised they've asked you back.'

'Maybe they're hoping I'll say no? I said I'd let him know by Monday.'

'Your call,' said Caroline.

'It might seem rude if I don't go.'

Caroline's eyes opened wide. 'Did I hear that correctly? Gavin Donnelly is worried about appearing rude?'

'Give me a break . . .'

Caroline moved in front of Gavin, smiling, and held both his arms at the elbows while she looked up into his face. 'I'm sorry,' she said.

Gavin, still with his arms pinned, brought his mouth down on hers in a long, hungry kiss. She didn't pull away, although there was a degree of uncertainty in her response. 'We agreed this was a bad idea,' she said when they finally parted.

'You agreed.'

'This is entirely the wrong time . . .'

'There's never a right time or a wrong time to fall in love with someone.'

'Please, Gavin, spare me the Christmas cracker philosophy. You're a fortnight early and my head's too full of other things right now.'

'Right.'

'And don't put on that hurt expression.'

'Right.'

'And don't agree with me so readily!'

Later, as Gavin lay in his bed looking at the moon, he wondered just how he was going to start a new investigation of Valdevan. Caroline's earlier assertion that even if the drug was reaching the tumours and was still active when it got there, it still didn't work, was finally getting through to him. She was right. He had made a breakthrough but it was an academic breakthrough, very satisfying but it wouldn't change anything for the patients who'd been treated with it. They would still be dead. But why? The drug *should* have destroyed their tumours. The more he wrestled with this, the more he understood Caroline's point that he had left himself with an even bigger problem than Grumman Schalk. They thought they knew what the problem was. He hadn't a clue.

The photographs in the company report had definitely shown an effect that could only have been caused by the drug affecting the S16 gene in the tumour cells, but this made him wonder about the photographs of healthy cells in the original papers he'd consulted about the drug: they hadn't shown any membrane aberration. Why not? Healthy cells and tumour cells were identical in terms of genetic make-up. Surely the drug should have affected the S16 gene in them too and caused the tell-tale pinching?

Gavin switched on the bedside lamp and got out of bed to start rummaging in the cardboard box he kept his reprints in. He started to shiver. A clear sky outside meant falling temperatures and the heating in the flat had been off for ages. Single glazing and the original, ill-fitting sash windows meant that the inside temperature became the outside one very quickly.

He found what he was looking for. It was a poor photocopy but the one he'd made on his first meeting with Caroline, when she'd loaned him her card. He searched in the pockets of his rucksack for his magnifying lens – which he'd bought the day before from Tom Brown's Stamp Shop in Merchiston Avenue – and then put the relevant page into the pool of light provided by his bedside lamp. The pictures hadn't improved any with the keeping but he was still pretty sure that there was no membrane alteration to the healthy cells.

Feeling mentally exhausted, he got back into bed, switched out the light and drew his knees up to his chest in an effort to get warm. The difference between tumour cells and healthy tissue cells was . . . division control. The tumour cells were undergoing uncontrolled cell division while the healthy cells were not . . . the tumour cells were showing membrane change but the healthy cells were not. There had to be a link – something that tied in with why Grumman Schalk had thought they had a specific drug against tumour cells. They must have seen tumour cells dying in the lab but healthy cells surviving. He would have to check out the effects of Valdevan on normal cells for himself. He couldn't just rely on old photographs. He would set up that experiment at the same time as running the last of the Valdevan concentration tests. He would go down to the tissue culture suite first thing in the morning and see about getting some healthy cell cultures.

He could hear tuneless singing coming from outside on the front street and echoing up over the tenement roofs as some night straggler from an office Christmas party informed the world that he had done it his way. It brought a smile to Gavin's lips. 'Sure you did,' he whispered, 'Thirty years with Standard Life and you did it your way . . .'

NINE

'Trish, I need some normal human cells. Any chance of getting some before the holidays?' asked Gavin, who had been waiting outside the Cell Culture Suite since 8.45 a.m.

A look of dismay came over the technician's face. 'You're kidding . . . no, you're not, you're serious.'

'There's some doubt about the behaviour of normal cells in the literature; I have to be sure.'

Trish looked uncertain. 'Shit, Gavin, we were actually counting on closing down the suite this afternoon and spending the last day just cleaning up and replenishing stock solutions.'

'I'll love you forever . . .'

'Not sure if that's a good enough . . . I'd have to check with the maternity unit to see if a placenta is liable to become available for amnion cells . . .'

'Forever and a day?'

Gavin followed Trish into her small office and stood by as she phoned the maternity unit. After a short conversation she said, 'They are expecting four births this afternoon.'

'Great.'

Trish broke into a resigned smile. 'You do realise this means I won't be going to the Christmas lunch with the girls?'

Gavin saw that she was serious. 'Shit, I'm sorry, I didn't realise it was that big a deal. Maybe this is something I could do myself if you pointed me at a book of instructions?'

'I won't pretend it's not tempting to walk off and leave you to it, but primary lines are a bit tricky if you've never done them before.'

Gavin grimaced.

'They're not like tumour cells which go on dividing forever as long as you feed them and dilute them. Healthy cells have a limited lifespan. We have to prepare them fresh each time and break down the tissue into component cells before we can even start.'

Gavin sighed. 'I'm sorry. I should have thought. I really didn't realise there was so much to it . . .'

'Having said that,' said Trish hesitantly. 'It's not impossible . . . providing the maternity unit comes up with the goods early enough. If they do, I'll set you up a batch before I go off.'

'You're an absolute ace person; I really won't forget this.'

'Yeah, yeah . . . I'll give you a call when they're ready or leave a message on your desk saying where you can find them.'

When Gavin returned upstairs to the lab he found a note on his desk from Frank Simmons, asking if he was coming to Christmas dinner or not. He had to know today. When Gavin went over to knock on Frank's door, Mary Hollis called out, 'He's not there. Sutcliffe's called a meeting of senior academic staff.'

'Was he wearing a Santa suit and carrying a sack?' asked Gavin sourly.

Mary broke into a smile. 'And just when I thought you were beginning to mellow . . .'

'You've not exactly been all sweetness and light yourself these past few weeks if I might say so,' said Gavin.

'Fair comment,' said Mary, her smile fading. 'Simon and I broke up. He found himself a blonde staff nurse with big tits.'

'Seems reasonable to me,' said Gavin with his back to Mary, but he was smiling, looking at the wall, waiting for the come-back.

Mary threw a box of tissues at him but she too managed a small grin. 'At least everyone knows where they are with you, Gavin. What you see is what you frighteningly get.'

'But really, I am sorry,' said Gavin, turning round to face her. 'You two looked good together, like it was the real thing.'

'It was for one of us.'

'I guess this has ruined your Christmas.'

'We'll see. I'm going home to Dublin to stay with Mum and Dad. My brother Pat is coming home from Germany, so it'll be nice to see them all again. I'll be leaving just after lunch. Tom's already gone off home to Bristol, and I think Frank said he was heading out to do his Christmas shopping after Sutcliffe's meeting. He probably won't be back this side of the New Year.'

'It's going to be lonely round here.'

'You've decided to work through the break?'

'They don't give you a Nobel Prize for eating Christmas pies.'

'So that's where I've been going wrong.'

Gavin scribbled a note saying that he would love to come to dinner on Christmas Day and sellotaped it to Simmons' door.

'Are you off out?' asked Mary.

'Just to an off-licence to get a bottle of wine for Trish. She's doing me a favour and setting up some human amnion cells for me.'

'You asked Trish for primary cells the day before we break up and she said yes?' exclaimed Mary.

'I told her I'd love her forever and she took pity on me.'

Mary seemed lost for words until she affected an exaggerated shake of the head and came out with, 'Men are something else.'

'Cancer doesn't stop for Christmas.'

'Neither does bullshit.'

———

Frank Simmons walked briskly along the corridor, determined for once not to be the last to arrive at the latest departmental meeting called by Professor Graham Sutcliffe. He had no idea what it was about – the memo hadn't said – but took comfort from the thought that his research group had done nothing lately to upset the smooth running of the department. Apart from that, it didn't take much for Sutcliffe, who saw communication as a great virtue and an essential element of academic life, to call a meeting. In Simmons' book this translated into nothing being too trivial to merit endless discussion.

Sutcliffe, wearing a light grey suit with a trouser waist that threatened his armpits and a university tie in deference to his later lunch appointment at Old College with the deans of the faculties, perched his reading glasses on the end of his nose and looked over the top at the people in front of him. He apologised for the short notice in calling the meeting. 'I understand that several of you have recently received letters from the pharmaceutical company Grumman Schalk, inviting you to apply for funding under a new research support scheme they have just announced?'

Five staff members, including Frank Simmons, agreed that this was so.

'Good. I thought that might be the case. As soon as I read the company's press release in *Nature*, I got in touch with the their administrators to ask for clarification about the wording concerning "special cases" and, without going into too much detail, it would appear that our department would almost certainly be viewed as a special case. The fact that we have so many distinguished researchers and an international reputation means that we could make a block grant application and expect to receive – assuming we were successful – a sum in excess of twenty million pounds sterling. A rough estimate says that that would be around twelve times as much as we could hope to achieve from the sum of individual applications. I've called this meeting to ask what you think about the idea.'

'There must be some serious conditions attached,' suggested Simmons.

'The company would want certain safeguards,' said Sutcliffe, as if to belittle the comment. 'It does not pretend to be a charity.'

'The power of veto over papers submitted for publication perhaps?' said Simmons.

Sutcliffe moved his feet uneasily. His voice took on a note of irritation. 'I should think that the company would almost certainly like to see such submissions before they were sent off, if only to check with their patents people in case something might require legal protection. Grumman Schalk would naturally want to protect their investment – perfectly reasonable in the circumstances, I think you would all agree?'

'Can you assure us that only their patent lawyers would want to examine submitted work? Their scientific directors wouldn't have the power of veto over results they didn't like or wouldn't want made public?'

Sutcliffe moved from irritation to exasperation. 'Look,' he snapped. 'It's early days to worry about things like that. Are we or are we not in favour of making a block grant application to Grumman Schalk? That's what we have to decide today. Competition is bound to be fierce. I know that Gerald Montague certainly intends to apply.'

The murmurs in the room seemed positive. Sutcliffe struck while the iron was hot. 'I need hardly point out that this would mean a considerable expansion of our department – certainly to a size where I think we could accommodate the creation of two more personal chairs . . .'

'Nice move,' thought Simmons. 'Money *and* personal advancement on offer.' He decided not to swim against the tide. It was unanimously decided to try for a block grant.

'Good, I'll formulate a first draft over the break and you can let me know your thoughts when you get back. It only remains for me to wish you all a very Happy Christmas and continued success in the New Year.'

Frank Simmons found Gavin's note stuck to his door. 'Ding dong,' he murmured, although his thoughts moved on quickly from 'Merrily on high' to 'Pussy's in the well' . . .

As it happened, Christmas Day passed without incident at the Simmons' house. Gavin turned up bearing books for the children and a bottle of Glayva liqueur for Frank and Jenny. He made a point of being careful over what he drank – sticking strictly to beer – and no reference at all was made to the events of his previous visit. Jenny's elderly parents, Tom and Matilda, were there, as was Frank's widowed father, Patrick, who had recently suffered a stroke and was showing frustration at not being able to express himself properly, nodding vigorously when someone filled in the blanks correctly, but shaking his head and slapping the arm of his chair when they got it wrong. There had been little opportunity to talk science – something that suited Gavin more than it did Frank, who kept looking for opportunities to question him about what he was doing in the lab. He finally succeeded when he found Gavin alone in the kitchen after gathering in empty glasses.

'So what are you up to in the lab?'

'Oh, you know, just trying out a few things: getting used to working with cell cultures on a regular basis . . .'

'With a view to starting the biochemistry of S23 cells, yes?'

'Actually . . . no,' confessed Gavin, stopping what he was doing and staring straight ahead at the wall in front of him. 'I thought I might try out one or two other things first . . . in my own time, so to speak.'

'Valdevan,' sighed Simmons. 'It's Christmas Day, Gavin, and I've no wish for us to fall out. But come the first day of the new term, I want to see you start work on the biochemistry of S23 cells. Understood?'

'Sure, Frank.'

Simmons put his arm round Gavin's shoulders. 'Fancy a whisky?'

'Maybe just a beer,' smiled Gavin.

'Let's join the others.'

Gavin got home just after seven and called Caroline.

'How's the cat?' she asked.

'Alive and well. Everything was fine. I've been on my best be-haviour all day but now I'm going to get guttered – Christ, I never knew behaving yourself could be so stressful. How was your day?'

'A nightmare of long silences and remembrances of times past. I didn't know cutlery could sound so loud on china. The sun came out for a little while this afternoon after we'd finished eating, so I took myself off for a walk in the woods.'

'And your mum?'

'She's started chemo and radiation therapy so she's very tired. She keeps trying to challenge fate by declaring that it's against her better judgement this time. How's the science been going?'

'Pretty good. I expect to get some results tomorrow from the primary cell lines I treated with Valdevan. Everything has been go-ing smoothly, except for the fact that I had to tell Frank I wasn't working on the biochemistry.'

'Shit,' said Caroline. 'How did that go down?'

'I guess he wasn't best pleased, but he didn't hit the roof or any-thing, and I am working in my own time . . .'

'But you're using up his resources,' countered Caroline.

'Yeah, I know, and he's been really good about it. On the other hand, he made it clear he wants me to start work on the biochemistry come the new term or I'm in deep shit.'

'Quite right too.'

'I could do with a little more support here.'

'We've been through all that.'

'Yeah, we have,' conceded Gavin. 'So what lies ahead for you?'

'An evening of Christmas telly stretches out before me like an ordeal by mirth,' said Caroline.

'Maybe it will take everyone's mind off things,' said Gavin.

'I'll feel guilty if I laugh.'

After a long pause Gavin said, 'Call you tomorrow?'

'Sure.'

Boxing Day was a landmark day in the lab for Gavin. Wearing two sweaters and a scarf against the cold and sitting at the inverted microscope, he got a nice clear answer to his question. Valdevan *did* affect normal cells. He could see distinct changes, and the typical membrane pinching that was now so familiar to him. But this, of course, was another conundrum.

After forty minutes of making absolutely sure, he rubbed his eyes and put his hands behind his head while he thought about his findings. Valdevan killed tumour cells in test tubes but not in the human body – although it caused membrane damage in both. It caused pinching but not death in healthy cells in test tubes, but had no effect at all on healthy cells in the body. Just what the hell was going on? What was the difference?

Gavin got up from the microscope and fetched a sterile glass beaker from the glassware cupboard. He filled it with cold tap water and placed it on a bench tripod before lighting a Bunsen burner below and adjusting the flame. Walking back to his desk, he brought out a small carton of tea bags he kept in the drawer and placed one in his Liverpool FC mug – noting that it could do with a clean: the mug was red but the inside was dark brown with tannin and coffee residue. But that was something that could wait for another day. Instead, he walked over to the window and looked out while he waited for the water to boil. There was very little traffic about, and he guessed that the cars that did pass by contained families on the way to visit relatives. *Your folks Christmas Day, mine Boxing Day.*

The water in the beaker started to bubble so he turned off the Bunsen and used an oven glove to lift it off and hold it while he filled his mug. He took a sip and gave a sigh of satisfaction which sounded unnaturally loud in his surroundings. Although it was cold in the lab – the heating had now been off for several days – it wasn't so much the temperature that was getting to him as the quietness. All the usual background sounds of heating and ventilation in the building were missing – it took their absence to make him notice – but other sounds were now more apparent. The on/off click of thermostats on incubators and water baths, the compressors on fridges and freezers cycling on and off as they kept their precious contents at steady temperature, unexplained creaks and moans from an old building. It started to rain as he drank his tea. The patter drew him back to the window. The glass had obviously not been cleaned in a long time; the rivulets followed a tortuous course down the tall panes, inviting parallels with life.

Gavin turned away. Maybe if he were to set up two cultures side by side – one tumour cells and the other normal, healthy cells – and added Valdevan to both at exactly the same time, he might be able to compare differences as and when they happened. He returned to the bench. This was what he'd do. He got out the necessary sterile glassware and checked the cultures he had available in the incubator. The tumour cells looked as if they needed diluting, so he fetched what he noted was the last bottle of tissue culture medium from the fridge. He sat it on the bench while he put on surgical gloves. As he did so, he noticed a slight tear in one of the gloves and made to strip it off. The tightness of the fit and the sudden movement of his arm when the glove finally gave way caused his elbow to hit the bottle of tissue culture medium and send it crashing to the floor, where it shattered and left him looking down at a spreading red puddle round his feet.

'Sweet Jesus,' he exclaimed. 'The last bottle . . .' He stared at the puddle as if unable to believe his appalling luck. 'Of all the fucking rotten . . .'

The tableau continued in silence for a few moments before he realised that it wasn't quite the end of the world he'd imagined it to be. There was nothing to stop him making up some more. He had the recipes Trish had given him and a good range of chemicals in the lab cupboards. All it would take was time and he had plenty of that: no one was waiting for him at home.

He looked at his watch and reckoned that it would be well after eleven before he'd be finished, but there was a chip shop on his way home which he knew stayed open until midnight. This was now his goal, something to look forward to. He would treat himself to steak pie and chips, and maybe even a large pickled onion.

He found everything he needed in the chemicals cupboard and lab fridges except for one ingredient, human serum. There was none in the freezer where it was usually stored, and now he remembered Trish saying that getting it at this time of year was always difficult, if not impossible. He wondered if the tissue culture medium would support growth without the addition of serum but was doubtful – human serum was a very rich source of nutrients. But Trish had given him recipes for a variety of different tissue culture media and he was pretty sure that at least one of them didn't list human serum as an ingredient. He rifled through his desk drawer until he found the relevant notes and checked through all the formulae. 'You beauty,' he murmured as he found the one he was looking for. He didn't need serum. He had everything he needed.

TEN

Gavin was back in the lab by nine next morning, although it was too early, of course, to expect results: he was just checking that the cell cultures were showing no sign of contamination. The fact that they appeared perfectly healthy gave him the peace of mind he was looking for and every reason to take the day off.

The sky was blue and the sunshine perceptibly warm on his cheek as he stood on the pavement outside the medical school and, for once, noticed that there was no wind to speak of in a city that could give Chicago a run for its money. On the spur of the moment he decided that he would go for a walk in the hills. In Edinburgh, he was spoiled for choice: the Braid Hills, Corstorphine Hill, Blackford Hill and the long-extinct volcano, Arthur's Seat, were all within city limits. On a bigger scale, the Pentland Hills stretched out along the southern boundaries of the city and well into the neighbouring county of West Lothian. He finally opted for the Pentlands because he felt like a longish out-and-back walk rather than a simple up and down.

He bought a couple of sandwiches and a chocolate bar from a sandwich shop at the foot of Lauriston Place and stuffed them into his rucksack as he made his way to the bus stop to catch the number 10 bus at Tollcross. Caroline had mentioned a few weeks ago when talking about Sunday walks that it was easy to get into the Pentlands from Colinton, the leafy suburb in the south-west of the city and the destination of the number 10, although on that particular occasion they had ended up walking by the shores of the Forth at Cramond.

The early view of the hills Gavin got from the top deck as the bus wound its way up Colinton Road whetted his appetite for the walk ahead. There was nothing like a bit of frost and snow for bringing drama and quality to the most mundane of slopes. Two dimensions suddenly became three.

The newsagent's shop in Colinton Village was open when he got off the bus, so he bought a newspaper and picked up a map of the Pentlands at the same time – they had been placed in a rack near the till. This would now make it much easier to plan his day. As he came out of the shop he noticed that the Colinton Inn was open for business, so it occurred to him that he could not only plan a route, he could have a beer at the same time.

With the folded map in his left hand and his rucksack swung over his right shoulder, Gavin walked up Bonaly Road until the road became a track and the track a path as it wound its way steeply uphill through a pine tree plantation. He paused when he reached the eastern fringes of a small reservoir to check where he was on the map and catch his breath, and noted that if he headed west – up and over Harbour Hill – he would come to a meeting of four paths at a spot marked as Maiden's Cleugh. This would be as good a place as any to pause and decide on what to do next.

He was breathing heavily by the time he reached the top of Harbour Hill, something that reminded him that he didn't get enough exercise, although walking to and from the medical school had been doing something to counteract too much beer and crisps in his life. He rested his hands on the boundary fence to take in the impressive view over the city to the Firth of Forth and the hills beyond and found himself wishing that Caroline was standing beside him. It would have been a good moment to share.

He started to feel guilty about enjoying himself so much while Caroline was going through hell, although in reality there was nothing he could do to help. He suspected he was going to feel like this a lot until the inevitable happened, something that led to yet more feelings of guilt as he wished this to be sooner rather than later for everyone's sake.

As he came down off the hill and joined the main path, he started to meet other walkers and began to feel self-conscious about what he was wearing. They all appeared to be dressed for a major Himalayan expedition in winter – a mobile montage of colourful Gor-Tex strung out across the white landscape. His own attire of denim jacket, jeans and trainers made him feel as if he had turned up at a funeral wearing a red plastic nose – *A member of the Pentland Hills mountain rescue team declared Mr Donnelly to be improperly attired for the rigours of the hills at this time of year . . . A nation shook its head in condemnation . . .*

Gavin sought out a quiet hollow in the hill in which to eat his sandwiches – well back from the path to avoid human contact. As a natural loner this was the usual thing for him to do, but today it made him stop and think. He found himself facing up to the fact that even out here in the hills he felt and behaved like an outsider and, for once, invoking Sartre's maxim that 'Hell is other people' wasn't working as well as it usually did. It had supported him well through Cambridge, but just recently, the combined efforts of Mary in the lab and Caroline, as well as other kindnesses he had encountered, were exposing flaws in the philosophy. If he wanted his relationship with Caroline to progress – and he did – he would have to do something about changing his outlook. He would not desert his principles, but he would have to consider seeking a happy medium. This was also true in professional relationships. The screw-the-world philosophy had worked throughout his undergraduate years because he had been simply acquiring knowledge that was already accessible without any real need for human contact. Books had told him what he needed to know, and his natural intelligence had enabled him to understand, use and interpret what he'd read.

Postgraduate study, however, was different. Although there was still much to absorb from the scientific knowledge base, he was now a researcher in his own right and therefore expected to increase that knowledge base by contributing to it. While it was not inconceivable that he could do this as a loner, it would be that much more difficult unless he was a genius, and he wasn't. He smiled wryly as he got to his feet and fastened the straps on his rucksack. Maybe Gavin Donnelly would make some New Year's resolutions. The thought gave him a fit of the giggles as he started climbing the next hill.

If anything, the view from the top of Bell's Hill was even better, affording him as it did the sight of the winter sun sparkling off the waters of Threipmuir Reservoir far below and stretching out to the west. The feeling of well-being that he was getting from the physical effort of the climb and the beautiful views was doing much to make this a memorable day. He abandoned his earlier plan to start heading back when he reached the reservoir crossing at Black Springs, and instead continued west on what appeared to be a little-used path along the north side of Black Hill. The new plan was to continue on up to a spot marked on the map as Green Cleugh where he would start heading back via the Red Moss nature reserve.

Later, as he waited for the bus back to town, the fading of the light and the reddening sky signalled the end of the day and reminded Gavin that they had just passed the winter solstice. They were a very long way from spring. The temperature was falling, heralding another frosty night, and grit-spreading vehicles were out on the roads of the city.

Caroline called Gavin to say that she would be back on 30 December, and he was there to meet her at Waverley station when her train pulled in. They walked down Waverley Bridge and turned into Market Street, heading for a coffee shop attached to an art gallery that they often used when they were in town.

'How's your mother?'

'Sick as a dog, hair falling out, becoming more bitter and twisted by the day, just what you'd expect, but let's not dwell on it,' said Caroline, clearly uncomfortable at discussing it. 'Tell me about something else. How have you been getting on?'

'Okay, I guess.' Gavin gave a half-hearted smile before diverting his eyes to look down at the table.

'What's wrong?'

'Nothing, everything's fine . . .'

'Out with it.'

'Oh, I've got some results I don't understand and it's sort of getting to me.'

'So tell me about it. I need distraction.'

'Where do I begin?' exclaimed Gavin, spreading his hands in a gesture of hopelessness. 'I suppose it all boils down to the results I'm getting this time not being the same as the ones I got last time.'

'Irreproducible data.' Caroline intoned it like a death sentence. 'Not good.'

'It's crazy. The results I got first time were exactly the same as the people at Grumman Schalk got but now, suddenly, everything's different.'

'So something must have changed.'

'I had to make up some new cell culture fluid.'

'There you are then. The cells don't like it. They're not growing properly.'

'But they are. The control cultures are growing and dividing perfectly normally. Trouble is, so are the ones with the drug in them.'

'You mean Valdevan isn't killing them any more?'

'You got it.'

'Maybe the drug's gone off . . . an old solution?'

'That would be good if it was true,' agreed Gavin. 'But the cells are showing membrane damage. The drug's working okay.'

'I seem to remember you saying something like that once before. Isn't that what happens in the body?'

'Exactly,' said Gavin. 'The tumour cells show membrane damage in the body but they don't die . . . it's never happened in the lab before, though.'

Caroline took in the worried look on Gavin's face and leaned towards him. 'This may not be all bad,' she said. 'Look at it this way. Instead of a bad result, you have – inadvertently, I grant you – created the very problem that exists in the body. What's more, you've done it in the lab which is a much better place to study it, isn't it?'

'I suppose . . .'

'No suppose about it. You have, haven't you?'

'Okay, you could be right.'

'So wipe that miserable look off your face and let's start making plans for the fireworks tomorrow. Where shall we go to watch them?'

'I thought you had tickets for Princes Street?'

'I have and it's the best place, but we'll be packed like sardines.'

'But if it's ticketed, surely it won't be too bad?'

'It was ticketed last year,' said Caroline. 'But they give all the sardines tickets. It's a big television event so the city bosses want the world to see thousands and thousands of people, packed together, convincing the world they're having a good time.'

'When they're not?'

'The fireworks are brilliant, make no mistake about it, but having drunks slobber over you at midnight, wading through broken glass and having people pee on your shoes tends to detract . . .'

'Jesus.'

'We can watch them from somewhere else if you'd rather,' said Caroline, seeing the alarm on Gavin's face. 'They say the view you get from the Botanic Gardens down at Inverleith is pretty good and it's not nearly so crowded . . . or even Blackford Hill? That shouldn't be too bad.'

'I think we should head for the heart of the party,' said Gavin, with a conviction he hoped didn't sound too false.

'If you're sure?' Caroline sounded far from certain.

'You bet.' Inside his head Gavin was already steeling himself for the nightmare ahead and planning a master class in turning the other cheek, but Caroline needed something to cheer her up and she was so looking forward to the fireworks. He mustn't ruin it with his hatred of crowds. 'I'll give you a hand with your stuff back to Pollock Halls.'

'I'm not going to Pollock,' said Caroline. 'I'm staying with Gina, one of my classmates. She's got a flat in Polwarth Gardens. Two of her flatmates are away and won't be back until the 3rd.'

—

'Well, I think I'm going to go in to the lab for a while,' said Gavin once Caroline was settled into her room in the Polwarth flat. He was looking out of the third-floor window at the Christmas trees in many of the windows of the flats opposite while she unpacked her rucksack. He felt that they probably reflected their owners every bit as much as the cars parked in the street below, and mentally matched the artificial black one with the minimalist white lighting to the Audi, while the bushy Norway spruce with its flashing coloured lights went with the Fiat Punto.

'You don't mind, do you?'

'Of course not. I think I'll have a bath, wash my hair, phone home to see how things are, and then have an early night if we're going to be out partying tomorrow. By the way, Gina's invited us to a party at her boyfriend's flat across the street after the fireworks. '

Gavin nodded. 'Sounds good.'

'Don't stay too late,' said Caroline as she saw Gavin to the door.

She reached up and brought his mouth down on hers to give him a long kiss. 'Thanks, Gavin,' she said.

'For what?'

'Being there.'

'Well . . . don't mention it . . . I can be there any time . . . middle of the night no problem, just call me.'

'G'night, Gavin.'

Gavin caught the 27 bus outside the building and sat up front on the top deck. He was feeling good, mainly because of the spontaneous kiss that Caroline had given him, but also because he was now thinking about what she'd said about his experimental results. The cultures *were* displaying the behaviour of treated tumour cells in the body and she was right; this would enable him to investigate the problem in the lab, but only if the effect was real. There was still a big question mark over the change. It might well be due to some artefact, and Caroline could still be right about the Valdevan solution not being as active as before. It had been stored in the fridge, but all drug solutions did go off after a time. The membrane changes suggested that it had still been active but the concentration might have dropped slightly. He would have to make up fresh stuff and repeat the experiment.

The bus slowed to a halt as it joined a long queue of traffic in Gilmore Place. At first, Gavin couldn't see the cause of the problem, but as they inched closer to the junction with Home Street, it became obvious that the pantomime at the King's Theatre was the cause of the tailback. A string of coaches, delivering school children and pensioners' outings to the front doors for the evening performance, was causing gridlock. Gavin smiled at the excited looks on the children's faces as they were herded into reluctant order by accompanying adults. An emotional roller-coaster was in store for them but, in the end, Cinderella would go to the ball, lose her prince, find him again, marry and be happy ever after. The bus driver hit the horn and swore as a small car cut in front of him.

Gavin found the lab cold, dark and unwelcoming. Even the fluorescent lights seemed reluctant to respond and took what seemed an eternity to stutter into life. It made him wonder what the medical school must have been like when gas lighting had been the order of the day, but he quickly reminded himself that a Liverpool paddy wouldn't have had the chance to find out in those far-off times. In fact, he wouldn't have had the chance a few years hence, as the medical school and the hospital next door were moving to a new site on the south side of the city. He liked the old building. Fate had been kind in affording him the opportunity.

He lit several Bunsen burners in an attempt to take the chill off the room and settled down to examine his cell cultures. There had been no change during the course of the day. There was still no sign of cell death, although there was marked pinching of the membranes. With a heavy heart he returned them to the incubator and set about making up a fresh solution of Valdevan. Four hours later he had set up the experiment all over again. He had now used up his entire stock of cell cultures. 'Please God, this time,' he murmured, as he secured the clasp on the incubator door and set about clearing his bench. He spun round as the lab door opened, startling him. It was the night security man.

'Will you be stayin' much longer?'

'No, just going.'

'You've no' had much of a Christmas.'

ELEVEN

Gavin met Caroline in Doctors as arranged. The place was buzzing, as were the streets outside, in anticipation of the city's Hogmanay party. It seemed that the prospect of heralding in the New Year with pop music and fireworks had gripped the imagination of everyone – certainly everyone under thirty. Two taxis drew up outside the pub and disgorged a crowd of young men wearing Scotland rugby jerseys and kilts. As they entered the bar, Gavin noted that three of them were carrying golfing umbrellas. He pondered on the image of a Jacobite with an umbrella.

'Maybe we should start making our way down town,' said Caroline. 'Find a good place to stand?'

'Right,' agreed Gavin, who had little heart for joining the four-deep throng at the bar in the competition to get served again. He gulped down the last of his beer, his insides churning in anticipation of the test to come.

'Perhaps we should go to the loo first? It could be a while.'

Gavin nodded and made sideways progress through the throng, using his trailing arm as an umbilical for Caroline. There was a queue outside the Ladies and Caroline said, 'This could take time. Why don't you make your way to the door when you come out and I'll see you outside?'

It was chilly and there was a definite hint of rain in the air when Gavin came out of the bar, but he found it infinitely preferable to the crush inside. He paced slowly up and down a fifty-metre beat of Teviot Place with his hands in his pockets, before being forced to take refuge in a shop doorway directly opposite the medical school as the rain suddenly started to get heavier. He looked up at the darkened windows and couldn't help but wonder how the new cells were growing, although he didn't know quite what to hope for. If they survived, he would have a phenomenon on his hands – very interesting, but time for investigation was running out fast: the new term started in a week's time. On the other hand, if they died, he still wouldn't know for sure what had gone wrong last time.

Caroline joined him in the doorway, fastening her collar and pulling her hat down over her ears.

Gavin smiled and hugged her. 'Well, what d'you think?' he asked, holding a hand out to feel the rain, which seemed to be slackening again. He looked up at the night sky.

'It was just a passing shower. Trust me,' said Caroline.

Gavin became ever more quiet and withdrawn as they walked towards Princes Street with more and more people joining them along the way, until half-way down the Mound the throng slowed to a slow shuffle.

Caroline noted the tautness in his features when she had to come close to his ear to make herself heard above the noise of the pop concert in the Gardens, which was being relayed to speakers erected at intervals all over the centre of town. 'How are you doing?'

'I'm fine,' Gavin assured her with a forced smile. In truth he would rather have been crossing the Sahara on a pogo stick at that particular moment, but his resolve not to let Caroline see his discomfort remained firm. 'Good band.' He stiffened as someone bumped into him from behind uttering a slurred, 'Sorry, mate.'

'No problem,' said Gavin, now on self-imposed good behaviour auto-pilot.

'Look! I think we can make it through to the railings,' said Caroline. She pulled Gavin off to the left into a space just vacated by an anxious girl leading away her boyfriend who looked deathly pale. 'I told you to stay off the vodka,' Gavin heard her say as they brushed past. 'Now we're going to miss the whole bloody lot because of you . . .'

'Perfect,' said Caroline, stepping up on to the low wall that supported the railings surrounding Princes Street Gardens and gripping a railing with either hand. Gavin cloaked her like a protective shield with his arms stretched outside hers, gripping the railings on either side. All he had to do now was stand here until it was all over. Fear of the unknown in a moving crowd had been taken out of the equation. He even joined in the orchestrated countdown to the New Year when it came, culminating in a lingering kiss from Caroline and a mutual sip of Ardbeg whisky from the hip flask in his pocket as the bells rang out and the sky was split by shooting stars and flashing lights. The noise was deafening but no one needed or wanted to speak as the heavens became a kaleidoscope of ever-changing colour and pattern. Oohs and Aahs were the only language required.

There was a sudden sense of anticlimax when the fireworks came to an end, the noise stopped, and the smell of smoke drifting in the air was the only thing left of what had gone before. Caroline broke the silence. 'That was absolutely fantastic, don't you think?'

'Great,' smiled Gavin, feeling both pleased and relieved to see that Caroline had enjoyed herself. Mission accomplished.

'I suggest we stay put until it gets easier to move.'

Gavin nodded and hugged her shoulders as they turned their attention away from the castle and gardens to rest their backs on the railings and watch the crowd disperse as police barriers were removed to open up arteries in all directions. He felt a sense of inner calm and almost exhaustion as he saw clear areas of pavement appear around him. Concrete had never looked so lovely.

'Well, you did it,' said Caroline.

'Did what?'

'Don't think I don't know how awful that was for you.'

'Nonsense . . . I'm not that keen on crowds but . . .'

Caroline put a finger to his lips. 'Thank you.'

'It was really great.'

'God forgive you.'

'Time to head for your Polwarth party?' Gavin was eyeing up the rapidly emptying streets as people headed off for parties of their own.

Caroline looked at him for what Gavin thought was an unnervingly long time. 'What's wrong?' he asked.

'I don't think I feel much like going to a party.'

'When it comes to bad nights to choose for an early night in Scotland . . .'

'It wasn't so much an early night I was thinking of, just somewhere quiet where we could be alone? What's going on at your place?'

'I think they were all going out . . .'

—

Gavin and Caroline spent New Year's Day together – or what was left of it by the time they got up – visiting Caroline's friends and generally eating and drinking too much. Gavin didn't say a lot. Caroline's friends were almost exclusively medical students and from similar backgrounds. He was aware of one in particular paying her a lot of attention, following her around the room in almost proprietorial fashion as she caught up with what friends had been doing over the break. He was tall and confident and clearly keen on her. Gavin held out the drink he'd been fetching for Caroline.

'Marcus, you haven't met my boyfriend, have you? This is Gavin. He's in cancer research.'

'Really, what particular aspect?' asked Marcus, appearing less than overjoyed at the news.

'Curing it,' said Gavin, shaking hands with Marcus but not bothering to smile.

Marcus seemed unsure. He'd thought it a joke, but on the other hand Gavin wasn't sending out the right vibes. 'Good show,' he said with a quick glance at Caroline. 'I'm sure we'll all be in your debt.'

Caroline gave Gavin a warning look.

'And what are your plans, Marcus?' asked Gavin.

'Any job that pays pots of money, I should think. Cosmetic surgery seems to be the thing.'

'Nice to have a vocation.'

'Oh, er, very good, yes. I suppose I asked for that.' He turned to Caroline. 'Carrie darling, I simply must go and say hello to Katrina . . .'

'Am I in for a bollocking?' asked Gavin, staring straight ahead as Marcus left them.

'I haven't quite decided,' replied Caroline thoughtfully. She took up stance beside him, also staring straight ahead. 'I suppose for you that was really quite restrained . . . but you were rude and Marcus is a friend.'

'I was jealous,' confessed Gavin.

'I know you were. That's why I'm going to let you off, but be warned, I don't want to end up friendless. They may be idiots in your book but they're *my* idiots and I like them. They may have had an easier start in life than you, but now you've joined them on equal terms. We're all privileged here and working-class resentment can be very boring, especially when there's no call for it.'

'Yes, Ma'am.'

Caroline looked at Gavin out of the corner of her eye.

'Time to go?'

'I think so.'

—

Gavin's cells were alive. The discovery, made on the morning of 3 January, left him staring over the top of the microscope at the rain on the lab windows. Something had changed in the experimental conditions that had allowed the tumour cells to survive in the presence of Valdevan, when in the past, they had always died.

'Shit,' he murmured as he leaned back in his swivel chair and crossed his arms. The change in culture medium must hold the key, but he still couldn't see how and he was rapidly running out of time. Such a pity, because he must be so close to unravelling a mystery that had persisted for twenty years. Understanding the nature of a problem was always the first step on the road to solving it and if – and he realised it was a big if – he could explain the changing behaviour of the drug, the end result might well be what the pharmaceutical company had hoped for all those years ago: a drug that specifically attacked cancer cells – the stuff that dreams were made of.

The phone rang and brought him out of his reverie. It was Caroline.

'Well, what happened?'

'They survived.'

'Damn, so it wasn't a low drug concentration after all?'

'Nope.'

'Is that good or bad?'

'I think it's good, and I feel I'm really close to understanding what's going on, but I need a bit more time and that's the one thing I haven't got.'

'It'll probably come to you in the bath and you can run stark naked up and down Dundas Street shouting eureka!'

'If it doesn't, I've got months of bloody biochemistry to look forward to. It's so frustrating. I know I'm that close, and if I can just come up with the reason . . . this could be really big.'

'You could try talking to Frank?'

'I think I've pushed my luck as far as it'll go.'

'It's still worth a try.'

'I'll think about it. Are you going home this weekend?'

'It'll be my last chance before the new term starts. What'll you do?'

'Hit the library and think. Could be my last chance too.'

The Sunday before the start of term had a depressing feel to it. Christmas, with its overtones of warmth and light, imagined stage-coaches and equally imaginary snow, seemed such a long way away, as did New Year with its alcohol-fuelled bonhomie and false prom-ises of new beginnings. What was left was reality, a wet Sunday in January and a biting east wind. But however unpleasant the weath-er, Gavin felt he had to get out. He had spent nearly every wak-ing hour of the weekend in the medical library, reading up on the kinetics of tumour cell growth – a task made even more unpleasant by the fact that the heating in the library, like all the other univer-sity buildings, had been turned off until the start of term. He had learned a lot about cell growth, but nothing that had shed any light on the Valdevan problem.

Now, clad in lightweight waterproof overtrousers and a hooded top, he set out to walk along the banks of the Union Canal. He wanted nothing but the sky above him and the smell of wet winter grass in his nostrils.

He started at the canal basin at Lochrin where in a different century, according to the tourist info he'd read, horse-drawn barges had come into the heart of the city from the west along a route excavated by mainly Irish labourers. Among them had been Burke and Hare, the infamous body-snatchers who had once supplied Professor Robert Knox and the university's anatomy department with cadavers taken from fresh graves under cover of darkness, but later, as demand outgrew supply, with the corpses of those they had murdered to keep up the supply.

Gavin found himself enjoying the walk. The bad weather had kept Sunday strollers, joggers and lycra-clad cyclists at home, and apart from the occasional intrepid dog walker, he met no one along the way. The going was easy as the Union Canal followed a contour line without the need for locks and level changes, and the wind coming from behind kept his hood up without the need to struggle with cords and toggles. There was even a lightness in his step as he thought about Caroline and how their relationship had grown.

He still couldn't believe his luck. Despite what she said about their priorities being to get their degrees, he was convinced that Caroline was the woman he wanted to spend the rest of his life with. They would be happy and successful and have lots of children. He'd take them on long walks and play games with them – not the ones he'd played in Liverpool's back streets, but proper childhood games like the ones in all the nice story books . . . like the one with sticks, he thought, as he came to a bridge over the canal at Redhall . . . Poohsticks, that was it.

Looking round to make sure he was alone, he decided to give it a go. He gathered some twigs from below the hedges at the side of the towpath and snapped them into little bunches before climbing up the muddy path and on to the bridge. He recognised that this game really required a flowing river, but a canal with a wind on it would have to do. He dropped the first group of four into the water on the windward side and then moved over to the other parapet to await their reappearance.

It took some time, but when the biggest one bobbed into view in the lead, he felt such a sense of achievement at having played Poohsticks for the very first time in his life. After a third race he broke out in a broad smile when he thought what he'd be telling Caroline later when she asked what he'd been doing. He left the towpath where it came close to the road at Sighthill and caught a bus back to town.

TWELVE

Gavin couldn't sleep. His mind was like a busy road junction, only it was information that was the problem, not traffic. A jumble of images and data about tumour cell growth and regulation – much of which he had absorbed at the library over the past few days – was vying for his attention. He had learned a lot in a short time, but the difficulty came in trying to put it into any structured form. He didn't know the nature of the problem so he couldn't decide which bits were relevant or which were not. There was no way round this.

He threw his head from side to side on the pillow, trying to escape the images and find peace of mind, but without success. Poohsticks floated into the troubled mix to drift with the cells that floated before his eyes in a race from one side of a microscope slide to the other. The biggest Poohstick always won, followed by the biggest cell, and then the race started all over again.

In his fitful state, Gavin construed this as survival of the fittest – the fastest and strongest winning – before having to concede that Poohsticks were inanimate: Darwinian rules didn't apply. He didn't know much about sailing, which was about as foreign to back-street Liverpool as three-day eventing, but did seem to recall hearing once that the longer the hull of a boat the faster it would go through the water. He pondered this, before wondering why on earth he was thinking about hydrodynamics in the small hours of this or any other morning. But as soon as he closed his eyes, the cells swam back into view, the big ones nudging the small out of the way – the fastest, the strongest, the fittest . . . That was it!

Gavin sat bolt upright in bed as the pieces of the puzzle fell into place. The eureka moment had arrived. Cell *growth rate* was the key to the whole puzzle. When he'd been forced to change the cell culture medium, he'd made up one that wasn't as rich as the original: it hadn't contained human serum. The cells would therefore have grown more slowly. There was a direct relationship between cell growth rate and size – the slower they grew, the smaller they'd be.

Cells growing in the poorer medium had shown the membrane blips associated with Valdevan. They'd been damaged, but they had survived because they were smaller and therefore . . . more stable. It was as simple as that. He had the key to the riddle. Cells growing in a rich medium would be bigger, so, when Valdevan damaged their membranes, they became unstable and burst. Tumour cells grew slowly in the body compared to cells growing in the lab, so they would be smaller and therefore remain stable too. It all made sense.

The bottom line was that Valdevan didn't kill cells at all; it caused membrane changes which slow-growing cells could accommodate but fast-growing cells could not. This was why it killed cells in the lab but not the body. The S16 gene was not essential: it was a stability problem associated with size that caused cell death.

Gavin turned on the bedside light as everything became beautifully clear. As Trish in the tissue culture lab had pointed out, everyone wanted their cells to grow as fast as possible because they were anxious to get results. The same would have been true for the scientists at Grumman Schalk. They would have used the best culture medium available. If they had tested their drug on slow-growing cells they would have got a completely different result, and possibly saved themselves twenty million dollars.

Gavin wanted to call Caroline and tell her about his discovery, but realised as he picked up his mobile that waking her at three in the morning to tell her why Valdevan hadn't worked might not be such a good idea, particularly as it would involve a short introductory lecture on cell growth and division kinetics before he could deliver the punch line. He got out of bed and shivered as he turned on the fire. He had to write all this down, just in case it still had elements of a dream about it which might not transfer to conscious memory.

On the first Monday morning of the new term, Frank Simmons drove to the medical school feeling relieved that the long break was over. It had been nice to spend time with his family and enjoy his kids' delight at Christmas, but always at the back of his mind was the thought that the research effort had stopped. Now, things could get back to normal. He found people gathered in the corridors, standing in small groups, telling tales of what they'd been doing over the break and exchanging New Year greetings. Cheek-kissing and handshakes were the order of the day. He opened the door of the lab and was surprised to find Gavin there.

Gavin got up, shook hands with him and wished him a happy new year before asking, 'Can we talk?'

Simmons was a little taken aback at the sudden end to small talk. 'Sure,' he agreed. 'Just let me get my coat off . . .' He shrugged off his overcoat and hung it on a hook behind his office door before settling in behind the desk. He crumpled up an old desk calendar and threw it in the bucket. 'Out with the old, eh? What's on your mind?'

'I know exactly why Valdevan didn't work.'

Simmons had to deal with a host of competing emotions ranging from surprise to disbelief. Apart from that, being wrong was never a good feeling. Was it really possible that this boy had succeeded where one of the biggest pharmaceutical companies in the world had failed? He would happily have bet his house against the possibility. He distilled his thoughts into, 'I'm all ears.'

Gavin told Simmons about his experimental work over the

vacation and what he had discovered, ending with, 'So you see, it all makes perfect sense.'

Simmons smiled, conceding that the science had been good and the logic flawless. The pleasure he took from this did much to wipe out the other things he'd been feeling. Scientific truth had a beauty all of its own. 'It does, and I'm sure you're right,' he said. 'Congratulations, that was a first-class piece of work. In fact, it was better than that; it was bloody brilliant.'

'Thanks, Frank,' said Gavin. 'It just sort of fell into place . . .'

'My God, Grumman Schalk will have a fit when they hear about this. How many millions did they flush down the drain?

'Twenty, I think.'

'And that was twenty years ago . . .'

Simmons looked thoughtful for a moment, leaning back in his chair and fiddling with his pen before saying, 'I think you should write this up immediately and chalk up your first publication. My inclination would be to submit to *Antibiotic and Chemotherapy* but we can have a think about that. In the meantime, as you've now shown that knocking out the S16 gene is *not* lethal, there's nothing to stop you reverting to our original plan and working on Valdevan-treated cells. All you have to do is keep the growth rate slow.'

Gavin adopted a slight grimace. 'Actually,' he began hesitantly. 'I was wondering if you might give me a bit more time to work on Valdevan treatment of tumours?'

'But you've just shown why it didn't work and never could,' exclaimed Simmons. 'Game set and match to you. What's left to do?'

'I think there may be some more mileage in it. I'm not sure but I'd really like to do a few more experiments.'

Simmons was doubtful. 'What did you have in mind?'

Gavin, who had not yet formulated a definite plan of action, shrugged uncomfortably. 'I'm not quite sure yet . . . We know that the faster cells grow, the more unstable they become in the presence of Valdevan, and we know that tumour cells grow faster in the body than normal cells, so . . .'

'There's no way on earth you're going to make tumour cells grow as fast in the body as they do in the lab,' interrupted Simmons.

'No, of course not, I accept that – but there just might be some other way to exploit the difference.'

'Like what?'

'I don't know yet . . . I need to get a feel for it.'

Simmons felt sceptical but then said, 'I was about to lecture you again about heading up blind alleys, but that's what I thought last time and I was wrong.' He paused for a moment to assess Gavin's likely disappointed reaction if he turned him down, before saying, 'Look, I'll make a deal with you. If you'll agree to give a seminar to the department about your work, I'll give you three weeks to chase rainbows. Deal?'

'Deal.'

Gavin was talking to Mary Hollis when Simmons returned from lunch. He glanced in Gavin's direction and said, 'I told Jack, Thursday at 1 p.m. if that's all right?'

Gavin nodded.

'What was all that about?' asked Mary.

'I'm giving a seminar, on Thursday apparently.'

'You? A seminar? Now I've heard it all. Is this something to do with a new you or does Frank have some dodgy negatives?'

'Neither. One forty-minute seminar gets me three more precious weeks to work on Valdevan.'

'But you've just told me why it can never work. What are you going to do?'

'Make it work.'

Mary's jaw fell open as she saw Gavin was serious. 'Ye gods, Gavin. You're nothing if not ambitious. Can I ask how, or is that a secret?'

'I haven't worked that out yet,' said Gavin, holding up and examining the plastic bottle he'd just removed from the fridge door. 'In fact, the only thing I'm sure of right now is that I'm going to need more Valdevan. I wonder if Frank would ask his contact. It would be quicker than writing.'

Gavin turned away and left Mary looking after him with an amused smile while he went to make his request to Simmons, who said that he'd actually been intending to call Grumman Schalk anyway. There were things he needed to ask about their new research grants scheme. He'd do it before lunch.

Gavin went on down to the tissue culture suite to wish the staff a happy new year and put in an order for more cell cultures.

'Did you use all the ones I made for you just before the break?' asked Trish.

'Every last one,' said Gavin, 'And like I said, I'll love you forever.'

'And a day,' Trish reminded him.

'And a fortnight if you like. I got some really good results and you'll be top of the acknowledgement list when the paper gets written.'

'Always nice to be appreciated,' said Trish, her cheeks colouring slightly. 'I'll give you a call when your cultures are ready. I take it you need both tumour and primary cells?'

'That would be great.'

Frank Simmons' intended phone call to Grumman Schalk had been precipitated by an internal mail message from Graham Sutcliffe to all academic staff, announcing a meeting on Tuesday to discuss their application for a block grant. Sutcliffe had formulated a draft over the break, but said he wanted to discuss it with his colleagues and add the finishing touches to it before sending it off. Time was of the essence, he stressed. Simmons took this to mean that any discussion would not be lengthy: Sutcliffe was looking for a rubber stamp. He thought that he might have more success in finding out about the conditions attached to such grants by asking Max Ehrman directly about company policy.

Simmons paused as he lifted the phone and wondered for a moment how much he should tell Ehrman about Gavin's discovery. There was a need for tact and diplomacy over it. He didn't know if Ehrman had had any personal involvement in the Valdevan project – probably not, but he wouldn't be human if he didn't feel some embarrassment, and maybe even a little resentment towards a first-year postgrad student who had succeeded where his company and all its resources had failed. He decided he'd have to play it by ear.

Max Ehrman was his usual helpful self, and proved only too happy to fill Simmons in on the conditions attached to his company's new research grants scheme. As Simmons had suspected, the company *would* insist on the final say in whether or not results could be published. Simmons' silence when Ehrman told him this prompted Ehrman to add, 'This hasn't proved to be too much of a problem in the past, Frank.'

'I suppose it's more potential problems I'm worried about.'

'Well, there has to be some degree of symbiosis in all this,' said Ehrman. 'We're not philanthropists and don't pretend to be: we're in the business to make money. On the other hand, we're not monsters either. New discoveries can bring glory to researchers, relief to sufferers and profits to drug companies. Everybody wins.'

'In a perfect world,' said Simmons.

'You worry too much, Frank,' said Ehrman. 'The chances are that such a conflict will never arise, and if it should, it would be resolved without bad blood.'

'Mmm.'

'How is your student getting along, the one who asked us for Valdevan?'

Simmons' pulse rate rose a little and he felt his mouth go dry. 'Fine, very well in fact. As we thought, it seems clear that the drug does target the S16 gene. Actually, I was just about to ask you for some more of the drug if that's possible? Gavin mentioned this morning that he's running low.'

'Of course it is,' laughed Ehrman. 'We're renowned for our generosity here at Grumman Schalk. By the way, I'm going to be coming to Edinburgh shortly. I'm attending the conference at Heriot Watt University at the beginning of February, and I'm also taking part in some TV programme that your BBC are doing. They've asked me to say something about the company's range of anti-cancer drugs. No doubt we will be cast in the role of big bad profit-maker, but we're used to that. I'll do my best to convince them otherwise. Maybe we could meet up at some point and I could talk to your student?'

'Of course. I'll look forward to that. Our department is going to be involved in the programme too,' said Simmons. 'It would be really nice if we could all sit round the table and talk . . . maybe over some dinner?'

'Great. I'll keep you informed about dates.'

Simmons felt relieved. It would be much better to discuss Gavin's work with him present and with everyone face to face in the same room.

A knock came at the door. It was Jack Martin. 'I take it you've had Sutcliffe's letter?'

Simmons nodded.

'Ever felt you were being steam-rollered into something?'

'I phoned Grumman Schalk this morning. If we got the block grant, all research carried out using their funding would have to be submitted to them for approval before we could publish.'

'Just like you thought, so what do we do?'

'Difficult. Sutcliffe wants to empire build and he's really got the hots for Grumman Schalk money. He's dangling the prospect of a couple of personal chairs in front of the senior staff to keep them onside, and the young ones will be keen to grab research money wherever it comes from, so he's virtually got all the backing he needs. Any objections from us will go down like the *Titanic*.'

'So what do we do?'

'Be pragmatic,' sighed Simmons. 'Don't get into a fight we can't win?'

'I suppose,' agreed Martin. 'Maybe brave gestures are best left to the young anyway. Has he said anything about a personal chair to you?'

Simmons shook his head. 'You?'

Martin said not.

'It's my guess he'll want to keep everyone guessing. If he picks two out at this stage he'll figure the rest of us might gang up on him – for the most noble of reasons, of course.'

'You know, for such a nice guy you really have quite an impressive grasp of human nature,' said Martin.

'And it doesn't make for pretty reading.'

'You'll probably find a few more pointers at the meeting tomorrow. Did you tell your Gavin that he's giving the internal seminar this week?'

'I did.'

'You don't think he's going to call off at the last minute with a headache?'

Simmons shook his head. 'If he does, the trade-off gets cancelled. I said he could have another three weeks to work on his pet theories if he gave a seminar to the department.'

'Like I said, an impressive grasp . . . How's his work coming along?'

'Brilliantly; you'll hear all about it at the seminar.'

⁕

Gavin met Caroline at seven and they went to eat at a Mexican restaurant in Victoria Street, starting with margaritas while they waited.

'I nearly called you at three this morning.'

'I'm awfully glad you didn't,' said Caroline. 'What did you want?'

'I worked out why Valdevan didn't work on cancer patients.'

'You're kidding,' said Caroline, pausing in mid-sip and licking the salt off her upper lip. 'You have to be.'

'I'm not.'

'Bloody hell, I'm impressed. Tell me more.'

Gavin explained his discovery over a nachos starter, pausing at intervals to wrestle with strands of melted cheese that were reluctant to part from the bowl.

'It seems so simple now,' said Caroline when he'd finished. 'But then so did DNA once Crick and Watson had worked it out. That was a brilliant piece of work, Gavin, but . . .'

'But what?'

Caroline appeared uncomfortable. 'I really mean it when I say it's a brilliant piece of work, but the bottom line is that you have found out why Valdevan didn't work . . . I mean . . . it still doesn't, right?'

'No,' agreed Gavin. 'But Frank's agreed to give me three more weeks to work on that.'

'Three weeks?'

'To make it over the next hurdle, then maybe he'll give me some more time. That's how I see it.'

Caroline looked at him. 'My God, you're determined. I'll give you that. You've come this far against all the odds and in spite of all the doubters, including me. Sometimes I wonder what I've got myself into.'

'A love affair,' smiled Gavin.

'Is that what it is?' teased Caroline.

'Yep, and it's going to be the longest, most beautiful love affair in the history of love affairs. It will go on to the end of time and our children and our children's children will speak of it long after we are dead and walking hand in hand along the road to eternity knowing we'll be together for ever.'

'Oh well . . . if you say so.'

'I do.'

'Two burritos,' said the waitress.

—

Gavin spent Tuesday going through the Grumman Schalk report again. Although no longer interested in anything they had done, or their reasons for doing it, he was looking for something that might help him decide on the concentration of the drug to use, to induce membrane damage in tumour cells but not in healthy ones. He found what he was looking for in a case report on biopsy material taken from a patient with lung cancer. Under his magnifying lens the photographs clearly showed that the tumour cells were displaying membrane blips, while the adjacent healthy tissue looked unaffected. Gavin noted the patient number and traced his finger down the column of relevant drug levels. Patient 2453F had shown a steady level of 25 micrograms per millilitre of blood. The suffix, F, told him she had been female. 'Thank you, patient 2453F, aged 43,' murmured Gavin. 'RIP.'

THIRTEEN

The weekly internal seminars in the department usually attracted an audience of around thirty – about half of those eligible to attend. It was generally accepted that what was being reported would be of a 'work in progress' nature: 'middles', rather than a complete story with a beginning, a middle and an end. But the programme gave experience in public speaking to the postgraduate students who comprised the bulk of the speakers, although group leaders also participated from time to time, usually giving overviews of their group's work. These tended to be more popular than the 'middles', which really only appealed to those already familiar with the specialised nature of the work being reported.

Today there were over sixty people packed into the small seminar room to hear what Gavin Donnelly had to say. His reputation had gone before him, and ensured that not all of them were there in a supportive capacity. Those who had fallen foul of his quick tongue in the past were attending in the hope of seeing him fall flat on his face.

As usual, the front row was occupied by senior members of staff with Graham Sutcliffe in the centre, legs crossed, interlaced fingers resting on his stomach, a man at ease with his position in the great scheme of things. To his immediate left sat Malcolm Maclean with two of his students, including Peter Morton-Brown. To his right, Frank Simmons and Jack Martin who, as organiser, checked behind him to see that everyone seemed settled before vacating his seat to indicate to someone at the back that the door be closed.

Frank Simmons couldn't take his eyes off Gavin, who was fiddling with his notes and showing signs of nerves as he sat, waiting to be introduced. He hoped to make eye contact with him to give him some gesture of reassurance, but Gavin didn't look up.

Martin cleared his throat and started to speak. 'It's a rather unusual occurrence for us to have a first-term postgrad student speak about his work – most postgrads spend their first term finding a place to stay' – polite laughter – 'but Frank Simmons tells me that Gavin has made such good progress that we should all hear about it. We are therefore delighted to have him here today to tell us what he's been doing.'

Gavin, unused to public speaking, in fact not used to speaking very much at all, started out on a mumbled introduction which was immediately interrupted by someone at the back calling out, 'Can you speak up, please!'

Gavin raised his voice a little, but continued to look down at the floor. 'As I was saying, the main thrust of my research concerns the genes associated with membrane integrity . . .'

'Might one ask why?' interrupted Graham Sutcliffe, his loud, confident voice contrasting with Gavin's nervous delivery.

Simmons felt a sense of alarm. The last thing Gavin needed was constant interruption. He noted that Sutcliffe's lips were smiling but his eyes were as cold as ice, and suspected that it was payback time for Gavin's refusal to participate in the postgrad teaching rota.

'I would have thought that was obvious,' said Gavin, making Simmons close his eyes in trepidation of what might happen next.

Luckily, Gavin seemed to realise that he was walking into the trap that Sutcliffe was laying for him, and sought to move quickly on and limit the damage. 'I mean, there is likely to be a link between the genes affecting cell division and those concerned with membrane growth and integrity. It's a fair bet the processes are co-ordinated.'

'A fair bet . . .' intoned Sutcliffe.

'Don't you think, Professor?'

'I wonder if Copernicus ever thought it "a fair bet" that the earth went round the sun,' said Sutcliffe. The comment attracted a ripple of sycophantic laughter.

'Is it the science or the linguistics you're objecting to, Professor?' asked Gavin, albeit in more controlled tones this time, but he noticed Frank Simmons close his eyes again as if in silent prayer.

'I haven't heard any science yet,' said Sutcliffe coldly.

Simmons prayed that Gavin was not about to suggest that he might if only he shut his mouth and listened.

'Then I'd best begin,' said Gavin. He started reading from prepared text. 'My project concerns the genes which affect membrane architecture. At the outset, my supervisor, Dr Frank Simmons, thought it might be a good idea to mutate one of these, the S16 gene, in order to establish whether or not the gene was essential. If not, we thought we might be able to detect useful differences in cell wall structure in the absence of the gene which might prove useful in an immunological sense. Luckily however, I noticed a paper in a recent edition of *Cell* which made passing reference to the likely mode of action of an old cancer drug named Valdevan. This in turn suggested to me an alternative approach to the project which would obviate the need for employing mutation.'

'That's the cancer drug which never worked?' interrupted Peter Morton-Brown, sounding both smug and loud.

'Sneaky little . . .' murmured Mary Hollis to Tom Baxter, who was sitting beside her three rows from the back. She knew that Morton-Brown had never heard of Valdevan before she told him about it that morning, when he'd stopped to ask her in the corridor what Gavin would be talking about.

'It was the proposed mode of action of the drug that was interesting, Peter, not its therapeutic history,' said Gavin. 'Can I take it you're familiar with the latest thinking about that?'

Morton-Brown had to admit not, his lip twitching uncomfortably between a scowl and a smile. 'Not entirely. . .'

'*Not entirely*,' scoffed Mary, in a whisper.

Gavin, his prepared script now abandoned and his earlier discomfort fading, was gaining confidence with each passing minute.
He explained the action of the drug and how he had applied it to
his work. His enthusiasm for his subject and the facts and figures
he had amassed to support his experimental work were making
things clear to all, even if his Liverpool accent had become more
pronounced than ever with his accelerating delivery.

There were no more interruptions and he concluded with, 'So
you see, Valdevan did not fail for any of the reasons Grumman
Schalk imagined – although it should be said that, at the time, they
didn't, of course, have the knowledge we now have. They took the
only course of action open to them.'

'How very charitable of you, Gavin,' said Sutcliffe, attracting
an irritated look from Frank Simmons. 'You'll pardon me for saying so, but we've known for twenty years that Valdevan didn't work
. . . and now you have worked out why . . . a personal triumph no
doubt, but for the life of me, I fail to see . . . the point?'

Once again, and much to Frank Simmons' relief, Gavin didn't
rise to the bait. He simply said, 'Well, from our point of view, Professor, establishing exactly why Valdevan failed has demonstrated
to us that the S16 gene is not essential. This gives us a possible approach to the problem of distinguishing tumour cells from healthy
cells.'

'But surely that's just where you started out from?' exclaimed
Peter Morton-Brown, adopting an exaggeratedly puzzled expression and glancing at Sutcliffe as if to align himself as an ally. 'Just
thinking about the possibility of using S16 mutants for the study?'

'Apart from the one year we've saved by not having to carry
out mutagenesis, Peter,' said Gavin, delivering a torpedo with a
Liverpudlian accent.

A suppressed titter of laughter ran round the room and Morton-Brown's cheeks coloured.

Jack Martin got quickly to his feet to thank Gavin for 'an extremely interesting talk', and brought the seminar to a close.

Mary Hollis and Tom Baxter came to the front to reassure Gavin that it had gone well, and he was grateful for friendly faces after what had gone before. 'Let's go get some lunch,' suggested Mary.

'As long as it involves beer,' said Gavin.

Simmons watched them depart and was joined by Jack Martin as the room emptied. 'I feel like I've been watching someone walk through a minefield for the past hour,' said Simmons. 'Just waiting for the explosion to happen.'

'He did well, but Graham really was a bastard to him,' said Martin. 'Gavin'll have to watch himself. Graham Sutcliffe could damage his future career if he puts his mind to it. Mind you, your reservations about his block grant proposal the other day didn't endear you to our leader either.'

'He shouldn't take that out on the students,' said Simmons.

'With Gavin, I think it's personal. He's a bit different from the norm . . .'

'I noticed Morton-Brown picking up brownie points. That bloke's turning brown-nosing into an art form,' said Simmons.

'He only succeeded in making a fool of himself. All in all I think your lad did well, and the science was first class. You're entitled to feel pleased.'

'Let's not go as far as pleased. Relieved is just fine. Gavin can be a real loose cannon.'

'He's getting better,' said Martin.

'It's his girlfriend: she's a good influence.'

———

January in Edinburgh was, as always, a cold, dark and almost constantly wet month, which ensured that smiles were hard to find on city streets and people developed an involuntary stoop as they habitually bowed their heads in an attempt to avoid biting winds and icy rain. The prospect of a similar February to come did little to lift spirits but much to support those who cited a lack of sunshine for their general low energy levels and absence of *joie de vivre*.

Gavin spent his three weeks of grace confirming his theory on the link between Valdevan's action and cell growth rate, and verifying that there was a concentration which would damage tumour cell membranes but leave healthy cells unaffected – although his satisfaction in doing this was countered by the fact that he couldn't, as yet, think of a way of utilising it. The confirmation of the growth rate data, however, pleased Frank Simmons and left him feeling more confident about telling Max Ehrman when he arrived in Edinburgh on the Friday of that week. This was two days before the conference at Heriot Watt University was due to begin, but Ehrman had expressed the wish to Simmons that he wanted to see a bit of the city before registration on the Sunday. He had suggested that he come in to the department some time on Friday morning and Simmons had readily agreed, something that Graham Sutcliffe was clearly annoyed about when he found out. He entered Simmons' office without knocking and said, 'Liz has just told me that Professor Ehrman from Grumman Schalk will be in the department on Friday. Why wasn't I informed?'

'It's not any kind of official visit, Graham. He's coming a couple of days early to see the sights and we're going to have a talk about Valdevan. It has no bearing on your grant application if that's what you're concerned about. He wants an update on what we've been doing and wants to meet Gavin.'

'Can't imagine why,' said Sutcliffe *sotto voce*, something that attracted a cold stare from Simmons. 'I still think I should have been informed. Professor Ehrman is a distinguished visitor, whatever the reason for his presence. Perhaps I could invite him to dinner after your meeting.'

'We've already agreed on an informal meal to talk further about cell division.'

Sutcliffe didn't try to hide his annoyance. He was determined not to be stymied. 'I still feel the department should welcome him properly, particularly at a time when Grumman Schalk is set to play an important part in our future and that of the university. Perhaps it's not too late to lay on a lunch up at Old College. I think I'll see what Liz can do.' Sutcliffe turned and left, totally preoccupied with the details of his proposed lunch. Simmons was left sitting at his desk, looking over his glasses at the departing figure who didn't close the door. 'Bonne chance, mon général,' he murmured.

Max Ehrman called on Thursday afternoon to say he would be arriving in Edinburgh on the first shuttle up from Heathrow in the morning. He declined Simmons' offer to pick him up at the airport, preferring instead to make his own way into the city, but said that he would call him from his hotel – the Balmoral in Princes Street – as soon as he got there. When he did, Simmons told him about Sutcliffe's plan to lay on a special lunch for him at Old College.

Ehrman let out a sigh that spoke of frustration with well-meaning people. 'That's very kind of him, but frankly I would have been just as happy with coffee and a sandwich and a chat round the table with you and your student.'

'I'm sorry,' said Simmons. 'That was the way it was going to be until the powers-that-be found out about your visit. I'm afraid it's now out of my hands. Our head of department insists on honouring you.'

'You mean he hopes to help pave the way to a big block grant for his department,' said Ehrman.

'That too,' agreed Simmons.

'Do you think we'll get a chance to talk at all today?'

'It's my guess that the great and the good will take up most of your afternoon, but I could book a table for dinner – just you, me and Gavin, if you haven't had enough of Edinburgh academics by then.'

'I'll look forward to it.'

'Any requests about food?'

'I suggest we let your student decide.'

'Fine. We'll pick you up at your hotel at eight.'

Gavin opted for Chinese so Simmons booked a table at the Orchid Lodge in Castle Street, thinking that it would be within walking distance for both the Balmoral Hotel and Gavin's flat in Dundas Street. He, living out of town, would, as usual, have to drive and not drink, but he'd walk down to the Balmoral from the medical school and then back again after the meal to avoid parking problems in the centre of town.

—

Later that morning, Simmons met Max Ehrman for the first time, in a situation that both of them found slightly bizarre and warranting knowing smiles, as they were introduced to each other by Graham Sutcliffe who had hijacked Ehrman on his arrival and subjected him to a half-hour monologue on the strengths of the department before conducting him on a whistle-stop tour of the labs.

'Hello, Frank,' said Ehrman, extending his hand.

'Nice to meet you, Max. Come and meet my students.'

'Actually, Frank,' interrupted Sutcliffe, looking at his watch with the exaggeration of a bad actor, 'We're rather pushed for time. Maybe later?' His hand was already on the door handle.

'As you wish,' said Simmons coldly. 'Mustn't let the soup get cold.'

Sutcliffe shot Simmons a look of disapproval.

'See you later, Frank,' said Ehrman as he turned to leave, his awareness of tension in the room bordering on slight embarrassment.

Gavin was still in the lab at seven thirty so he and Simmons walked down town together, cutting along Chambers Street to join North Bridge – another connecting link between the Old and New

Towns, which in turn led down to the Balmoral Hotel at the junction with Princes Street.

'So, what's the plan, how do we tell him?' asked Gavin.

'We tell Professor Ehrman that his company wasted twenty million dollars . . . with great tact and diplomacy, Gavin,' said Simmons. 'Rubbing his nose in it is a definite no-no. Can we agree on that at the outset?'

'Sure.'

The doorman at the Balmoral, wearing some marketing man's idea of traditional Scottish dress, opened the door for them, but gave Gavin the once-over as he passed by, his carefully honed powers of observation taking in that Gavin's denims were more functional than trendy.

Ehrman was waiting for them in the lobby. His jeans *were* trendy, a fact the designer label endorsed, and his soft leather blouson had *expensive* written all over it. 'You must be Gavin,' he said with a smile. 'Good to meet you.' He turned to Simmons. 'Hello, Frank, finally we get to talk, huh?'

'How was your day?' asked Simmons.

'I've had worse. I kind of liked Old College. It carries the weight of its history well and the Playfair Library – well, that was something else. Where are we off to?'

'Gavin decided on Chinese. It's a ten-minute walk to the restaurant.'

They walked west along Princes Street with Ehrman cooing appreciatively about the views of the castle and asking about the Scott Monument, built to commemorate Sir Walter Scott.

'One of Scotland's literary greats, but not as well known as Robert Burns,' said Simmons.

'Now, I've heard of *him*,' said Ehrman. 'Can't say the same about Scott though.'

'At least Scott's intelligible,' said Gavin. 'Burns could be writing in Serbo-Croat as far as I'm concerned.'

'Gavin is English,' Simmons explained in a stage whisper.

'Ah, the English and the Scots . . .'

———

Frank joined Ehrman in a gin and tonic, his rationale being that the measures served in Scottish hotels and restaurants wouldn't push a gnat over the limit when it came to breath tests, but he would still have only the one. Gavin had a bottle of German beer.

'So how have you been getting on with your Valdevan experiments?' Ehrman asked Gavin as he snapped a piece off a prawn cracker.

Gavin stole a quick glance at Simmons who gave him a nod of encouragement. 'Okay. In fact, we've got some news for you.'

'Really?'

Simmons had a mental image of someone lighting a fuse.

'We've found out why Valdevan didn't work all these years ago,' said Gavin.

Ehrman took a sip of his drink and snapped another cracker. 'Oh, yes?'

'It's all to do with growth rate.'

Gavin's enthusiasm took over and he gave Ehrman a comprehensive account of his work and the conclusions he'd reached.

'Well, well, well,' said Ehrman when he'd finished. 'I don't know whether to laugh or cry. It seems so obvious now.'

'Were you involved in the original work on the drug, Max?' asked Simmons.

'It was a good bit before my time but still . . . for the company to be upstaged in this way . . . is a bit embarrassing to say the least.'

'There was a big element of luck in it,' said Gavin. 'If I hadn't been working out of term and the lab hadn't run out of human serum there would have been no need for me to make up a new growth medium, and I would never have stumbled across the truth.'

Ehrman smiled wryly. 'A familiar story. Be in the right place at the right time . . . and the prize will be yours.'

Simmons nodded. 'I think Gavin's being too modest. He's a bright, dedicated student who chose to work through the Christmas break when others were out having a good time – including me, I have to say.'

'Well, it's all water under the bridge now,' said Ehrman. 'The company recovered from that painful episode to regain its place as a world leader and, with the latest initiative, we aim to be a major force in supporting medical research in European and American universities. As for you, Gavin, I've just been discussing with your head of department our continuing requirement for bright postdoctoral workers. I should think in time your credentials might prove . . . irresistible to us. What say you, Frank?'

They all laughed and Simmons was relieved that such a difficult bridge had been crossed. He was particularly pleased that Gavin had handled things so well. He had stuck to the science and the logic behind it in as cold and dispassionate a way as he could have hoped for. Ehrman, to his credit, had not made any attempt to dispute the results, accepting immediately that Gavin's hypothesis was beyond argument. He could now enjoy his dinner. In fact, they all enjoyed their dinner, and had what they would remember as a very pleasant evening.

The three men parted company at the foot of the Mound. Gavin headed north to Dundas Street, Ehrman east to the Balmoral and Frank south, up over the Mound, to the medical school car park.

Gavin called Caroline as soon as he got in, as they had arranged.

'Well, how did it go?'

'Really well. I think Frank was a bit nervous, but the big bad wolf from the drug company just accepted it all as "water under the bridge", to use his expression.'

'I'm so glad.'

'He more or less offered me a job when I'm through here.'

'Brilliant. How do you feel about that?'

'Not for me.'

FOURTEEN

On the following Monday, Gavin started out on the biochemistry of cells treated with Valdevan. He had little heart for it, but a deal was a deal.

The department was unusually quiet because of the conference at Heriot Watt, with staff sneaking out at intervals to cross the city and attend only lectures they were interested in, rather than register – and pay – for the whole conference programme. Frank Simmons had gone along to hear a talk on growth kinetics given by Professor Hans Lieberman from the Max Plank Institute in Berlin and Mary had joined him, leaving Gavin alone in the lab until Tom came back from a meeting that Sutcliffe had called for all senior postgrad students.

'What was all that about?' Gavin asked.

'Grumman Schalk are on an early recruiting drive. They're signing up postdoctoral workers for next year. Sutcliffe was asking if anyone was interested.'

'Are you?'

'I didn't think I was until I heard the salary they were offering, then I was very interested. I've put my name down.'

'Anyone else keen on what Mammon has to offer?'

'Peter Morton-Brown and a couple of others said they'd give it some serious thought.'

'You're selling your soul,' said Gavin.

'If it turns out you don't have one, that could be a pretty good deal,' replied Tom. 'Besides, there's not much room on the moral high-ground for the likes of me, with you occupying it all the time.'

'Ouch,' said Gavin, but he smiled and asked, 'How many are Grumman taking on?'

'Sutcliffe seemed to think about twenty.'

'Then you should have a good chance.'

Tom smiled and said conspiratorially, 'Between you and me, Professor Ehrman told Sutcliffe that it's pretty much in the bag. Good salary, new labs, nice working conditions, lots of fringe benefits. I can't believe my luck.'

'But can you really see yourself wearing a suit and driving a Mercedes, Tom?' asked Gavin, tongue in cheek.

'Damn right.'

The conference at Heriot Watt finished on Tuesday evening so the department filled up again on Wednesday and was positively crowded by the afternoon, when the BBC arrived to discuss details of their planned programme, along with the scientists from other universities and institutes who would be taking part and who had stayed on after the conference. The large meeting room with its table for thirty people had been pressed into use with Graham Sutcliffe at its head. For the BBC, the producer of the programme, two production assistants, two presenters and camera and lighting advisors were present. Sutcliffe had invited all his senior staff and they had been joined by Professors Gerald Montague from the University of Leicester, Rosie Kilbane from the Medical Research Council labs in Cambridge and Donald Freeman from the Cancer Research Campaign in London, along with Max Ehrman from Grumman Schalk. Three others were to join in by live video link: a consultant radiologist from the Radcliffe Infirmary in Oxford, an expert in chemotherapy, and a consultant in palliative care from one of the large UK hospices. Representatives from the Department of Health would be interviewed separately to give their views on current cancer care initiatives.

Sutcliffe got to his feet and formally introduced the scientists. The BBC producer, Steve Paxton, a short man in his late thirties with a high forehead, and wearing glasses with brown and white striped frames which Simmons felt were being worn to divert attention from his lack of height, did likewise for the programme makers before going on to give an outline of what he thought the programme might reflect. 'We all know that great strides have been made in the field of cancer treatment in the past few years. What we would like you folks to do is spell out for the benefit of the man in the street just what they are and what their significance will be to cancer sufferers in the short, medium and long terms.'

'A toughie,' murmured Simmons to Jack Martin.

'Pity the poor bugger who gets the short term,' Martin whispered back.

'Well, how long have you got?' exclaimed Gerald Montague. 'I think we could go on all night about the strides we've been making in terms of our understanding of the disease and the wide range of approaches we are pursuing. I'm sure the same applies to the clinicians and radiologists when it comes to treating the disease. Radiotherapy can now be given with pinpoint accuracy and new drugs which extend life expectancy are coming on to the market all the time . . .'

Frank Simmons, who had been prepared to sit through Montague's 'act' in silence, adopting his usual neutral but polite expression, suddenly found that what he was hearing was pushing him over the edge. He conceded that it might have had something to do with the way he had been feeling about cancer research in general for the past few months, or maybe even Gavin's less than complimentary views about the man in particular, but he found that he couldn't take any more. He got to his feet and interrupted. 'But they don't cure the disease. They extend the course of it. They *permit* the patients to suffer for longer.'

Simmons spoke loudly and clearly, but he could feel the pulse beating in his neck. He waited until the hubbub died down and a heavy silence had enveloped him like a cold, wet mist before continuing. 'The truth of the matter is that after all these years, we still really don't understand cancer that well and we certainly can't cure it.'

Gerald Montague took on an air of righteous indignation. 'Personally, I find that an extremely negative view of things and even downright insulting to the many excellent scientists who dedicate themselves to the cure of this dreadful disease,' he said.

'Hear, hear,' agreed Graham Sutcliffe.

Steven Paxton appeared bemused. 'I'm sorry. I suppose I assumed that the programme would automatically reflect a positive attitude. I didn't realise there was disagreement. We hear such a lot about breakthroughs these days.'

'They're usually diagnostic,' said Simmons flatly. 'Medical science can tell you sooner that you have an incurable disease, but still can't do anything about it.'

'But . . .'

'Science, like so many other professions these days, has discovered that image can triumph over substance and is a damned sight easier to generate. Many scientists are dressing up largely technical progress as 'breakthroughs', when they are not what the public understand by 'breakthroughs', and certainly not what disease sufferers understand by the term. They announce their findings and hit all the right buttons so the press will pick up on it, but if you look carefully at the text, you'll come across give-aways like *Work is at a very early stage* and *Hopefully within three to five years this will lead to improved treatments* – three to five years being the average span of the new research grant that they are really angling for – and the chances are that it won't.'

'What an utterly cynical view,' said Sutcliffe.

'I call it realistic.'

'I agree with Frank,' said Jack Martin, attracting a look of gratitude from Simmons, to whom the rest of the room now appeared hostile. 'Real progress when it comes to cancer has been extremely limited.'

'Are either of you willing to put this point of view across on the programme?' asked Paxton. There was another deathly silence in the room.

'No,' said Simmons. 'It was never my intention to take part in the programme. I have nothing positive to report, but I felt compelled to try and put the brakes on those who would have the public believe that a cure is just around the corner. It isn't. On the other hand, I recognise that being negative could be as damaging to patient morale as being absurdly positive without cause. It would serve no point to say what I really think on air.'

'Then I would have thought that your being here any longer serves no purpose,' said Sutcliffe, clearly angry at what had gone before.

Both Simmons and Martin left the room.

'You might have warned me you were going to do that,' hissed Martin when the door closed behind them.

Simmons shook his head. 'I'm sorry, Jack. I didn't mean to. It was just that Montague hitting the bullshit button so soon really got to me.'

'You didn't make many friends in there.'

'I don't care,' said Simmons. 'I feel better, as if I'd just owned up to something that's been bugging me for ages and now I'm out in the open about it. Incidentally, I'm grateful for the way you backed me up.'

'You can't argue with the truth. Catch you later.'

Simmons watched Martin walk off before returning to the lab, collecting his things and going home. He told the others in the lab that he wasn't feeling well – not untrue, although there was nothing *physically* wrong with him.

Jenny was having a sandwich for lunch after her morning stint at the surgery and was sitting in the kitchen when he got in. She was flicking through the previous weekend's copy of a Sunday supplement.

'Smug bastards,' she said. 'Look at them, sitting on their cream leather sofas on their reclaimed wooden flooring, looking pleased with themselves, bleating about the old mill they've just rescued which has been lying derelict since the fifth century BC.'

'I get jealous too,' said Simmons.

'So what are you doing home at this time?'

'My tongue ran away with me.'

'Oh dear. Dare I ask?'

Simmons told her what he had said at the meeting and Jenny shrugged, 'Well, it was true, wasn't it?'

'I think so.'

'So what's to feel bad about?'

'Nothing, I suppose, when you put it that way. I was expecting you to give me a lecture about learning to live in the real world and keeping my mouth shut where authority is concerned – like you keep saying Gavin should do.'

'There's a world of difference between expressing genuine concern and what Gavin comes out with simply because he has a chip on his shoulder about being working class in a middle-class environment.'

'Strikes me he's getting better and I'm getting worse.'

'You'll probably end up meeting in the middle and becoming lifelong buddies.'

'Gavin's okay. Different, but okay.'

'Yes, dear. Did anyone support you this morning?'

'Jack Martin.'

'Good for him. I'm surprised you didn't go off to the pub with him instead of coming home.'

'Maybe it's a different kind of comfort I'm looking for . . .' said Simmons. He reached out and caressed the outline of Jenny's bottom as she stood with her back to him.

'Oh, is it?' she said, not sounding entirely averse to the idea.

Simmons squeezed her bottom.

'Will you buy me an old mill and furnish it with leather sofas and reclaimed wooden flooring?'

'Yes.'

'Liar,' giggled Jenny. 'Whatever happened to the high moral values of a moment ago?'

'A regrettable lapse,' replied Simmons, getting to his feet and escorting her towards the stairs.

———

Gavin finished the first part of the biochemistry protocol he was following and put the beaker containing his cell preparation in the fridge. It was just after four o'clock so he thought he'd take a chance and phone Caroline.

'What are you doing?' he asked.

'Conception,' she replied.

'What?'

'Conception, growth and development. I've got an exam tomorrow.'

'Oh, I see. I'm just clearing up. I thought you might fancy a coffee?'

'Could do, I could do with a break, but then I'll have to spend the rest of the evening on this stuff.'

'Let's go up to that little café in the High Street – the one that does the good scones?'

Caroline agreed, and they arranged to meet in ten minutes outside the medical school. It was another ten-minute walk to the café and Caroline was rubbing her hands in deference to the cold by the time they arrived. 'Hope it's warm in here,' she said as she gripped the door handle.

It was, and the air was full of the comforting smell of home baking. Only two of the ten or so tables were occupied, one by an elderly couple who had kept on all their outdoor clothing, including hats and scarves, and the other by a mother with a two-year-old sitting in a push-chair beside her. She was keeping the child amused by blowing bubbles from a toy that comprised a plastic battery-operated fan and a small tub of soap solution. The child squealed with delight each time a stream of bubbles left the soap-filled loop. Gavin and Caroline found the laughter infectious: Gavin pretended to try to catch the bubble that drifted briefly in his direction and caused yet more laughter as he feigned complete incompetence.

A waitress, who seemed immune to childish laughter and to whom smiling would have required maxillofacial surgery, brought a tray with their coffee and fruit scones on it and laid it down without comment. Gavin made a face behind her back and the child giggled.

'You'd cause trouble in an empty house,' said Caroline.

Gavin munched on his scone. 'Don't know what you mean.'

'What's been happening?'

The BBC was in the department, talking about some cancer programme they're planning.'

'Is Frank going to be in it?'

Gavin shook his head. 'He was asked, apparently, but declined – said he's got nothing worth reporting.'

'So who has?'

'Ain't that the big question?' replied Gavin. 'There were plenty of big names around.' He paused to make a funny face at the child, who had been strapped into his pram and was being wheeled to the door. 'As for big results . . . it's my guess the big discoveries will all be round the next corner as usual. And like tomorrow . . . they'll never come.'

'You'll change all that,' said Caroline.

'I love you,' said Gavin.

'I love you too, but right now I have to get down to some serious study of the process of conception if I'm to pass this exam tomorrow and move on to neurological and musculoskeletal.'

'Well, if I can be of any assistance in the study of conception . . .'

'Watch it.'

As they walked back to the medical school, Caroline said, 'You like children, don't you?'

'I suppose. What made you say that?'

'The child in the café.'

'He was a lot more fun than the waitress. Did you see the look in his eyes when he saw the bubbles? I like that, a mixture of joy and wonder. You don't see it in adults. Too many other things pop up in their heads at the same time – it's a trick; it's a trap; there must be a logical explanation.'

'I liked the expression on his face when you tried to catch them.'

'When there was more chance of catching the moon.'

'But he thought you could do it.'

Gavin stopped walking and stared straight ahead.

'What's the matter? . . Gavin, what's the matter?'

'The bubbles . . .'

'What about them?'

'The bubbles were so fragile that they ruptured at the slightest contact. If something came along to disrupt an already damaged membrane . . . the cell might rupture and die . . .'

'Gavin, would you please tell me what you're talking about, instead of behaving as if you're getting messages from Mars?'

Gavin looked at her, but still seemed distant and preoccupied. 'Valdevan causes damage to the cell membrane. These little blips could be vulnerable areas: they might cause the cells to explode like the bubbles did if they came into contact with . . . something . . . but only the cells that had them would die. There's a concentration of Valdevan which only produces blips in tumour cells. We might be able to kill these cells off without damaging the healthy ones!'

'Wow,' said Caroline. 'But cells aren't soap bubbles.'

'In effect they are. They have a thin phospholipid membrane that keeps them intact despite the fact they are under quite a bit of internal pressure. If anything should rupture the membrane they'll explode.'

'But how would you make them . . . explode?'

Gavin wrapped his arms round her and said, 'That's what I have to find out.' He kissed her forehead and ran off, saying that he was going to the medical library. He'd call her tomorrow. 'Good luck with the exam!'

After four hours of flitting between internet searches on the library computer and the pharmaceutical bookshelves, Gavin decided that cationic detergent drugs – in particular the polymyxins – might be his best bet for some initial experiments, but his problem might be getting his hands on some. He had two choices. One, he could confide in Frank Simmons and hope that he might be enthusiastic enough to let him order some on the lab grant and carry out preliminary work on the idea or, two, he could try to obtain some on his own and perform a couple of trial experiments at night before he said anything to anyone. He thought the latter possible because he had just read that polymyxin was not only used as a drug, it was also used by microscopists as a spreading agent. There was a good chance that the microscope lab downstairs in the medical school might have some.

FIFTEEN

Gavin was standing outside the locked double doors of the microscopy suite in the medical school when Norman Singleton, the chief microscopy technician, arrived. 'Samples for EM?' he asked. 'There's a basket just round the corner. You can leave them there with a request form.'

'No, I'm on the scrounge,' said Gavin. 'I need some polymyxin. I thought you guys might have some?'

'You just might be in luck there,' said Singleton, unlocking the doors and leading the way inside. Gavin followed him through the reception area and across a green-lit room where two electron microscopes sat like periscopes rising from their control desks.

'Through here,' said Singleton, leading the way into a smaller lab where two expensive-looking Zeiss light microscopes sat side by side on a bench, one with a conventional, tungsten light source attached, the other emitting a violet glow from the UV lamp secured to its base. 'I used some recently for a nuclear prep I did for the Jackson group. Here we are,' he said, opening a fridge door and taking out a small bottle. 'polymyxin B. How much do you need?'

Gavin shrugged his shoulders. 'Not sure to be quite honest. Depends if it works for what I have in mind.'

'Why don't you take the bottle?' suggested Singleton. 'We don't use the stuff a lot. If I need it, I'll get back to you.'

Gavin was whistling when he reached the lab. This drew a disapproving look from Tom Baxter and the comment, 'God protect me from happy people. What have you got to be so cheerful about?'

'Guess I'm just a happy-go-lucky sort of a guy,' said Gavin.

Mary and Tom exchanged glances of exaggerated disbelief.

'Or maybe . . .' Gavin paused while he took out the cell preparation from the previous day from the fridge, 'it's just the prospect of biochemistry for the next six months that's pushing me over the edge . . .'

The other two seemed more comfortable with this suggestion.

Gavin slipped the polymyxin B inside a plastic box in the fridge with his name scrawled in marker-pen on the lid and closed the door. Periodically throughout the day, when he had a lull in the biochemistry protocol he was following, he would gather things together for the evening's work ahead. He had cell cultures of both tumour and normal cells growing in the incubator: he had Valdevan and polymyxin and he had a good supply of sterile glassware.

The excitement he felt at the prospect of stepping into the unknown caused several more outbreaks of whistling throughout the day, before night fell and people started to go home.

'Going to be here long?' asked Mary as she put on her coat.

'Another hour or so,' replied Gavin. 'Everything takes so long with biochemistry.'

'It'll be worth it in the end.'

Tom had already left for a dental appointment. Frank Simmons was the next to leave at a quarter to six. 'How's it going?' he asked as he came out his office with his coat on and carrying his briefcase.

'No problems, pretty straightforward really. It's just the waiting between reactions that's the bummer . . .'

'It was ever thus,' smiled Simmons. 'Take my advice and buy a book of crossword puzzles. You'll get pretty good at them before the project's over.'

Gavin smiled and felt a tingle of excitement as the door closed and he was finally alone in the lab. He brought out the drugs from the fridge and made up sterile solutions – seeing it as the first step on the road . . . to what? But this was why he'd gone into research. This was the tingle that said it was the best job in the world. Ultimately, it would be researchers who would uncover the secrets of life on earth. It would be they who'd uncover the meaning of it all – where we came from, where we were going and, even more importantly, why. As far as Gavin was concerned, every other job on the planet was just part of a network of service industries, required only to keep the machinery of discovery moving along.

There was a limit to how much he could do on this, his first evening. It was more a case of getting things up and running, but taking the first step of any journey was exciting. Before he could test the action of polymyxin on tumour cells he would need a supply of them, treated with Valdevan and displaying the characteristic membrane blips. This would take a couple of days, but they should be ready by the weekend when the lab would be quiet and he would have more time to experiment without anyone asking what he was doing. Everything was up and running by eight thirty. The Valdevan-treated cells had been placed in the incubator and a range of polymyxin solutions sat in the fridge.

He would have enough in the way of cell cultures for the initial experiments, but would have to order up some more from Trish for the next stage. The tumour cells, which he was also using for the biochemistry, would not pose a problem. Ordering up supplies of normal cells might raise an eyebrow or two when the monthly grant accounts came in, but he would cross that bridge when he came to it. In any case, he would have his results by then.

He called Caroline to ask how her exam had gone.

'Okay, I think,' she replied. 'I must have taken in more than I thought.'

'Look, I'm sort of assuming you're going home this weekend?' he added tentatively.

'Sounds like you're planning to work,' said Caroline, but not unkindly. 'But yes, I think I will. I'll be starting a new module next week so it's probably a good time to go. How did it go this evening?'

'Things are up and running but it'll take a couple of days before the cells are ready to test. That's what I'll be doing at the weekend.'

'God, it would be so fantastic if it worked.'

'Fingers crossed.'

———

Gavin was in the lab by 6 a.m. on Saturday morning when he knew it would be quiet. Others – mainly grad students – would come in and out throughout the day to check on experiments and set up cultures, but that probably wouldn't start happening until after ten. Student Saturdays usually started with hangovers. His heart was in his mouth when he took out the Valdevan cultures and examined them under the inverted microscope, but everything was fine. He could see the membrane blips.

It was time for the moment of truth. He took the polymyxin solution from the fridge and filled a small syringe, knowing exactly how much he was going to inject because he'd done the calculation in his head a hundred times since Wednesday. He pressed the plunger and rocked the tube gently to and fro before placing it back under the scope.

'Sweet Jesus,' he exclaimed as he watched the tumour cells rupture and die before his eyes. Within seconds he was left with little more than rafts of cell debris drifting across his field of view among the ghosts of the membranes which had once contained it. 'I don't believe it,' he murmured. 'Things this good don't happen to me . . .'

Gavin controlled his impulse to get up and dance around the lab but recognised that he had only cleared the first hurdle. The Valdevan-treated cells were wonderfully sensitive to damage by polymyxin but the question now was, were they more sensitive than normal cells? If healthy cells should behave in the same way, there was nothing to get excited about and it would all be a wild goose chase, but polymyxin-based drugs had been used in the past to treat bacterial infections without any report of tissue damage, although they had shown other toxic side effects – the reason their use had largely been confined to topical application in modern times.

First, he would establish the minimum concentration of poly-myxin necessary to kill tumour cells. He brought out another cell culture and this time injected it with a smaller dose – half the previous concentration, but the result was the same. Keeping a grip on his emotions was proving more and more difficult as he halved the concentration yet again and still saw immediate signs of cell death. Surely healthy cells could not possibly behave this way in the presence of so little drug?

Gavin couldn't resist finding out any longer. He fetched one of the primary cell cultures from the incubator and injected it with the smallest dose of polymyxin he'd used so far. There was absolutely no reaction: the healthy cells remained completely unaffected.

He was aware of the thump of his heart as he doubled the concentration and got the same result. 'Bingo!' he exclaimed. There was a big difference between the sensitivity of tumour cells and normal ones. Right now, he could do what no one else in the world could do. He could specifically target and kill cancer cells.

He allowed himself to ponder this for more than a minute, savouring the moment and revelling in the feeling of achievement, before looking for reasons not to believe his results. He couldn't think of any off-hand, although he did recognise that this was lab science and still might not translate into the treatment of patients, but this was a dream start.

He couldn't resist carrying out one more 'show-biz' experiment before going back to the discipline of establishing the minimum dose of polymyxin necessary to kill cancer cells. This was to mix tumour and normal cells together in the same test tube and add polymyxin. It worked like a dream. The tumour cells with the membrane blips died: the healthy cells without the blips did not.

Gavin called Caroline on her mobile. 'Where are you?'

'Waverley station. Where are you?'

'In the lab. It works! I can kill tumour cells without damaging healthy ones.'

'Oh, Gavin, I'm so pleased for you. That is bloody brilliant,' exclaimed Caroline. 'I'm so sorry for ever doubting you.'

Gavin found himself competing with the station announcer who was announcing a London train departure. 'It works like a dream!' he shouted.

'That's absolutely wonderful, Gavin. I'm so glad for you. Call me later and tell me all about it. Oh, I'm so pleased for you, Gav. Got to run; my train's leaving.'

'Love you.'

'Love you too.'

Gavin got up from his seat, clenched his fists together, looked up at the ceiling and yelled out, 'Bloody brilliant!'

'What is?' asked Mary Hollis as she came in through the door.

Gavin was overcome by embarrassment. 'I just got a good result,' he stammered.

Mary looked puzzled. 'Already? You only started the biochemistry on Monday.'

Gavin's silence brought a suspicious look to Mary's eyes. She saw the cell cultures sitting on Gavin's bench. 'You're not still working on Valdevan, are you?' she asked in disbelief.

Gavin shrugged. 'Just at evenings and weekends,' he tried, with a mock apologetic look, and Mary smiled. 'Gavin, you really are something else.'

'I'm just curious.'

'So what's so "bloody brilliant" or shouldn't I ask?'

Gavin looked at her for a moment as if undecided whether to

say anything or not. 'I think I know how to kill tumours without harming healthy tissue.'

This seemed a bit much for Mary who sank down into her seat. 'Just like that,' she said. 'You're telling me you can cure cancer?'

Gavin made a face. 'Seems like it.'

'Well, don't keep me in suspense. Tell me!'

Gavin outlined what he had been doing and showed her the cultures he'd been looking at.

After a couple of minutes Mary looked up from the microscope and said, 'I'd like to say something like, *it's far too soon to be sure*, or *you're reading far too much into this*, but I can't. This is absolutely fantastic: there's no other word for it. Does Frank know about this?'

'Not yet, I wanted to be sure of my ground. 'I've got a few more things to check out. I'll speak to him first thing on Monday.'

'You do realise that if this works *in vivo*, it's going to be the biggest single advance in cancer treatment . . . ever?'

'It may have crossed my mind,' said Gavin.

'Sorry,' said Mary. 'Of course you know it. What a bloody stupid thing to say.'

Gavin smiled affectionately at her. 'Don't apologise. You're one of the good guys.'

'The whole scientific world will be queuing up to be your friend,' said Mary. 'And Graham Sutcliffe will be leading the applause.'

Gavin laughed out loud at the notion. 'That'll be worth seeing on its own. So, why are *you* here this morning?'

'I'm looking for a bit of peace and quiet to write up my paper. My flatmates had other ideas.'

'I'll only be here for another half hour and then I'll leave you in peace,' said Gavin.

'I'm really pleased for you, Gavin.'

Gavin could see that she meant it. He smiled and nodded and then, after a moment's hesitation, he went over to her and kissed her on the cheek. 'Thanks for being so nice to me.'

Mary smiled at the clumsiness of the gesture.

Gavin finished establishing the minimum dose of polymyxin needed to kill tumour cells and cleared his bench. Life was good. It was to get even better on Sunday evening when Gavin met Caroline off the train and she told him that her mother had entered a period of remission. She had been in good form at the weekend and was almost back to being her old self. 'God, it was so nice to hear her laugh again. She always could be so funny. She has a wicked tongue when she puts her mind to it.'

Caroline picked up on Gavin's muted response and said, 'All right, I know it's just a pause in the nightmare and it will come back, but it was just so good to see her without that terrible barely suppressed bitterness for once. It seemed like . . . we were friends again.'

They went back to Gavin's flat where he served up spaghetti bolognese and a bottle of Valpolicella he'd bought from Safeways.

'Why don't we get a flat together?' asked Gavin when they had finished.

Caroline shook her head. 'We're fine the way we are. If we move in together we'll have all the baggage that goes with that – laundry, bills, who does this, who does that – I don't think I could cope with all that right now. Doesn't mean to say I don't love you.'

'That's all that matters.'

—

Frank Simmons noticed Mary and Gavin deep in conversation when he came into the lab. Both turned and said 'Good morning', before apparently having trouble suppressing laughter over something. He closed the door of his office, thinking that laughter was good in the lab. It was the pained silence that followed squabbles that was the enemy of progress. He sat down and started opening his mail when a knock came at the door and Gavin came in.

'How was your weekend, Frank?'

'Crap, if you must know. Our babysitter didn't turn up on

Friday night so Jenny was in a bad mood all day Saturday. We took the kids to a country park on Sunday and they squabbled all the way there and all the way back. Domestic bliss. How was yours?'

'You can do what?' exclaimed Simmons when Gavin told him about his weekend work.

'I can kill cancer without damaging healthy tissue. All you have to do is pre-treat the tumours with Valdevan and this makes them hypersensitive to cationic detergent drugs like polymyxin.' Gavin explained his rationale for trying this in the first place and his subsequent findings.

'This is absolutely incredible,' exclaimed Simmons. 'If you're right . . . and I'm not suggesting for a moment that you're not . . . this is going to . . . Christ, I don't know.' He threw his hands in the air. 'Revolutionise cancer treatment.'

'Music to my ears,' said Gavin. 'I'm sorry I went behind your back to do the experiments. I just couldn't let it go.'

Simmons waved away the apology with a hand gesture. 'In this case, the end has justified any means used to achieve it. Who have you told about this, Gavin?'

'You, Mary, my girlfriend Caroline, that's about it.'

Simmons nodded. He was finding it difficult to keep his emotions in check. He wanted to dance around the lab.

'What happens now?' asked Gavin.

'That's just what I'm wondering,' said Simmons, tapping the end of his pen on his desk. 'My instinct is to tell Grumman Schalk that their drug, Valdevan, can be a wonder drug after all. What do you think?'

'Seems only fair.'

'Hang on a minute though,' said Simmons, remembering something. 'I don't think you can give patients polymyxin-based drugs any more. They were very toxic as I remember . . .'

'I checked up on that,' said Gavin. 'They were used to treat bacterial infections when they first came out and you're right, they did prove to be very toxic, but the level of the drug needed to kill the tumours is way below the dose needed to kill bacteria. I think there's a good chance that patients won't experience any side-effects at all.'

'You seem to have thought of everything,' smiled Simmons. 'So who's going to tell the company, me or you? I take that back; it should be you. Give Max Ehrman a call. Bloody hell, this is going to be the mother and father of all phone calls.'

'Thanks, Frank.'

'Gavin? What a pleasant surprise. What can I do for you? More Valdevan?'

'Actually, no, I have some news for you, Professor.'

'Max, please.'

'Max, I think it might be possible to use Valdevan after all.'

'I'm sorry? Use Valdevan? For what?'

'To treat cancer, just as you guys hoped all these years ago.'

'Are you kidding? It didn't work then and it doesn't work now, and you were instrumental in showing us why not.'

'I know, but we can exploit the membrane damage it causes in tumour cells.' Gavin went on to explain his findings.

Ehrman seemed stunned. The silence seemed to go on for ever.

'Max?'

'I'm still here. Well, you've really given me something to think about, Gavin. I think I'd like to get back to you later if that's all right. I need to discuss this with my colleagues. But congratulations on an intriguing piece of work.'

Gavin felt deflated. He'd expected a bit more enthusiasm from Ehrman, but told himself that this would probably come later when the company had had time to digest what he'd discovered. Frank

Simmons wasn't in his office when Gavin went to tell him about the call, but he returned shortly afterwards with Graham Sutcliffe in tow. 'I thought you should tell Graham about your discovery,' said Simmons. 'It's going to affect everyone.'

'Sure,' said Gavin, noting again the coldness in Sutcliffe's eyes, although he was affecting a smile.

The three men sat in Simmons' office while once more Gavin went through his work. Simmons looked to Sutcliffe for a response when he was finished.

'Well, I must say, this is all very interesting,' said Sutcliffe, giving the impression that he didn't know quite what to say and needed time to get his thoughts in order – not that this stopped him talking. 'Of course, I need hardly say . . . I must advise caution at this stage. These are lab results . . . and as such, are a world away from the human situation . . . or even animal trials . . . and as you yourselves say, they are also based on two drugs, one of which has already failed and another which has proved to be highly toxic . . .'

'This is a brilliant finding,' said Simmons.

'It's very encouraging,' conceded Sutcliffe.

Gavin watched and listened to the verbal battle without contributing to it. Frank kept trying to ignite the flames of enthusiasm in Sutcliffe, while Sutcliffe kept dousing the fire with negativity.

'This is the sort of thing that should be in your BBC programme. This is real breakthrough material,' said Simmons, still trying to persuade Sutcliffe.

'I take it you have informed Grumman Schalk?' Sutcliffe asked Gavin.

'I've just spoken to Professor Ehrman. He's going to confer with his colleagues and get back to me.'

'Let's wait for that then, shall we?'

Seeing that Gavin was looking a bit down when Sutcliffe left the room, Simmons said, 'The professor comes from a background where showing any kind of emotion is a no-no.'

'Public school tosser,' said Gavin.

'Not exactly what I meant,' said Simmons. 'But perhaps something along those lines.

'Don't let it get to you, Gavin. Both Valdevan and the polymyxin drugs have already been through the trials and licensing process. They don't need to go through it again to be used together or consecutively. It just needs Grumman Schalk to put Valdevan back into production and then the medics can try it out.'

Gavin cheered up noticeably.

'Let me know when Max has been back in touch.'

SIXTEEN

Gavin reappeared in Frank Simmons' office shortly after 4 p.m. He looked ashen.

'What's wrong?'

'I can't believe it. Grumman Schalk say we should forget the whole thing.'

Simmons' mouth fell open. 'You have to be joking.'

'They say that it's probably just a lab artefact and that there's no way they'd ever consider putting Valdevan back into production. Apart from that, they say that treating patients with polymyxin would be a non-starter because of the toxicity. The bottom line is that I should forget the whole thing and "move on".'

'No way,' exclaimed Simmons. 'What the hell are they playing at? Didn't you tell them that it would only be a low dose of polymyxin that would be required?'

Gavin nodded. 'Several times. They didn't seem to want to know.'

'This is crazy.'

A knock came at the door and Jack Martin came in with the new term's seminar schedule. 'Long faces,' he said as he laid a copy on Simmons' desk.

'Sit down and listen to this,' said Simmons. 'We've just had Grumman Schalk's response to Gavin's discovery.'

Gavin told him what the company had said.

'You're kidding,' exclaimed Martin. 'Ye gods, you'd think they'd be jumping down your throat to get something like this up and running.'

'I just don't get it,' said Simmons, getting to his feet and looking as if he didn't know what to do with his arms. 'How can one of the biggest drug companies in the world not be interested in curing cancer?'

'Who did you speak to at GS?' Martin asked Gavin.

'Max Ehrman.'

'Then it wasn't as if you were speaking to the office boy.'

The three men lapsed into silence before Martin suddenly said, 'Wait a minute; how old is Valdevan?'

'I don't know, maybe something like twenty to twenty five years since it first hit the market. Why?' said Simmons.

'It's out of patent!' exclaimed Martin, as if he'd just solved a particularly difficult crossword clue. The others just looked at him.

'I'm trying to think like a businessman,' explained Martin. 'Apart from the obvious difficulties of trying to reintroduce a product that's already failed, the drug's out of patent. That's why they don't want to hear anything about it. Any company could make it now. They've no longer got the monopoly on Valdevan. It's anybody's to manufacture!'

Simmons looked at him incredulously. 'You're saying that they're not interested in a potential cure for cancer because they can't make money out of it?'

'That's about the size of it.'

'What about saving lives? Doesn't that matter to them?'

There was another silence in the room.

'I've heard some stories about drug companies, but this is outrageous. We can't let them get away with this,' said Simmons angrily. 'For God's sake, their whole business is curing disease.'

Martin shook his head indulgently. 'No, Frank, their whole business is making money and keeping their shareholders happy, just like any other commercial concern.'

'Then we'll hunt around and get another company to make the stuff if it's out of patent like you say.'

Martin looked doubtful. 'It's my bet that none of them will touch it. They've got too much to lose. Think about it. What do you think will happen to sales of their current chemotherapy drugs if you go wiping out cancer with a compound that anyone can make? They all stand to lose a bundle. Incurable disease and chronic illness are big earners for the pharmaceutical industry, much more so than any condition they can cure.'

'Couldn't we get the government to make the stuff?' asked Gavin.

'That might be your only hope,' agreed Martin. 'Why don't you guys talk to Unived? They're supposed to be the bridge in this university between academic discovery and the wicked world of commerce, but you'd better keep Graham informed of what you're doing. That's one loop he wouldn't care to be left out of.'

'Thanks, Jack,' said Simmons. 'We'll do that.'

Martin left to continue his rounds with the seminar lists, Gavin returned to the lab and Simmons picked up the internal phone book.

'Unived. How can I help?' asked a pleasant female voice.

'This is Dr Frank Simmons at the med school. I need to speak to someone about some work one of my postgraduate students has been doing.'

'One moment. I'll put you through to Mr Chalmers.'

A pause, then, 'John Chalmers.'

'Mr Chalmers? I'll come straight to the point. I think one of my students has come up with a possible cure for cancer. Can we talk?'

There was another slight pause before the reply came. 'You know, I think I've been waiting all my career for a call like this.'

A meeting was set up for the following morning.

⬥

Simmons and Gavin drove over in Simmons' car to the Unived offices on the university's science campus at King's Buildings. They made the journey in silence, in the aftermath of an early morning meeting with Graham Sutcliffe, who had appeared to be siding with Grumman Schalk. 'It stands to reason that you can't go injecting all sorts of failed rubbish and toxic compounds into people simply because you saw something in a test tube,' he had maintained. 'It's far too early to go over the top about this. There are proper procedures to be followed, permissions to be obtained, trials to be set up.'

Simmons felt he couldn't say what he really thought about Sutcliffe's stance to a postgraduate student, and Gavin kept quiet for similar reasons of protocol, although he did permit himself the occasional sigh and shake of the head as thoughts of the meeting continued to prey on his mind.

John Chalmers, an overweight, avuncular man dressed in a smart suit and tie – in contrast to Gavin and Simmons in their denim jeans and open-necked shirts – welcomed them to his well-appointed office which, as Simmons noticed, was remarkably free of the clutter he was used to in his own office, and where venetian blinds offered striped shade from the morning sunshine. They were served coffee and Gavin was invited to tell all.

'Sounds absolutely wonderful,' said Chalmers. 'A historic moment, you might say. But let me get this straight . . . neither of these drugs is new?'

'They've both been around for a very long time,' said Simmons. 'It's the way of using them that would be new, and the theory behind it.'

'Mmm,' said Chalmers. 'So it's not a new treatment we'd be selling . . . it's a new technique . . . a new idea . . .'

'We're not interested in selling anything,' said Simmons curtly. 'We'd like to see the medics try this out as quickly as possible.'

'Of course you would,' said Chalmers, smiling indulgently as if the two men in front of him were babes in his particular wood. 'But outside your ivory tower, chaps, things are different. Some of us have to live . . .'

'In the real world. Yes, whatever that is,' interrupted Simmons. 'We just want this treatment to be given its chance.'

'Of course, of course, I understand that,' said Chalmers, holding up his hands. 'But you must appreciate that it's my job to protect the university's financial interests in all of this. I would be failing in my job if I didn't put certain safeguards in place. There are a lot of sharks out there.'

Simmons kept his tongue in check and Gavin managed to do the same, although the look in his eyes suggested it might be a close-run thing. 'Of course,' he said.

'It seems to me that even if we have no right to patent any single component of the new treatment, there might well be a case for patenting the intellectual property – the idea if you like – but I'm no lawyer. I'll have to pass this on to my colleagues, but I promise you I'll do this as quickly as possible and get straight back to you. All right?'

'I suppose it'll have to be,' said Simmons.

As they got into the car to drive back to the medical school, Simmons turned to Gavin and said, 'Well done.'

'What for?'

'Not decking him.'

'Only because I thought you were going to,' said Gavin.

It brought the first and only laugh of the day.

It was Wednesday afternoon when Chalmers called back. 'I've just had the report from our legal eagles. They think it might fly, but intellectual property is a tricky area. They're going to have to refer the whole thing to specialist lawyers.'

'Good,' said Simmons. 'How long will this take?'

'Hard to say, but first things first, we need to get university approval for the application. Patent lawyers don't come cheap. I'll have to request the official go-ahead from Old College.'

'Jesus,' sighed Simmons. 'And how long will that take?'

'End of the week if I stress the urgency.'

'I take it you heard that?' Simmons asked Gavin who was sitting in his office. Gavin nodded. 'Good to hear he's going to stress the urgency,' he said flatly.

'Well, we'll just have to grin and bear it. I suggest you go on with your experiments – establish the lowest doses possible of both drugs, and try to calculate the doses necessary to give to patients to achieve these levels. See what you can glean from old papers on polymyxin.'

'Will do,' said Gavin.

'I'm going to try and persuade Graham to incorporate your stuff in the BBC programme. There's nothing like a bit of publicity for concentrating people's minds.'

It was late afternoon before Simmons could see Graham Sutcliffe, who had been acting as co-examiner in a PhD viva exam for one of the students downstairs. On hearing Simmons' request he immediately voiced his reservations again, insisting that publicity would be premature and that proper procedures had to be followed.

Simmons listened politely until impatience overtook him and he interrupted. 'I'm sorry, Graham, but you are missing the point here. Both Valdevan and polymyxin already have licences for human use – they've been through clinical trials and have been licensed for use both here and by the FDA in the USA. There is nothing to stop physicians trying this new treatment – if only they could get their hands on a supply of clinical grade Valdevan.'

'Which Grumman Schalk have refused to provide.'

'Exactly – and that's why I'm asking you to include Gavin's work in the television programme. We need to put pressure on the company. Public opinion can be a pretty strong weapon; it would level the playing field a bit.'

Sutcliffe appeared uncomfortable, but couldn't think of a cogent argument against this. 'I'm really not sure,' was the best he could offer.

'But you will consider it?'

'We have until Thursday of next week before we have to agree the programme's final format. I need hardly point out that if we were to incorporate Gavin's work, someone else would have to stand down . . .'

'How about Gerald Montague?' said Simmons, almost immediately regretting letting his tongue run away with him.

Sutcliffe's face darkened. 'Gerald's work on the temperature sensitive differences between tumour cells and healthy ones is showing great promise. Gerald Montague is a most distinguished researcher.'

Simmons remained silent.

'I'll let you know my decision.'

Simmons took this as his cue to leave. He stopped beside Gavin in the lab to say, 'Graham will let us know about the TV programme,' before going into his office and calling Jack Martin. 'I need a beer.'

———

'Drinking again?' asked Jenny when her husband arrived home a little after seven.

'Just the one, Constable . . .'

'Lor luv us. Whatever's going to become of me and the children?' said Jenny, affecting a cockney flower-girl accent. 'I take it Graham wasn't too enthusiastic?'

'He didn't say no, but he would have liked to. I just don't understand why everyone is being so negative about something that has the potential to be the first real breakthrough in years. It's almost as if they see it as a threat.'

'It is,' said Jenny. 'If you wipe out cancer, what are cancer researchers going to do? Thousands of people will be out of a job.'

Simmons, who obviously hadn't looked at it in this way, stared at her for a moment before saying, 'Jesus, I don't even want to go there.' He slumped down into a chair and held his head in his hands as he stared at the floor.

Jenny got up and stood behind him, massaging his shoulders. 'Why don't you take your shoes off and I'll fix you a large whisky . . . which I bought instead of food for the children . . .'

Simmons put back his head and closed his eyes. 'Time they were up chimneys anyway, earning their keep.'

———

'How's Gavin taking all this?' asked Jenny, when they had finished their evening meal.

'Pretty well, considering. He's never exactly been a fan of the establishment, but I don't think even he thought it could be this bad. He's kept his cool this far, but he might snap if all this gets bogged down in the offices of patent lawyers.'

'What about the TV programme?'

'I might snap if they put in Gerald Montague's crap instead of Gavin's work. It's our best chance of putting pressure on Grumman Schalk to start making Valdevan available again.'

'What's Montague's stuff about anyway?'

'He thinks tumour cells are more sensitive to heat than normal cells and has produced a million graphs and given a hundred seminars to show it.'

'So, where's he going with it?'

'Nowhere, unless he intends dropping cancer patients in boiling water.'

'But I take it no one will be pointing this out on the programme?'

'You take it right,' snorted Simmons. 'His peers will nod sagely and pronounce the distinguished professor's work to be extremely interesting.'

'I hate to see you down like this.'

'God, it's ironic when you think about it. This is the sort of moment we've all been working towards for years. We could be on the very brink of a cure for cancer and we're all at each other's throats. Crazy.'

'Let's watch some shit television. It'll take our minds off things.'

'Look, Gavin,' said Caroline. 'I hate to say this, but maybe they're right and maybe you *are* rushing things a bit? It doesn't necessarily mean they're dismissing the whole idea out of hand.'

They were talking at a table in Doctors. Gavin was rotating his beer glass constantly, in a nervous gesture which was beginning to annoy Caroline. She put her hand on his wrist to stop him.

'You didn't hear what Ehrman said.'

'No, I didn't – but if what Jack Martin says is true, about Valdevan being out of patent, Grumman Schalk are not in any position to have the final say anyway.'

'Not on paper,' agreed Gavin. 'But he seemed pretty sure the other companies would toe the line, so it comes to the same thing in the end.'

'A bit of publicity will soon put a stop to that.'

'We'll see.'

'Cheer up, Gav. Nothing worthwhile ever comes easy, but when you publish your findings, the scientific and medical community will draw their own conclusions and start asking questions. A torrent of angry letters to the *BMJ* should help Valdevan make a comeback. And you could always canvass the support of the cancer charities.'

'I think Frank's pinning all his hopes on this BBC TV programme, but you're right; it wouldn't do any harm to have a backup plan.'

'From what you've said, the main objections are that Valdevan didn't work the first time around and polymyxin is toxic. The first is irrelevant – you were the one who showed them exactly why

Valdevan didn't work – and, in any case, you're not trying to use it to kill tumour cells. The second is probably not valid because of the reduced dosage you'd be using. Actually, maybe it would be useful to demonstrate that?'

'How?'

'Ask for volunteers to take a reduced dosage of polymyxin, measure their blood levels to see if they're achieving the level you need, and monitor them for side-effects.'

'Why the hell didn't I think of that?' exclaimed Gavin. 'It wouldn't be like trying out a new drug, so none of the legal restrictions would apply. If no one showed any ill effects, it would scupper any objections along those lines. Brilliant!'

Caroline made an all-in-a-day's-work gesture and asked, 'What kind of reduced dosage are we talking about here?'

'The sums say that a quarter of the normal dose should give a high enough level to kill off damaged tumour cells.'

'That's a big reduction, so there shouldn't really be a problem. Want me to ask my classmates?'

'That'd be brilliant. I'll talk to Frank about this in the morning.'

On Thursday morning Frank Simmons was called to Graham Sutcliffe's office. He was surprised to meet Jack Martin on the way and learn that he'd also been summonsed.

Sutcliffe seemed in a good mood when they entered, and Liz served up coffee with a knowing smile on her lips.

'I've had a call from Grumman Schalk,' said Sutcliffe, sitting back in his chair and making a steeple with his fingers. 'It's good news: nothing in black and white yet, but it seems we're almost certain to get the block grant.'

'Congratulations,' echoed Martin and Simmons.

'Congratulations to all of us, I think. This means a considerable expansion for our department and, as I mentioned at the outset, justification for the creation of two new personal chairs . . .' Sutcliffe paused to give his words time to take effect. 'I have decided that you two should be the members of staff to benefit from this. I take it neither of you would have any objection to becoming Professors Simmons and Martin?'

'None at all,' said Jack Martin.

'I'd be honoured,' said Simmons. 'But I think I would still like your assurance that we will have the chance to debate the conditions attached to the Grumman Schalk award.'

'You have it, Frank,' smiled Sutcliffe. 'All I ask is that you do not dig your heels in on a matter of principle and refuse to budge, without looking at things in the wider context. Consider the advantages as well as the disadvantages.'

Simmons nodded.

'I must ask you to keep this under your hats for the moment, just until the paperwork appears and it all becomes official.'

'Of course.'

'That was a surprise,' said Jack Martin as he and Simmons walked back along the corridor. 'I thought we were in for some kind of bollocking.'

'It's the squeaky wheel that gets the grease,' said Simmons.

'What's that supposed to mean?'

'He's buying us off. We're the only two to have raised any question about Grumman's editorial control over what we publish in future. Now it's a case of keep your mouths shut and you'll both get personal chairs.'

Martin let out a long sigh. 'I think that's going a bit far, Frank. Graham's right about viewing everything in context. The block grant money will make an enormous difference to this place, and we are probably the two most senior members of staff.'

'Maybe.'

'Heard anything back from Unived?'

'Maybe tomorrow.'

Simmons closed the door of his office behind him a bit more roughly than he'd intended, but it reflected his mood. He'd just been told that he was about to be made a full professor and he felt bad. He was angry at feeling bad when he should be feeling good and thinking of celebration, but the suspicion that he was being bought off just wouldn't go away. Maybe it was him? Maybe he expected too much of other people? Maybe this was just the way the world worked? This line of thought only evoked memories of Mary lecturing Gavin on the subject, which didn't help. He was glad when a knock came at his door. He needed distraction.

Gavin told Simmons about Caroline's suggestion.

'Good idea. I don't see anything wrong in principle,' said Simmons. 'Although we'll probably have to pay for the polymyxin and to have the blood tests done. I think we should probably bring in the University Medical Centre on this. We'll need them to administer the drug, and they'll probably want disclaimers signed, but if the dose is to be a quarter of what patients have been given before, I don't foresee any great difficulty. I'll ask them if you like. '

'Thanks, Frank. I'll start asking around for volunteers.'

SEVENTEEN

Frank Simmons took a call from John Chalmers at Unived at ten on Friday morning.

'I'm afraid there's been a slight hitch. Old College have deferred a decision.'

'What on earth for?' asked Simmons, his tone betraying the frustration he was welling up inside him.

'They need clarification.'

'Of what?'

'Whether Valdevan is going to be available should the university fund a successful application for intellectual property rights.'

'There's no need to worry on that score. Over the past few days we've managed to establish that Jack Martin was quite correct in his suspicion that Valdevan is out of patent. Anyone can make it.'

'Anyone with the facilities of a large pharmaceutical company, that is,' said Chalmers.

'Anyone who has an interest in treating cancer,' snapped Simmons. 'How long is this delay going to go on?'

'I'll pass on what you've said about the drug and get back to you when I hear something.'

Simmons put the phone down and rested his elbows on his desk while he massaged his temples. 'Bugger . . . bugger, bugger.'

He was about to go through to the lab to tell Gavin when the phone rang again. It was a Dr Colin Mears at the University Medical Centre. 'It's about this small drug trial you've asked us to administer.'

'Is there a problem?'

'No problem, but you do know that it's no longer usual to give polymyxin by injection? Side-effects and all that.'

'We know, but we're using a quarter of the recommended dose.'

'Won't that defeat the purpose?' asked Mears.

'We don't intend using it to fight bacterial infection.'

'Fair enough . . .' said Mears, with the air of a man who had thought about asking more but had decided not to. 'There are still certain people we will have to exclude – anyone with a history of kidney problems and anyone prone to allergies. These were the groups shown in the past to suffer the worst side-effects.'

'We'll screen the volunteers,' said Simmons.

'Then we can start whenever you like,' said Mears.

—

Simmons passed on the bad news to Gavin about the delay to the patent application and asked how the search for volunteers was coming along.

'We've got twelve,' said Gavin. 'Six medical students from my girlfriend's class including Caroline herself. Mary, Tom, Trish from tissue culture, Jack Martin and yourself.'

Simmons told him what Mears had said about exclusions.

'I'll check.'

'I suggest we make a start on Monday morning. That should give us the data by the end of the week, and we should know about both the TV programme and when they're going to submit the patent application by then.'

'Sounds good,' said Gavin.

'Could be a big week.'

—

On Sunday, Gavin and Caroline took the bus down to Leith, once an independent and busy port, but now swallowed up to become

Edinburgh-by-the-sea where the docks and shipyards of the past had given way to the flats and bistros of modern times. They had lunch in a waterside bar before starting a slow walk back to the city on the walkway which traced the course of the Water of Leith up through the heart of the city and out to the west. Both were excited at the prospects of the week ahead, and what the future might bring once Gavin's discovery was put to the test.

'I can't believe it's only a few months since I thought you were a complete bullshitter,' said Caroline.

'Thanks for that.'

'You know what I mean,' said Caroline, squeezing his arm. 'If someone suggests they're going to cure cancer, the last thing in the world you'd expect them to do is . . . cure cancer. God, this is so exciting.'

'Still a way to go,' said Gavin.

'That doesn't sound like you. What made you say that?'

'I've seen the early opposition. It can only get worse.'

'But Frank's on your side . . .'

'He's been brilliant. I couldn't have asked for more support, but maybe even he doesn't realise what he's up against.'

'And you do?' challenged Caroline.

'I was the one who spoke to Ehrman,' said Gavin.

'And?'

Gavin sighed. 'That guy was as nice as ninepence when we met in Edinburgh, but when he got back to me after supposedly discussing my results with his colleagues, he was as cold as ice. I got the impression he would have signed my death warrant without batting an eye.'

'Well, screw him. He's in no position to do anything to stop you, so he'd better get used to the idea,' said Caroline. 'Your idea is going to work.'

'Mmm,' said Gavin.

'I think you have to wear a morning suit when they give you a Nobel Prize,' said Caroline.

'Best get mine off to the dry-cleaners then,' said Gavin.

Only one of the original volunteers had to be replaced on Monday morning. One of Caroline's medical student classmates confessed to suffering from a range of allergies including one to penicillin. He was replaced at the last moment by his girlfriend – also a medical student – and all twelve volunteers were given their first injection of polymyxin. This was followed an hour later by the taking of a blood sample from each to assess the levels of the drug present at that time. The week continued with regular injections and blood sampling until by Wednesday there was enough data to make a preliminary judgement on how things were going. None of the volunteers had suffered any side-effects, and all of them had achieved blood levels of the drug above that required to destroy Valdevan-treated tumour cells.

'Looks good,' said Simmons.

'Looks great,' said Gavin.

There was a bad moment on Thursday morning when Tom Baxter appeared in the lab looking very ill, but close questioning revealed that he had been out on the town the night before, celebrating the success of one of his friends in gaining his PhD in biochemistry. His 'illness' had more to do with alcohol than with polymyxin.

The relief, however, was short-lived when Simmons took a call from John Chalmers. He took it in the open lab so that the others heard one side of the conversation.

'I'm sorry; they've decided not to go ahead with the application.'

'Why not?' exclaimed Simmons, feeling the numbness of disappointment invade his limbs.

'When push came to shove, Old College felt they had a duty not to waste university funds, and the risk inherent in applying for intellectual copyright over something that could not be guaranteed to be made available was deemed too great. I'm sorry.'

'And where do people with cancer come into all this?'

'I'm sorry?'

Simmons put down the phone.

Gavin took the news like a punch in the stomach. He turned on his heel and left the room without comment.

'What are they playing at?' said Mary, shaking her head. 'Why is everyone solely concerned with money, with something like this at stake?'

'I'll go see if Gavin's okay,' said Tom.

Gavin had escaped to the Meadows. His first impulse had been to seek out a pub where he could spend the rest of the day drinking in an attempt to numb the feelings of frustration and helplessness that were threatening to overwhelm him, but thoughts of what Caroline might say acted as a deterrent. Instead he walked and walked, all the while cursing an establishment that couldn't see further than the end of its cheque book. When he'd calmed down, he came round to wondering what to do next. If the university wouldn't provide any support, surely there was someone else out there who would.

He came round to considering the very people who were funding his studies, the Medical Research Council. They should certainly be interested in a new treatment for cancer. In fact, this sort of thing should be more up their street than the University's when all was said and done. He had the number of the MRC's head office in London entered in his mobile phone, so he brought it up on the screen and called it. After saying who he was, he asked if the Council had any sort of interface between its researchers and the commercial world.

'We certainly do,' came the reply.

'Brilliant,' said Gavin, asking for details, punching in the number, and making sure there was no misunderstanding by asking about the function of the unit.

'Its remit is to make sure that the work of the Council's research-ers is brought to the attention of possible developers and manufac-turers, and to safeguard the Council's interests,' said the woman.

Gavin thought he heard warning bells ring in the last phrase, but he called the number and asked to speak to the person in charge.

'That would be Dr Welsh. May I ask what it's about?'

'A cure for cancer.'

'I beg your pardon?'

'A possible cure for cancer.'

'One moment, please.'

Gavin shifted his weight from foot to foot as he waited, mainly to keep warm, but nerves were also playing a part.

'Graham Welsh; who is this, please?'

Gavin said who and what he was, and gave a brief outline of his research work on Valdevan.

'Can I just stop you there?' said Welsh. 'You say you have already contacted the makers of the drug?'

'Yes, it was the first thing we did. We thought they'd be pleased with our findings.' Gavin grimaced at the hollow sound his words had now.

'Telling them was a mistake,' said Welsh. 'Once you've done that it's no longer possible to patent your idea.'

'I don't want to patent it,' exclaimed Gavin. 'I want someone to try it out.'

'I can understand that,' said Welsh. 'But I'm afraid that's some-thing we really can't help you with. It's outwith our remit.'

'Outwith your remit,' echoed Gavin. 'You mean, if you can't sell it, you're not interested?'

'I wouldn't put it quite like that.'

'How would you put it? Christ, you're the Medical Research Council! Isn't there a wee clue in the name?'

'Does your supervisor know you're making this call?'

'Do they stick batteries up your arse in the morning?'

Gavin walked back to the med school, still fuming. He was met on the stairs by Tom Baxter who said, 'I've been looking for you all over the place. Sutcliffe wants to see you and Frank.'

Simmons, who had been waiting for Gavin to turn up, was checking his watch and on the point of leaving the lab when Gavin appeared. They hurried along the corridor to Sutcliffe's office together, only to be told by Liz that the time for a private meeting had passed. The departmental meeting about the BBC programme was now in progress in the small seminar room.

Simmons inclined his head towards Gavin as if asking a silent question, and Liz went on, 'Graham said you should both attend.'

They entered to find Graham Sutcliffe and the academic staff in the early stages of discussing the programme format.

'Ah, there you are,' said Sutcliffe. 'I did want to have a word in private with you two before the start of this meeting but . . . you weren't available. Anyway, not to put too fine a point on it, I have decided that Gavin's work, laudable though it is, should not be included in the programme at this particular moment in time.'

There was a hush in the room. 'Why not?' asked Simmons. 'It has all the signs of being the most significant development in cancer research for years.'

'It has potential, I'll grant you, but all the objections I raised at the outset still stand, I'm afraid.'

'Except one,' said Simmons. 'We've been running a trial on low-dose polymyxin treatment over the past week. Twelve volunteers were injected with the drug at the low dosage required and we've seen no side-effects . . . None at all.'

'Be that as it may . . .'

'Don't dismiss it lightly, Graham; that was one of your major objections,' said Simmons.

'One of them,' countered Sutcliffe.

'Perhaps you'd care to remind everyone of the others?'

'I will not be cross-examined in this manner,' snapped Sutcliffe.

'It's important that we all know,' said Simmons, as calmly as he could with a racing pulse and the feeling that he had just crossed the Rubicon uppermost in his mind.

'I will not be party to anything that promises false hope to vulnerable people,' announced Sutcliffe.

'It's real hope, Graham. It's what you plan to put in the programme that's going nowhere. I don't mind the old boys patting each other on the back and calling each other distinguished, even dishing out prizes to one another, but not at the expense of the exclusion of something like this. If you won't include Gavin Donnelly's work in the programme, I'll seek publicity for it elsewhere.'

'Which would be totally irresponsible and might well be construed as bringing this university into disrepute,' stormed Sutcliffe.

Simmons noted the threat of bigger guns being brought to bear on him, but did not react.

'I urge you to think again,' continued Sutcliffe. 'To announce publicly that an untried –'

'We are not exactly getting the chance to try it, are we?' interrupted Simmons.

Sutcliffe continued unabashed. 'By announcing that an untried and untested treatment could be their salvation would be putting the health and welfare of thousands of vulnerable people at risk.'

Simmons snapped. With a preliminary glance at the heavens as if seeking divine help, he leaned forward and fixed Sutcliffe with blazing eyes. 'THEY'RE DYING OF CANCER, FOR FUCK'S SAKE! THEY DON'T HAVE ANY FUCKING HEALTH AND WELFARE ISSUES. THEY ARE DYING, OR HAD THAT ESCAPED YOUR ATTENTION?'

Jack Martin leapt to his feet, holding up his hands in an attempt to interrupt proceedings and limit the damage. He was helped by the stunned silence that enveloped the audience. 'Gentlemen, this is getting us nowhere,' he pleaded. 'I suggest that we all calm down, get some coffee and reconvene in say, half an hour?'

People were ready to agree.

Gavin was back in the lab first. He told Mary and Tom what had happened. 'Frank lost it big time. What a hero. You should have seen Sutcliffe's face.'

'I really don't understand why Graham refuses to have your stuff in the programme, as a preliminary study if nothing else. You'd think it would do the department nothing but good,' said Mary.

'It's personal,' suggested Tom. 'He really doesn't like you.'

This brought a smile of resignation from Gavin just as Simmons came into the room. He looked slightly embarrassed. 'I don't think you should come back into the meeting, Gavin,' he said. 'Just in case the professor decides to make it a double crucifixion.'

'You were brilliant,' said Gavin.

'No, I wasn't,' insisted Simmons. 'I lost my temper and blew any chance we might have had of getting Professor Sutcliffe to change his mind.'

'He was never going to do that, Frank,' said Gavin.

'I don't think so either,' said Mary, and Tom nodded his agreement, adding, 'He hates Gavin.'

'All the same . . .' Simmons let out his breath in a long, weary sigh. 'Any coffee going?'

The four of them stood in the lab sipping coffee, Simmons preoccupied by what had happened and the others trying to think of something light to say. When all else failed, Gavin told Simmons of his earlier conversation with the head of the MRC technology transfer unit. Simmons shook his head. 'Christ, who would have thought that it would be so . . .' He let the slump in his shoulders say the rest.

Simmons suggested that Gavin maintain a low profile for the time being. He would call him when there had been some kind of resolution. He started out to return to the meeting when he

176

met Liz in the corridor. 'I heard what happened,' she whispered in confidential fashion. 'Graham's desperately afraid he'll lose it if you don't back down over Gavin,' she said.

'Lose what?'

'The block grant . . .'

Simmons' eyes opened wide. 'Are you saying that Grumman Schalk have been pressurising Graham?'

Liz looked alarmed. 'I thought you knew,' she murmured, as the enormity of her slip hit home to her. 'Oh, my God, what have I done?'

Simmons patted her arm, although his mind had just gone into overdrive. 'It's all right, Liz,' he said. 'Don't worry about it. It would have come out anyway . . .'

It was Jack Martin, not Graham Sutcliffe, who was first to speak when the meeting reconvened. It seemed only right as he had cast himself in the role of peacemaker before the break. He did his best to make light of what had gone before with references to passions running high and the 'emotional minefield' of a subject like cancer. He expressed the hope that they could put it all behind them.

Simmons' regret and embarrassment at his earlier outburst had now been replaced by an anger that smouldered inside him as he watched the head of department get to his feet.

Graham Sutcliffe began in conciliatory tone. 'I fully recognise the enthusiasm that some of you feel for Gavin Donnelly's work,' he said. 'But I must emphasise that my first consideration as head of this department has to be the reputation of the department and, indeed, the university. It would be foolish for us to go over the top about something which is, at this point, little more than an interesting observation in a test tube. It was for that reason that I decided that Donnelly's work will not be included in the BBC programme. I hope that after giving it some thought, you, my colleagues, will come to agree with me and not seek ill-advised publicity for what is after all –'

'A thorn in Grumman Schalk's side,' interrupted Simmons in a level monotone.

'I beg your pardon?'

Simmons' gaze did not waver as he asked, 'What was the threat, Graham? Keep the lid on Gavin's work or you lose the block grant?'

There were gasps in the room and all eyes were on Simmons, whose unwavering and accusing stare at Sutcliffe suggested a man very sure of his ground.

'How dare you!'

'No, how dare you, Graham? I was prepared for Grumman Schalk's interference in what we could or could not submit for publication if we accepted their money, but I didn't expect them to start running the department before we'd even got it.'

Sutcliffe was almost apoplectic.

'Will everyone please calm down,' appealed Jack Martin, above the hubbub which had broken out.

As order was restored, Martin looked at Simmons and said, 'That is a very serious accusation, Frank.'

'And I'm waiting for a response.'

Martin turned and looked almost apologetically at Sutcliffe, who took a deep breath and got to his feet. 'This is a total misrepresentation of the facts,' he said, but his words lacked conviction and the room sensed it. 'Quite understandably, Grumman Schalk, like me, believes that it is not in the interests of anyone to have publicity given to Donnelly's work at this stage.'

'Or any stage,' said Simmons coldly. 'Did they threaten to withdraw the offer of the block grant if you didn't play ball?'

There was a long pause while it seemed to Simmons that Sutcliffe was trying to work out just how much he knew. 'Not in so many words . . .'

All around the room eyes were cast downwards as Sutcliffe's answer was seen as an admission.

'Well, of course "not in so many words", Graham. How did they dress it up?'

'It's not a question of dressing anything up,' spluttered Sutcliffe. 'The company simply feels that if Donnelly's work were to be given undue publicity on such a programme as the BBC intends to produce, their refusal to put Valdevan back in production might lead to adverse publicity and – a misinterpretation of their motives – something that might well have financial repercussions for them –'

'And lead to a withdrawal of the grant offer,' completed Simmons.

'Which is a perfectly understandable point of view to those of us . . .'

Who have to live in the real world, thought Simmons as he saw it coming.

'Who have to live in the real world.'

Simmons left the room.

EIGHTEEN

Simmons was sitting alone in his office, feet up on the desk, head back, staring at the ceiling, when Jack Martin put his head round the door. 'So where do you go from here?'

Simmons sighed. 'I don't know, but I do know I'm not going to give up on this. If Sutcliffe won't put Gavin's work in the programme, I'm definitely going to seek exposure for it elsewhere.'

'In which case Grumman Schalk will definitely pull the plug on the grant.'

Simmons looked at Martin questioningly. 'What are you saying, Jack?'

Martin shrugged in a gesture of innocence. 'I'm just making sure that you know what you're getting yourself into. It's not just Sutcliffe who desperately wants the grant, it's the university. We're talking big bucks here, and Old College is like a thirsty sponge when it comes to cash.'

'Jesus! That's why they blocked the patent application!' exclaimed Simmons, as if suddenly realising it. 'It had nothing to do with them risking precious university funds. They were dancing to Grumman's tune too.'

'I should think you'll get quite a lot of fancy footwork for twenty million,' said Martin.

'And where do you stand on all of this, Jack?' asked Simmons, watching his friend's reactions. 'Presumably, no grant means no personal chairs?'

Martin gave a resigned shrug. 'Graham did make it pretty clear that they were dependent on the department getting Grumman Schalk money and expanding. Maybe I should get you to tell Lorraine the bad news instead of me. She was tickled pink at the idea of becoming the wife of a learned professor.'

The remark had been made light-heartedly but the message was there, thought Simmons. He took it as an early warning that Jack Martin had come as far as he was going to in the support stakes and could even be thinking about engaging reverse gear. He suddenly felt very alone. 'Well, I don't know about you, but I'm for home,' he said, changing the subject. 'It's been one hell of a day.'

'Fancy a drink?'

'Maybe not tonight, Jack.'

—

'So how serious is this?' asked Jenny when Simmons told her.

'It's me and Gavin against the rest of the world.'

'What about your drinking buddy?'

'Jack's starting to waver. Lorraine's been telling her pals at the lunch club that he's going to be made a professor.'

'Oh dear. Well, for what it's worth, I'm right behind you. I just can't believe that all these people are putting money before a possible cure for cancer. It's absolutely outrageous.'

'Thanks, but I don't think we should underestimate the strength of the opposition. Edinburgh may not be Sicily, but the Morningside mafia can hold their own with anyone when it comes to dirty tricks.'

Jenny ruffled Simmons' hair as she passed by. 'Right, so when the story breaks about you and the three call-girls in a bed . . .'

'You'll know I've been set up.'

'Either that or you invented the whole cancer cure business to cover it up . . .'

'Trust me to marry a clever woman.'

'If it's any help, I feel just as angry,' said Caroline. 'It's beginning to sound as if everyone is really quite happy with the way things are, and you're being cast in the role of troublemaker because you've dared to make progress and rocked their comfy little boat. How dare they!'

'If it wasn't for Frank standing up for me I think I'd be out on my ear and serving burgers in McDonald's by now.'

'So what are you two going to do?'

'I spoke to him on the phone. He says the main thing to do is to get the results into print. He thinks there's a good chance we'll be able to get the paper into a really prestigious journal like *Cell* or *Nature*. Once it's out there in the public domain things should get easier. We're hoping there will be an immediate demand for the reintroduction of Valdevan and for trials to begin on the new treatment.'

'You don't think the opposition will attempt to block publication?'

'I'm sure they will. That's why we'll have to make sure the data is absolutely watertight. We mustn't give the reviewers any reason at all to turn it down. I'm going to repeat all the experiments, starting tomorrow. Frank's going to investigate the possibility of setting up a couple of experiments to treat tumours in lab animals with what supplies of Valdevan we've got left – that would really make the point.'

'How much do you have?'

'They sent me six five-gram vials the last time I asked. I think we can safely assume that's the last they'll give us.'

'If the animal experiments work out, surely not even Grumman Schalk could go on ignoring it.'

'Don't you believe it. They'll probably say that experiments in animals are not necessary a valid indication of what will happen in humans. But we'll deal with that shit when it happens. Let's talk about something happy for a change.'

'What would make you happy, Gav?'

'Beer . . . bacon crisps . . . sex . . .'

'If you were a swimming pool, Gavin, you'd have two shallow ends,' said Caroline.

Something of a siege mentality developed over the following days and weeks in the Simmons lab. Whereas a few weeks before they had been fêted as the lab who'd come up with some really exciting results, they were now being regarded by others in the department as the group that was threatening a huge influx of research funds through their sheer obstinacy and unwillingness to see reason. Sure, Gavin Donnelly's experiments were interesting – possibly exciting – but one postgrad student's results were no reason to damage everyone else's research prospects. That was just plain selfish according to Peter Morton-Brown, who led the whispering campaign among the younger members of the department. Mary and Tom came under particular pressure in the common room to try to make Frank and Gavin see that delaying making their find-ings public until after the block grant had been agreed would be the decent, sensible thing to do.

'And how long do they imagine Grumman Schalk would like the delay to be?' was Simmons' icy response when Mary told him.

'Quite a while?'

'Try forever.'

'Maybe not,' said Gavin, who'd been working at the bench. The others turned to look at him. 'It's my bet that Grumman's people are already working night and day to come up with a single com-pound that exploits the idea behind the combination of Valdevan and polymyxin.'

'And make squillions,' said Mary.

'What d'you think their chances are?' asked Tom.

'Impossible to say,' said Gavin. 'If they could do it in a relatively short time, I think I'd be happy to chuck this in and say good luck to them. But there are no guarantees; it could be several years, maybe never. I don't want to go on sitting on this, knowing that folks could be benefiting from it right now.'

'Hear, hear,' said Mary.

⸺

Simmons had bad news for them the following day. 'The request for permission to carry out animal experiments has been declined.'

'Why?' asked Gavin.

'They say that the Valdevan we were given by Grumman Schalk is not for therapeutic use. It says so on the specification form that came with it.'

'But there's nothing wrong with it,' said Gavin. 'The spec sheet also shows that it passed all its purity tests. The warning is there just because they sent unsterile powder instead of a sealed injection vial. They must know that we would sterilise any solution before it was used.'

'Look, we all know this is an excuse,' said Simmons, holding up his hands. 'But there's absolutely nothing we can do about it. The powers that be have dug their heels in and that's that.'

'Shit,' said Gavin. 'Throw a six to restart.'

'We can still go to print. The animal experiments would have been a bonus, but the cell culture data will stand up on its own. How are the repeat experiments coming along?'

'No problems, exactly the same results as last time. The data's going to be rock solid.'

'When will you be finished?'

'End of next week.'

⸺

On the Wednesday of the following week Gavin let out a string of expletives as he routinely examined his Valdevan-treated cells before adding polymyxin. It was the final experiment, the final hurdle, and suddenly he felt himself falling. The tumour cells were already dead.

'What the . . . I don't believe it.'

Mary came across to take a look and then Tom.

'Not much doubt about that,' said Tom. 'Maybe the growth rate was too fast. Are you sure you didn't use the wrong culture medium?'

'No way,' said Gavin. 'I only use one these days and I make it up myself. There should only have been blips in the cell membrane . . . and no effect at all on normal cells . . .' He paused while he changed the culture under the microscope. 'Shit, they're dead too.'

'My God, this is a real show stopper,' murmured Mary. 'If there's any chance at all of killing normal cells with Valdevan . . . you can't use this. You'll kill the patients.'

Gavin looked bemused. 'I just don't understand it. This is just plain crazy.'

'Strikes me Valdevan has a history of throwing up odd results,' said Tom. 'You'd better tell Frank.'

Frank Simmons examined the cultures for himself and joined the long faces in the lab. 'I hope we all have a taste for penitence,' he said. 'If we can't explain this, we could be eating dirt round here for some time to come.' He looked at Gavin. 'Are you absolutely sure you couldn't have added too much drug or used the wrong culture medium?'

'I'm certain.'

'Couldn't you repeat it?' said Tom.

'No point,' said Simmons. 'Even if he did it a hundred more times and got the result he was looking for, it wouldn't make this result disappear. It's going to sit there in the data like an indelible stain, putting a stop to everything. It's an explanation that's needed. That's the only way to get rid of it.'

'I don't think I have one,' said Gavin.

'I don't suppose it was an old solution of the drug that could have broken down or something . . .' suggested Mary, without much conviction.

Gavin shook his head, but fetched the bottle from the fridge and read out the date he'd written on the label when he'd made it up. Almost automatically, he held up the bottle to the light and shook the contents to check how much was left. He was about to return it to the fridge when something made him repeat the gesture. He had a puzzled look on his face.

'What's wrong?' asked Mary.

'How much would you say was in there?'

Mary took the bottle. 'About 3 mil?' she said.

'That's too much,' said Gavin, apparently carrying out a quick calculation in his head. 'There shouldn't be that much.' He removed the top from the bottle and sniffed the contents. 'Smells of swimming pools . . . chlorine.'

The others agreed in turn.

'Indicator paper,' muttered Gavin, as he started a hunt through the lab drawers, 'We need indic . . .' He finally brought out a small book of pH indicator strips.

The others looked on as he used a Gilson pipette to remove a small sample of the solution and drop it on to a strip of the indicator paper. The immediate colour change was dramatic. Gavin compared it to the comparison chart and said, 'pH less than 2.5. It should be 7.2. Somebody's added acid to it . . . hydrochloric by the smell . . .'

'Well, well, well,' said Simmons, caught somewhere between bemusement, outrage and relief. 'What do you know? We have our explanation. It was a deliberate act of sabotage.'

Everyone seemed stunned. Mary was the first to break the silence. 'At least we don't have to search far for a motive. The department is full of people who don't want Gavin's work to be published.'

'But to go this far . . .' said Tom.

'Never underestimate human nature where money and self interest are concerned,' said Simmons. 'The next question is, what do we do about it?'

'Maybe it's a police matter?' said Mary cautiously, as if unwilling to make the suggestion but feeling that she should.

'No point,' said Gavin. 'The police would be like fish out of water in a place like this. They'd go through the motions, cause disruption everywhere and then piss off into the sunset with a couple of choruses of *Just One of Those Things*.'

'I'm afraid Gavin's right,' said Simmons. 'Interviewing the entire department would get us nowhere and just antagonise people even more. No, I suggest we do absolutely nothing and keep the whole thing to ourselves.'

Three pairs of eyebrows were raised.

'But this is a really serious matter,' said Mary.

Simmons nodded. 'It is, and you're right, but so is getting Gavin's work into print, and that has to be our main objective. Whoever did this has failed, and that's what's important right now. We know why the cells died; it was sabotage, so we can remove the rogue result from the data and complete the successful repetition of the tests. Finding out who did this can wait until we have more time to think about what kind of people we're working beside. Let's proceed as if nothing's happened . . . only we keep all relevant drugs and chemicals under lock and key from now on and make sure the lab is locked at night.'

Gavin, Mary and Tom all nodded.

'Good, not a word to anyone.'

—

The sabotage to Gavin's final experiment caused a week's delay while Trish and her colleagues in the tissue culture suite prepared new cell cultures for him.

'I thought you said you were finished,' said Trish when Gavin put in the request.

'So did I,' said Gavin. 'But when you've got a perfectionist for a boss . . .'

'Tell me about it,' murmured one of Trish's staff.

'I wonder who rattled her cage,' said Trish, but all three girls were smiling. 'I'll give you a call when they're ready.'

On the Monday of the following week the cell cultures arrived and Gavin prepared to set up the final repeat experiment. Frank Simmons had already written the main draft body of the paper and given it to Gavin to read over the weekend for comment.

'I see you're about to fill in the blanks,' said Simmons when he arrived in the lab and saw Gavin setting up his work bench. He was referring to the spaces he'd left for the results of last experiment. 'What did you think?'

'Reads well,' said Gavin. 'Thanks for putting my name first.'

'Whatever did you expect, Gavin?' said Simmons, exchanging a smile with Tom, who was waiting to have a word. 'I'm off to the library if anyone's looking for me.'

Gavin placed the instruments he would need in an alcohol-filled beaker ready for flame sterilisation when required and brought out the first of the cell cultures he would need. His mobile rang: it was Caroline and she was upset.

'Where are you?' he asked.

'Downstairs, can you come?'

Gavin changed out of his lab coat and hurried along the corridor to the lifts. As he got there, the door to one of them opened and Mary stepped out, freeing the scarf from her neck one-handedly and almost bumping into Gavin, who was attempting to sidle past. 'Where are you off to in such a hurry?' she exclaimed.

Gavin was about to say that he'd explain later when he suddenly remembered that he'd left his cell cultures lying out on the bench. With one hand holding the lift door open and the other clamped to his forehead, he told Mary what he'd done.

'No problem, I'll deal with it.'

Gavin blew her a kiss as the lift doors started to close. 'Carrie needs me. I'll be back as soon as I can.'

Gavin found Caroline waiting just outside the front doors. She looked pale and drawn. 'What's up?'

'It's Mum; she's really bad. I'm going to have to go down there. Dad phoned this morning.'

'End of the remission?'

'In a big way. Dad says she's in a lot of pain. Look, can we walk? I have to be at the station in half an hour.'

They crossed the road and started heading up George IV Bridge. 'I'm so sorry,' said Gavin, putting his arm around her shoulders.

'Dad wasn't planning on telling me just yet, but they put her on a new chemo schedule and she's been reacting really badly. They've had to up her radiation dose too.'

Gavin made a face.

'I know, I know . . .'

'Carrie, why are you going?'

Caroline withdrew a little and looked at him questioningly. 'What do you mean, why am I going?'

'What good can you do?'

'Gavin, she's my mother.'

'Yes, but you have to ask yourself, what good can you do?'

'Be there for her, damn it. Can you really not see that? What kind of person are you, for God's sake?'

They had stopped to face up to each other at the head of the Mound. Gavin held up his hands in a subconscious gesture of defence. 'Look, all I'm saying is that you can't do anything to help her, Carrie. She knows it; you know it. You'll be putting yourself through hell for no good reason other than the fact that you're do-ing what you think you should . . . your duty, if you like.'

'Damn right it's my duty.'

'Carrie, I really didn't mean to upset you,' pleaded Gavin. 'Honest, I'm just trying to stop you making yourself ill if you rush down there every time there's a bit of a crisis.'

'A bit of a crisis? You call my mother dying a bit of a crisis?'

'You know I didn't mean it that way. Don't do this to me, Carrie. We both know it's a one-way journey for her and it's downhill all the way.'

'Piss off, Gavin.'

'Let me see you to the station at least?'

'I said, piss off!'

Caroline turned on her heel and hurried off, leaving Gavin standing there feeling small and useless. 'Oh fuck,' he murmured, his feet turning to lead as he started slowly back towards the medi-cal school. At that moment, the black clouds that had been lurking over the city for the past few hours decided to turn threat into ac-tion, and large spots of rain started to pock-mark the pavement for a few moments before the heavens finally opened and sent people scurrying into shop doorways and under bus shelters in the mis-taken belief that rain that heavy couldn't last long. Gavin had too much on his mind to care. He was soaked through by the time he got back to the med school.

NINETEEN

Hair plastered to his head and clothes dripping, Gavin stepped out of the lift and started out along the corridor, studiously avoiding eye contact with anyone, although his dishevelled state was drawing unwanted attention to him. He didn't want to be there at all, but the final experiment had to be set up, otherwise the cultures would overgrow and cause yet further delay. He would do what he had to do and then leave.

He'd done it again, him and his big mouth. He hadn't meant to upset Carrie. He'd just said what he felt and . . . it had happened. God, how many times had he had to invoke that excuse in the past? Maybe there really was something wrong with him. Maybe he didn't see things like other people. All he'd wanted to do was point out the truth of the situation to Carrie because he thought she was too close to things to see for herself. He'd thought he was being objective, even helpful, but she had obviously seen things differently. She'd seen him as someone totally without feelings and possibly even someone she never wanted to see again . . . 'Shit, shit, shit.'

As he turned the final corner on the approach to the lab, he reached up to wipe some rain water from his forehead, just as a blinding flash filled the frosted glass panels on the door in front of him and a blast of burning hot air rushed past his cheeks, followed by the sound of screaming. It was the sort of screaming that made his blood run cold, and it was Mary Hollis.

Gavin recovered from his initial shock and blinked his eyes several times to make sure they had not been affected, before pushing open the lab doors to find half the lab on fire. Mary was writhing on the floor, holding her hands to her face. No one else appeared to be there. His first instinct was to fall to his knees to see what he could do to help – but common sense took over and he grabbed at the phone on the wall to call the university emergency number, requesting an ambulance and the fire brigade. He gave details of location and slammed down the phone before hitting the fire alarm and filling the air with electronic whooping.

A chemical bottle exploded as the flames licked up towards the gantries above the work benches, sending glass and its contents flying across the room and making Gavin duck before squatting down to slip his hands under Mary's arms, dragging her across the floor to the door. She had stopped screaming, but he found the animal-like whimper she was now making even more disturbing. Her lower limbs were jerking as if controlled by some deranged puppet master as successive waves of pain seemed to engulf her.

Gavin hadn't had time to assess the extent of Mary's injuries: he had been so intent on getting her out of the lab and shielding them both from fire and possible explosion. Now, safe for the moment behind the fire doors out in the corridor, he felt ill when he saw the state of her face and hands. 'Easy, Mary,' he murmured, cradling her as best he could, but the unevenness of his voice made it sound less than convincing. 'Everything is going to be okay. You're safe now. An ambulance is on its way. You'll be fine, Mary . . . you'll be fine . . .'

The horrified looks on the faces of the people hurrying towards the fire exits couldn't have disagreed more.

The senior technician from the Maclean lab and the first-aider for the floor appeared beside Gavin to see if she could help – an offer that froze on her lips when she saw Mary's face. She was carrying a small plastic box with a green cross on it, which Gavin saw as being ridiculously inadequate in the circumstances: an operating theatre and a team of plastic surgeons were what was needed.

Jack Martin was next to appear: he took in the situation quickly. 'We'll have to get her out of here fast. What's the story with the fire?'

Gavin said, 'I think it's containable if we get to it soon. It seems to be confined to one bench, although the chemicals are causing a problem. On the other hand, there hasn't been an explosion for the past few minutes. I'd like to have a go with the fire extinguishers. Maybe you and Ann can evacuate Mary while I try?'

'Regulations say we should all get out,' insisted Martin.

'I've got too much to lose,' said Gavin.

'One of them could be your life,' snapped Martin.

'Look, if it seems like it's getting any worse, I'll get my arse out of there. I just need to try.'

Martin acquiesced. 'All right, I'll join you when the other fire marshal appears. He's just making sure the floor's clear. He can give Ann a hand to get Mary downstairs.'

Gavin went back into the lab and grabbed a CO_2 extinguisher from the wall just inside the door. He wrenched out the retaining pin and squeezed the trigger to attack the flames in successive three- to four-second bursts. Luckily the fire still appeared to be largely confined to the one bench in the lab – his own. Jack Martin joined him a few moments later, and between them they brought the fire under control just as the sound of sirens bringing professional help reached them.

'Cavalry no longer required,' murmured Martin, wiping grime and sweat from his brow. 'Whose bench is this anyway?' He was looking at the charred, smouldering surface that had been the seat of the fire.

'Mine.'

'What happened?'

Gavin shook his head. 'I wasn't here. Mary seems to have been the only person in the lab at the time.' He told Martin about seeing the flash from out in the corridor as he returned.

'She was working at your bench?'

'Looks like it,' said Gavin.

'Any idea why?'

Gavin made a face. 'I can guess. I met her coming out the lift when I was leaving – I'd just had a phone call from my girlfriend: she was upset. I told Mary that I'd left some cell cultures lying on the bench and asked her if she'd put them back in the incubator for me. I wasn't sure when I was going to be back. It's my guess she decided to set up the experiment for me. It's the sort of thing she'd do.'

'What kind of experiment?

Gavin told Martin, adding, 'I'd left everything ready.'

'How could doing something like that start a fire . . . ?' murmured Martin as he continued to examine the blackened surface of Gavin's bench. 'You say you saw a flash. Was there an explosion?'

Gavin shook his head. 'Maybe a popping sound, but no big bang, just the flash I saw through the glass and then a sudden rush of hot air.'

They were interrupted when three firemen came into the lab in full fire-fighting gear. The senior man raised his visor and asked what had happened. Gavin had just started telling him what little he could when Frank Simmons joined them. 'I've just seen Mary off in the ambulance,' he said. 'I was down in the library. What in God's name happened?'

'As far as we can make out, Mary was alone in the lab when whatever it was happened,' said Jack Martin.

'But there must be some clue . . .'

'We've had a look around: there's nothing obvious,' said Martin. 'We may have to wait until she can tell us herself.'

Simmons shot him a glance. 'That could be some time. Did you see the state of her?'

Martin nodded. 'Poor lass.'

Simmons shook his head in frustration. 'There must be some clue. Her face and hands clearly took the brunt of it. But brunt of what? What was she doing?' He gave up the search for words as he examined the damage. 'But this is your bench, Gavin . . .' he said, looking at the blackened seat of the fire.

'We were just talking about that,' said Gavin. 'I think Mary may have been doing me a favour, setting up an experiment for me. I had a problem this morning: I had to go out for a while.'

The firemen finished checking the lab over and were making sure that there was no possibility of a further flare-up. 'Can I take it you guys know what happened here?' asked the senior man.

'We won't know for sure until we can speak to the injured girl,' said Simmons. 'But we know where it started.'

'Maybe we can have a copy of your internal report when it becomes available?'

'Of course, and thanks for coming so quickly.'

'That's what they pay us for,' said the fireman.

'Maybe, but thanks all the same.'

Simmons, Martin and Gavin were left alone in the lab, the atmosphere heavy with the smell of burnt wood and plastic. 'So, Mary would be sitting here,' said Simmons, attempting to reconstruct the scene. He picked up a stool, which was lying on its side, and placed it at the middle of the burnt bench, at the same time looking to either side of him. 'And the cell cultures would be where?'

'Just here,' said Gavin, indicating to a point on the bench to the right of the stool.

'So, she'd light the Bunsen, unless you'd left it on the pilot flame?'

'No, I hadn't lit it.'

Simmons nodded. 'She'd light the Bunsen . . . take a pair of forceps from the ethanol beaker . . . and flame them.'

There was a glass beaker lying on its side under the gantry. Simmons righted it and moved it beside his right hand. He mimed the action of taking the forceps from the beaker and flaming them. 'And then what?'

'She'd take the stopper out of the cell culture bottle and flame the neck before adding the Valdevan . . .'

'Where's the vial?' asked Simmons.

Gavin and the others started looking.

Eventually, it was Gavin, who had got down on his hands and knees, who recovered the vial and the melted plastic remains of an automatic pipette from below the bench. 'I probably knocked them off with the extinguisher,' he said.

'Still nothing to tell us what happened . . .' said Simmons.

'She could have knocked the beaker over with the pipette and set fire to the ethanol,' suggested Jack Martin. 'Wouldn't be the first time that's happened.'

'An ethanol fire wouldn't have caused a blast,' said Gavin. 'Or done so much damage so quickly. Something else must have been involved, something really volatile.'

'We have to remember that ethanol burns with an almost invisible blue flame,' said Martin. 'She may not have been aware of a small fire on the bench until it was too late and the flames set something else off.'

'But what?' said Simmons. 'What was lying around on the bench that would flare up like that?'

No suggestions were forthcoming.

'There's another smell in here,' said Simmons, sniffing the air.

'A number of chemical bottles exploded with the heat,' said Gavin. 'It could be that. I didn't see which ones. I was too busy ducking.'

Simmons took another exaggerated sniff of the air. 'I know that smell,' he said. 'I just can't put a name to it . . .' He went on a slow circular walk round the damaged area. 'It's the kind of smell you associate with . . . hospitals.'

'This is a medical school, Frank,' said Martin.

'No, it's something that takes me back to my childhood, something that once you smell it you always associate it with hospitals . . . ether! It's ether!'

196

'Now you come to mention it,' said Martin, taking in a long sniff of the air, 'you could be right.'

'Did you have a bottle of ether sitting on your bench, Gavin?'

'No.'

'You're sure?'

'Positive. I've had no reason to use it.'

Simmons went over to the metal cupboard on the floor under the fume cupboard where dangerous and inflammable chemicals were kept and squatted down to unlock it. There was a series of clunking glass sounds as he moved the stock bottles around. When he stood up, he was holding a one-litre, dark glass bottle. 'Ether. Half empty.' He read out the date on the label. 'Obtained from the stores two days ago . . . but already half empty?' He returned it to the cupboard. 'Ether vapour is notorious for causing flash fires,' he said, his voice a hoarse whisper. 'If you leave a container of ether open to the atmosphere for long enough you'll get an explosive mix of ether and air which would be heavier than air itself .'

Simmons walked back to the burnt bench. 'The fumes would have built up around Mary until the concentration became critical and the Bunsen flame would have set off a flash fire in her face.'

'Jesus Christ,' said Martin.

Simmons looked at Gavin and said, 'You say there was no ether on your bench . . . so the obvious explanation is that the beaker the instruments were sitting in – the beaker that Mary thought contained alcohol – actually contained ether.'

'No way,' said Gavin. 'I filled it myself this morning with ethanol.'

'The ethanol is kept in the same cupboard as the ether,' Simmons reminded him.

Gavin remained silent and didn't flinch.

'Is it not just possible that . . .'

'I didn't mix them up,' said Gavin, cutting off the question. 'No way.'

The haunted look had returned to Simmons' eyes. 'Then the alternative is just too awful to contemplate,' he said.

Martin voiced it. 'Someone meant this to happen? They deliberately substituted ether for ethanol, knowing that Mary would turn on the Bunsen near it?'

'No,' said Simmons. 'It's Gavin's bench. They thought it would be him.'

'Christ,' said Gavin.

'Shit,' said Martin. 'Attempted murder?'

Gavin could see that both Simmons and Martin were having trouble believing this. It was clearly a step too far for both of them. They would be much more comfortable with an explanation involving a mistake or an accident, and it was making him feel uneasy – like a schoolboy who wasn't being entirely believed by his elders. He found the silence threatening.

People were being allowed back into the building, and the corridor outside was busy and filled with the buzz of staff discussing what had happened. Ten minutes later Graham Sutcliffe came in and took in the scene imperiously, before asking Simmons, 'Do we know what happened here? Health and Safety are going to be crawling all over the place in the next hour or so.'

'It looks very much as if there was a flash fire in the lab resulting from ether fumes getting into the air,' said Simmons.

'How did they get into the air?'

'That's what we're trying to establish.'

'The university will be keen to –'

'Absolve themselves from all blame,' interrupted Simmons. 'Yes, I know. I think we've established it was either an accident . . . or a deliberate act of sabotage. Either way, Old College can rest easy in their beds. They weren't to blame.'

'This is hardly the time for levity,' said Sutcliffe.

Simmons ignored the rebuke. He looked at Gavin, adopting an exaggerated grimace of embarrassment, and said, 'Gavin, can we just assume for a moment . . .' He paused as if the words were causing him pain, '. . . that a mistake *was* made. You obviously didn't realise it, otherwise you would have changed the solution immediately, but will you at least consider the possibility that this could *conceivably* be what happened? I mean, we all make mistakes from time to time. It was just unfortunate that in this case it had such tragic consequences.'

'I did not make a mistake,' said Gavin flatly. He saw the look that Sutcliffe gave Martin. It suggested that this was exactly what he expected to hear from the Liverpool paddy. Blank denial when in the wrong.

'Then we are faced with the prospect of calling in the police,' said Simmons, after a long pause.

Gavin nodded his agreement. 'And if I can just remind you, it was my arse they were after.'

Sutcliffe rolled his eyes. 'Oh, come on, no one in their right mind would do something like this deliberately. It was clearly an accident caused by thoughtlessness, carelessness, kismet, call it what you will.'

'No, it was sabotage,' said Gavin. 'Someone wanted to put a stop to the Valdevan experiments.'

'What arrogant nonsense,' stormed Sutcliffe. 'What makes you think your piddling little experiments could possibly provoke criminal action like this?'

'The fact that they're not piddling little experiments,' said Gavin. He was angry but in control.

'Someone has already added hydrochloric acid to a drug solution in this lab in an attempt to wreck Gavin's experiments,' said Simmons. 'So there is precedent.'

Sutcliffe's mouth fell open and he waved his arms around in a gesture of utter bewilderment. 'What on earth is happening to this department?' he pleaded to the heavens. 'This beggars belief. We are a centre of excellence with a research record that stands comparison with that of any university in the world, and suddenly people are behaving like guttersnipes and talking about sabotaging each other's work.'

The look Sutcliffe gave Gavin left him in little doubt where he thought the blame lay.

'Has anyone phoned the hospital?' asked Jack Martin.

'I'm just about to do that,' said Simmons.

'Frankly, I am very reluctant to call in the police,' said Sutcliffe. He was speaking to Jack Martin while Simmons made the call. Gavin was examining the extent of the damage to the lab outside the immediate area of the flash fire. The electricity cable to the cell culture incubator had melted, fusing the plug and cutting off the power supply. The cultures inside were ruined. It would be back to square one again, but before that, there would have to be extensive repairs to the lab, which would take even more time. It was depressing and the conversation he was overhearing wasn't helping.

'I'm inclined to treat the matter as a tragic accident without apportioning blame,' said Sutcliffe.

'I agree,' said Martin.

'Perhaps you could put out a departmental circular, warning of the hazards of flammable chemicals in the lab and urging vigilance?'

'Of course.'

Simmons put down the phone and all eyes moved to him. 'They're moving her to a specialist burns unit.'

'But she's out of danger?' asked Sutcliffe.

Simmons looked at him as if his thoughts were a million miles away. 'She'll live. They've managed to save her sight but she's going to need extensive surgery. A long process, they say.'

There was silence in the room while everyone came to terms with the fact that Mary Hollis was going to be scarred for life.

'What a bloody awful thing to happen,' said Martin.

'It should have been me,' said Gavin quietly.

'Maybe we'll all be able to think more clearly in the morning,' said Sutcliffe. 'Life can be terribly cruel.'

Martin and Sutcliffe left the lab without saying anything more. Simmons went into his office to start gathering his things together. Gavin followed him. 'You do believe me, don't you, Frank? I didn't mix up the bottles.'

Simmons turned round. 'I'm sure you believe it, Gavin. Right now, I just want to go home and think about what I'm going to say to Mary's parents when they get here in the morning.'

'The hospital called them?'

'Yes.'

'I haven't seen Tom around. Does he know what's happened?'

'He told me earlier he was going to meet some relations at the airport and probably wouldn't be back. I suppose whoever's in first in the morning will have to tell him.'

'I know it's not exactly the time to talk about this . . . but what are we going to do about the final experiment for the paper?' said Gavin. 'All the cultures I set up are knackered.'

Simmons felt that he'd had all the emotional trauma he could take for one day. 'Tomorrow, Gavin. Let's leave it till tomorrow,' he said, collecting his things and preparing to leave. 'What a shit awful day.'

Gavin watched the door swing shut. He wasn't looking forward to telling Tom Baxter what had happened, but he suspected that he might have to if Frank were to go directly to the hospital in the morning.

An hour later, as Gavin himself was preparing to leave, the lab door opened and Peter Morton-Brown came in. He looked about him slowly, taking in the damage. 'I heard what happened to Mary.'

Gavin didn't respond. He just looked at him as if waiting for something more.

'You must be feeling like shit, old son.'

'I'm sorry?'

'Making a mistake like that, I mean. Could happen to any of us and you shouldn't feel bad about it . . . but all the same . . . what a bloody nightmare.'

'I didn't make any mistake.'

Peter adopted an exaggerated look of puzzlement. 'I'm sorry? That's what everyone's saying. If it wasn't a mistake . . . then what?'

'It was done deliberately. It was meant for me.'

Peter now put on a contrived look of shock. 'I see . . . but who would do something like that?'

'Someone determined to see that the Valdevan experiments didn't make it into print.'

Peter affected an amused smile. 'I've heard about delusions of grandeur, old son, but this takes the biscuit. Who the hell do you think you are?'

'The guy who's going to turn your smug, patrician nose into a mess of blood and snot if you don't sling your hook within the next ten seconds.'

'Ah,' said Peter. 'You don't think you've done enough damage for one day?'

Gavin felt himself on the edge of losing control, but he managed to confine himself to making one slight movement in Peter's direction. It was enough to send him scurrying out through the door.

'Bastard.'

TWENTY

Gavin was up at three in the morning being sick. It was the third time since coming home just after midnight, and now there was nothing left in his stomach to void. All the beer and junk food he'd consumed had been vomited, leaving only the painful spasmodic retching of an abused digestive system, which had to be endured until his body was satisfied that he had got the message. He rinsed his mouth out several times with cold water and then splashed some up into his face to combat the fuzziness. Was it worth it? He looked at himself in the mirror and defiantly concluded that it was. He'd managed to achieve a couple of hours of oblivion, an escape from the hell his life had become in the space of just twenty-four hours.

It seemed that the entire world saw him as an arrogant, insensitive nobody whose work was viewed as a threat to colleagues, to the department – even to the university – and whose carelessness had resulted in a colleague probably being disfigured for life. Even the girl he loved couldn't stand the sight of him.

There was a knock on the bathroom door.

'Are you all right in there, Gav?'

'Just pissed.'

'Then shut the fuck up, will you? Some of us have got work in the morning.'

Gavin mumbled an apology. A few minutes later he tiptoed back to his room and lay on top of the bed, looking up at the few stars he could make out in the sky through the pinkish glow of light pollution from the city. He got under the covers – as the temperature demanded he must – but stress had put sleep out of reach, making him toss and turn as he struggled to come to terms with what was happening. Worst of all was the feeling of helplessness he got when trying to fight back. It seemed that the best he could manage was an assertion that all he'd done was speak the truth. Why should that cause such problems? Why should that *always* cause such problems?

It wasn't in his nature to pussyfoot around. He couldn't pretend to Carrie that rushing off to the Lake District to be with her mother was going to do either of them any good when it clearly wasn't. Why couldn't she see that? Carrie was an intelligent woman; she had a mind of her own; she was studying medicine, for God's sake. Surely she must have realised that he'd just been telling the truth? But she hadn't wanted to hear that . . . she'd needed something else, something that he had failed to provide. Couldn't provide? Love? He loved her dearly and she knew that. Comfort? Reassurance? How could he offer these when it would just be empty, meaningless nonsense. And, coming from him, that's exactly what it would have sounded like. He screwed up his face as he recalled his pathetic attempts at reassuring Mary that everything was going to be all right when he'd held her in his arms after the fire. Now he hoped that she hadn't heard. Telling someone that everything was going to be fine and dandy when it wasn't was quite beyond him. It wasn't as if he didn't care. He did. He felt as deeply as anyone else. He just couldn't go through the motions of uttering meaningless crap with any great conviction. Nor was he able to concede to Frank Simmons' request that he consider the possibility of having made a mistake over the contents of the instrument beaker, when he was damned sure that he hadn't. This, of course, brought the unthinkable alternative back into focus. Someone had made a deliberate attempt on his life.

This was not a happy thought for someone giving birth to the mother and father of all headaches, involving, as it did, facing up to the sheer number of people in the department who disliked him, and questioning who among them might go so far as to cause him actual bodily harm. A brief flirtation with the notion that, having failed the first time, they might try again, he dismissed as being over the top. The person who'd done this was not some psychotic Mafia hit man; it was someone on the staff; someone who hated him; someone who had tried to harm him, but who had got it tragically wrong and devastated the life of someone else, someone everyone liked. Being inside his own head right now was bad enough, but he suspected that being in theirs must be even worse.

—

'Are you all right?' asked Jenny Simmons as her husband came back to bed. The green digits on the bedside clock said it was 4 a.m. She'd heard him get up about an hour before, and had been aware of him pacing around the house when she'd stirred at intervals from her own restless sleep.

'Sorry, I just can't stop thinking about Mary,' said Simmons, sitting on the edge of the bed. He shook his head.

'They can do wonders with plastic surgery these days.'

'No they can't,' said Simmons. 'That's something that everyone pretends, but ten years and twenty operations down the line she'll still not be right.'

Jenny sighed deeply. 'I know it's no help and a bit of a platitude, but these things happen, Frank. It was a tragic accident.'

'Gavin thinks not.'

'How very like Gavin not to face up to the possibility that he might not be infallible.'

'But if he's right . . .'

'You don't think he's right, do you?' asked Jenny, propping

herself up on the pillow on one elbow and rubbing her husband's shoulder.

'Maybe I don't want to think he's right.'

'It was an accident, Frank. Gavin screwed up but won't admit it.'

'Gavin's not a liar. I don't think he knows how.'

'But who in their right mind would do something like that deliberately?'

'No one said anything about right minds.'

'Are you saying you think there's a homicidal lunatic on the staff?'

'No, but you're assuming that whoever did it meant to inflict personal injury. It could have been a crude attempt to cause a fire in the lab that went wrong. Flash fires aren't predictable.'

'Even so, who would want to stop Gavin's research so much that they'd turn to fire-raising?'

'Most of the staff, the head of department, the university, one of the biggest drug companies in the world. How am I doing?'

'Going way over the top. Try to get some sleep. You're going to make yourself ill.'

Simmons swung his legs up on the bed then changed his mind. 'I'm going to have some coffee. Want some?'

'No.'

———

Gavin was in the lab by nine thirty, despite how bad he was feeling. He regarded the hangover, as he had so often in the past, as a penance to be paid without question. He knew he'd feel better as soon as the alcohol cleared from his system and, to start the process, he'd walked to work. His progress towards feeling better, however, was impeded when, on entering the building, at least three people blanked him in the corridor and, when he went down to the cell culture suite to ask for yet more cultures, Trish was cool, almost to the point of being aggressive.

'I don't think anyone expected to see *you* in here today,' she said.

'Why not?'

'I would have thought you'd have other things on your mind after what happened to Mary . . .' She half-turned to the other girls, who were looking daggers at Gavin. 'We all did.'

'It may suit the department to believe I was to blame for what happened to Mary yesterday, but I wasn't,' said Gavin, in as measured tones as he could manage.

'If you say so.'

'I do say so. Now, about these cell cultures . . .'

'I'm afraid we're really busy at the moment. Tell us what you want and you'll be put in the queue.'

'Any idea how long?'

'Not really.'

—

Gavin felt himself flush with anger and frustration as he walked back to the lab. He couldn't see a way out of the impasse. Whatever he said or did, the whole department from the top down was going to continue blaming him. He considered reporting the affair to the police himself, but knew that as soon as Sutcliffe and the academic staff let it be known that they thought him to blame, the police would be happy to go along with that. Like water running downhill, they would go for the easiest option.

The lab was full of men in suits when he got back. They were carrying clipboards, taking measurements and making notes. One was replacing the used fire extinguishers and checking the others by weight, using a spring balance. He too was making notes. There was a light on in Frank Simmons' office, so Gavin knocked on the door. As he did so, he heard one of the men say to another, 'Aye, some silly bugger made a mistake and a lassie got it in the face.'

Gavin screwed his eyes shut and fought the urge to snap back at him, while willing Simmons to respond quickly.

'Wait!' said Simmons from within.

Gavin couldn't remember him ever saying that before. He sat down at Mary's desk -his own was being used by the men in suits – and didn't quite know what to do with his hands. He was reluctant to touch anything. He looked along the neat row of A4 folders containing Mary's experimental notes: three years of work for a PhD, and the foundation of a research career that would be on hold for the foreseeable future. He subconsciously ran his fingers lightly over the skin on his face as he pondered yet again that it could have been – should have been – him.

Simmons' office door opened and Tom Baxter emerged, tears running down his face. He seemed too distraught to take in anything around him. 'I just need a bit of time,' he insisted as he shrugged off Frank Simmons' attempt to put a hand on his arm. Gavin got up to offer help, but Tom was already out the door. Simmons turned and motioned to him to come in.

'Tom's taking it very badly.'

'I can see that,' said Gavin.

'I didn't realise he and Mary were that close.'

'Everyone liked Mary . . . as I've been finding out to my cost.'

Simmons raised an eyebrow.

'People are blaming me. The tissue culture people have decided I'm to be at the back of the queue when it comes to supplying cell cultures. Others have decided that I don't exist any more.'

'They'll come round. People do.'

'I don't want them to come round,' said Gavin. 'I want them to believe that I had nothing to do with what happened.'

Simmons sighed. 'Of course, I forgot. You don't make mistakes.'

'Not that one.'

'Well, you'll just have to face up to the fact that people think otherwise. I think they'd be more sympathetic if you didn't keep denying even the possibility that you made a mistake.'

'Look, Frank, I didn't do it, and I'm going to keep on denying it, so where do we go from here?'

Simmons adopted a resigned smile. 'The works department tell me that it will take at least a month to put the lab back together again.'

'Maybe I'll have some cell cultures by then,' said Gavin sourly.

Simmons looked at his watch. 'I'll have to get myself out to the Burns Unit. Mary's parents are due there at eleven thirty. They're flying in from Dublin.'

'Have you heard how she is?'

'Not much change. Her life's not in danger, but she has yet to be told about the full extent of her injuries.'

Gavin nodded and looked around. 'Well, I guess there's nothing I can do here at the moment.'

'Best stay away for a bit.'

'Everyone would like that.'

Simmons shrugged, but felt he could offer no reassurance.

***

Outside in the lab, Gavin sat back down at Mary's desk, waiting until the men in suits had finished so that he could gather together some stuff to take home with him. If he was going to take time off, he'd need his notebooks and some relevant journals. He wondered briefly what else he should take, before deciding to move the Valdevan and polymyxin, in case anything 'unfortunate' happened to them. Ever since the episode with the acid contamination he had been hiding them in a plastic box with the contents labelled as something else in the big communal fridge out in the corridor. He'd be happier now with the box in the fridge at the flat. If anything happened to the Valdevan, the company certainly wouldn't give him any more. There would be no more experiments and possibly no published paper if the results had to depend on a single series of experiments.

Gavin fetched the box from the corridor fridge and removed the two bottles containing the drugs which he relocated in a small, thick-walled polystyrene container before adding ice to it and sealing it with tape. He packed it away in his rucksack.

The Works Department men had finished their work and were stuffing their clipboards back in their briefcases. Gavin watched as they filed out with a series of nods and smiles in his direction, of the type afforded to unknown people of unknown status.

Simmons came out of his office and said, 'I'm off to the hospital.'

Gavin, who was very much aware of the barrier that had come down between Frank and himself, said, 'Tell Mary . . . to hang in there.' He knew it sounded lame. He would send flowers on his way home.

Simmons nodded. 'Has Tom come back yet?'

Gavin said not.

'Maybe you could make sure he's all right before you go?'

'Sure, Frank.'

Simmons left and Gavin took a slow walk round the lab, tracing his hand over the charred surface of his bench. He had been so busy fending off the suggestion that it had all been his fault that he hadn't had time to consider exactly how an unknown third party could have done this. It wouldn't have been easy. If he had filled the beaker with ethanol – as he was sure he had on that morning – and then left the lab in response to Carrie's phone call, someone must have switched the ethanol for ether in the time between his leaving and Mary arriving. Frank had already gone off to the library and Tom had been about to leave for the airport . . . Gavin's throat tightened as he realised that Tom Baxter had been the only person in the lab at the critical time – and he, of course, would have had no idea that Mary was about to sit down at his bench and work there . . .

As if on cue, the lab door opened and Tom Baxter came in, looking deathly pale. He was holding a white envelope which he placed on Mary's desk, before looking at Gavin through dark, empty eyes. Gavin read in them all he needed to know.

'It was you, wasn't it?' he said hoarsely, now understanding why Tom was so upset over what had happened. 'You must have heard on the news last night that someone had been injured in a fire at the university but no name was mentioned. You thought it was me until Frank told you this morning.'

The blank stare did not change.

'Why, for Christ's sake?'

A look of utter disdain appeared on Tom's face. 'Have you any idea how much I loathe you?'

The look on Gavin's face said not.

'I have to work my butt off just to keep my head above water in this place, while everything comes so natural to you, Mr bloody know-it-all. If I forget something you'll know it. Any time I screw up, you'll be there to point it out. You do bugger all for weeks on end and then you make one suggestion and suddenly you're Frank's ace researcher. I get my one lucky break: Grumman Schalk are prepared to give me a job, a good job, much better than anything I was going to be getting on the poxy postdoc circuit for second-rate researchers like me – yes, you see, I do know my limitations. After that, I'd probably end up teaching biology in some bloody comprehensive to a bunch of teenage fuckwits who didn't want to know.'

Gavin was mesmerised by the change that had come over Tom Baxter. The body of the gangly, dishevelled student seemed to have been taken over by a spirit of malevolence and bitterness. Even his voice seemed different. The nervous pauses and unnecessary clearing of the throat were no longer in evidence.

'Then you have your big idea and fuck things up. Grumman are going to pull the plug on everything, including the job offers, because you won't stop fucking around with Valdevan – but what does that matter to the great Gavin Donnelly? He knows best. He always knows fucking best.'

Gavin tensed himself as Tom started to come towards him. He sensed that Tom's anger had reached the critical level where action

211

had to take over to provide some sort of release. He tried anticipating what he might do and noticed, with a frisson of horror, the scalpel lying on the island bench. It had a blade so sharp that it could open up his face before he realised anything had happened, and it was just about to be within Tom's reach.

Gavin's heart missed a beat when Tom paused next to it but, to his enormous relief, Tom didn't appear to see it. He didn't seem to see anything, and Gavin realised that he was lost in the nightmare of what he'd done.

'Mary . . . poor Mary,' Tom murmured. 'She just had to do you a good turn and . . . Christ, what have I done?' He put his hands to his face and his shoulders started to heave.

Gavin kept perfectly still, feeling that Tom was so unstable that anything could happen. He clearly couldn't come to terms with being the cause of Mary's disfigurement, so it was still possible that he might turn his anger and guilt on him in an effort to block out the pain. Any move he made, even a wrong word – and right now, they'd all be wrong – might trigger a sudden explosion of violence.

Tom brought his hands down slowly from his face and looked at Gavin, who felt himself tense again. He expected to see eyes filled with hatred, but that wasn't what was there. He saw nothing but emptiness: deep, dark, despairing emptiness. He sensed the danger had passed.

'And now I have to make it right . . .' murmured Tom as he turned away and made for the door. Gavin let out his breath and felt his shoulders relax. He considered going after him but dismissed the idea, recognising that he was the last person on earth that Tom would want near him. He assumed that his assertion about 'making it right' meant confession, giving himself up to the police, but he decided to call security anyway. 'Try to stop him leaving the building, will you? He's not well.'

'Do we call the police or an ambulance?'

'The police.'

Gavin slumped down into a chair, feeling the adrenalin drain from him. He started to take comfort from the silence in the lab, but only until somewhere out in the corridor a woman started screaming. It went on and on.

Gavin rushed out, as did others from the neighbouring labs, exchanging questioning looks as they followed the source of the sound. It was coming from behind the doors leading to the stairs. There they found a slight, blonde girl – one of the junior technicians from the Drummond lab – screaming hysterically as she pointed down into the stairwell. 'He just . . . went over . . .' she stammered as two of her colleagues wrapped their arms round her.

Gavin looked over the banister to see the body of Tom Baxter spread-eagled on the stone floor far below. Even at this height he could see that his skull had shattered. This was what Tom had meant by 'making it right'.

'What on earth's going on?' asked Jack Martin, appearing at the railings by Gavin's shoulder.

'Tom Baxter,' said Gavin.

Martin looked at him quizzically.

'He put the ether in the beaker. It was meant for me.'

'Baxter? Jesus Christ, what was he thinking about?'

'He thought my work was going to stop him getting his dream job with Grumman Schalk. He seemed to think the company was going to withdraw the postdoc job offers as well as the grant.' Gavin looked directly at Martin, making it a question.

'There has been some talk along those lines,' conceded Martin.

'First they threaten the university with withdrawal of funds if work on Valdevan doesn't stop, then they tell the postgrad students that their jobs are going down the tubes as well. Nice people.'

'Where's Frank?' asked Martin, clearly not wanting to be drawn.

213

'He went to meet Mary's parents at the hospital.'

'Shit. Now he has this to come back to.'

Both men looked down again at Tom Baxter's body, which had now been covered by a white plastic sheet. The police had arrived.

TWENTY-ONE

Gavin couldn't bear to be in the lab any longer. He knew that the police would want to speak to him, but at that precise moment, he didn't want to speak to them, or anyone else for that matter. His world had collapsed and he needed to be away from the epicentre of the disaster. He collected his rucksack and left the building by the back stairs, where he paused for a moment, undecided as to which direction to take until he remembered the package in his rucksack. He would have to go back to the flat and put the drugs in the fridge before he did anything else.

As he crossed the road, he saw a number 27 bus coming up Lauriston Place and sprinted to the stop in Forrest Road where he got on board, fumbling in successive jacket pockets for his travel pass, to the annoyance of the driver, who sucked his teeth and tapped his fingers on the wheel.

Back at the flat, Gavin removed the ice from the polystyrene box, resealed it carefully with tape and put it in the fridge. He was out again within five minutes and, after a short walk, standing in the Abbotsford in Rose Street, where he had two packets of crisps and a pint of lager for lunch. It was still early: the bar was quiet. Another half hour and it would be buzzing with the atmosphere Gavin liked so much, but not today.

'Day off?' asked the barman, wiping the bar top.

'You could say,' replied Gavin, putting an end to conversation. Normally, he welcomed talk with strangers, often finding it, as most people did, easier than with people he knew, but today he needed to be somewhere where he could think clearly and without distraction. A pub wasn't going to fit the bill. He drained his glass and left, still not sure about where he was going.

He joined Princes Street at its east end and started walking west past a row of buses, waiting line astern like a string of sausages as they took it in turn to move in to their appointed stops. The one at their head had 'North Berwick' on its destination board. On impulse, Gavin got on. He'd never been there, but he knew that it was beside the sea and about twenty miles or so east of the city. The plan was to find a beach and start walking. On a cold day in February this should afford him the solitude he needed.

There was an icy wind coming from the east so he decided to walk in the opposite direction, so that he would have it behind him. The tide was out, so he was able to walk on firm wet sand instead of the strength-sapping soft stuff at the head of the beach, something which also meant that he wasn't forced to adhere strictly to the line of the shore and could cut across small bays and inlets at will, making straight lines out of curves.

His attention was drawn to a big rock situated about a hundred metres out from the shoreline. It was over two metres high, but had barnacles all over it, suggesting that it was routinely covered at high tide. Feeling drawn to it, Gavin went over, doing his best to avoid the puddles and rivulets left by the receding water, which threatened to swamp his trainers. He rested his hands on the surface, very conscious of the weight of its years.

'Well, big rock,' he murmured. 'What are you saying? I'd appreciate your input. You were here a long time before I was born, and you'll be here a long time after I die. What's it all about, eh? Why do we do what we do?'

Gavin found a smooth section to rest his cheek against while he looked idly at the water, which was lapping the sand with a sluggishness that suggested extreme cold.

'Nothing to say, huh? Maybe you don't know either.'

As he turned away, Gavin looked back and said, 'You're quite right: saying nothing is probably the best policy. That way, you don't upset anybody . . .'

Gavin had been walking for just under an hour when he came across a log that had been washed ashore and sat down on it for a few minutes to give his legs a rest. Almost immediately, he felt himself grow colder as the wind caught his right side, making him pull up the collar of his denim jacket and fold his arms, although this had little effect. It was less than five minutes before he decided that he had to start moving again, but as he stood up, his mobile rang. He could see on the screen it was Carrie. It had rung four times before he summoned up the courage to answer.

'Hello.'

'Gavin? Can you talk?'

'Sure.'

'What's that sound in the background? Where are you?'

'It's the wind. I'm on the beach.'

'Where?'

'Somewhere near North Berwick.'

'What's going on, Gavin?'

'Where do I begin? There was a fire at the lab – Mary was burned: she'll probably be scarred for life. Tom Baxter has committed suicide because he caused the fire. He meant it for me. Apart from that . . .'

'Stop it, Gavin! Talk sense.'

Gavin took a moment to pull himself together. The enormity of all that had happened had given him a strange feeling of detachment which, even in his upset state, he recognised as an escape mechanism from the hell of reality. 'Tom thought my research was going to screw up his job prospects with Grumman Schalk, so he set me up to have an accident in the lab.'

'An accident?'

'A flash fire involving ether, only Mary Hollis got it instead. She was doing me a good turn – setting up some cultures for me. She

217

was badly burned: she's in intensive care. When he realised what he'd done, Tom couldn't handle it. He threw himself down the stairwell. End of story.'

'Oh, my God.'

'Why did you phone?' asked Gavin, closing his eyes.

'I need to talk to you.'

'It's bye bye Gavin time, right?'

'No, you idiot, I just need to talk.'

'I'm not dumped?'

'You can be a prat at times, but I still love you.'

'You do? Christ, I thought it was all over.'

'No, but I do need to talk to you, although, after what you've just told me, this is probably not the best time.'

'No one else wants to talk to me. I think even Frank wishes he'd never laid eyes on me. If I hadn't come to his lab none of this would have happened.'

'Don't blame yourself, Gavin. None of this was your fault.'

'What was it you want to talk about?'

'My mother.'

'I'm sorry I said all those hurtful things. I wasn't thinking straight.'

'Oh yes you were,' said Caroline. 'It's just that sometimes it's so painful to be confronted with the truth. It can be so cold and unforgiving, not what you want to hear at all . . .'

'I guess.'

'Let's not talk over the phone. Maybe we can meet up later? I came back this morning. I'm in Edinburgh.'

'Sure. Eight o'clock in Doctors?'

'Fine.'

Gavin, seeing signs of habitation, turned inland, climbing up through the sand dunes and plantations of stabilising marram grass to find the village of Gullane, which didn't take long to impress its comfortable middle-class and golfing credentials on him, as he made his way up to the main street looking for a bus stop. He had less than fifteen minutes to wait before he was on his way back to the city.

—

Jenny Simmons found her husband sitting in the house when she got in from work at the surgery. He had his back to her and was looking out of the window. 'This is becoming a habit,' she said. 'Not sex again?'

'No,' sighed Simmons, 'Nothing like that.'

'Oh,' said Jenny feigning disappointment. 'I didn't think it was that bad last time . . .' The smile faded from her face when she saw the look in her husband's eyes. 'Oh, my God, Frank, what's the matter?' she asked, sinking to her knees beside him.

Simmons told her what had happened to Tom Baxter and why. 'Christ, Jenny, what a mess.'

'I really don't know what to say,' said Jenny. 'I thought things couldn't possibly get any worse after yesterday.'

'Tom's dead, Mary is going to be disfigured for life, and my lab is in ruins. To top it off, everyone wishes the one remaining member of my group had never been born . . . and all because he came up with something that looks like a cure for cancer.'

Simmons looked at his wife in wide-eyed disbelief. 'Can you believe it?'

Jenny shook her head. 'It's crazy.'

'I'm desperately trying to find something positive to concentrate on,' said Simmons. 'But I'm damned if I can find anything. Help me?'

'I wish I could, Frank,' said Jenny, hugging him. 'Maybe when the awfulness of what's happened to Mary and Tom . . . passes . . . you'll be able to concentrate on Gavin's research again . . . and the good that can come from it?'

Simmons felt himself go tense.

'I know . . . I know that's what caused all of this but . . . nevertheless . . .'

'Maybe,' agreed Simmons.

'I think you should call the doctor and get something to help you sleep. You didn't get much last night,' said Jenny.

Simmons waved away the suggestion.

The phone rang and Jenny answered it. She turned and said, 'It's Graham Sutcliffe. Do you want to speak to him?'

Simmons took the phone.

Jenny couldn't tell anything from her husband's expression, which seemed to stay blank throughout the short conversation. 'Well?' she asked.

'He wants a meeting.'

'Tonight?' exclaimed Jenny.

Simmons nodded. 'At Old College.'

'Of all the insensitive . . .'

'They'll probably want to discuss damage limitation over Tom's death.'

———

Gavin met Caroline outside the pub just before eight. He took her in his arms and felt a wave of emotion overcome him as he held her close. 'God, it's so good to see you.'

'You too. You've been through such a lot since I last saw you. I'm still finding it hard to believe what happened in the lab.'

'Let's not go there,' said Gavin. 'I've been over it so many times in my head that I don't want to talk about it any more. Instead, you can tell me what's troubling you.'

'Is it that obvious?'

'To someone who loves you.'

'My mother's asked me to help her.'

Gavin closed his eyes as it dawned on him what Caroline meant. 'Oh, God,' he murmured.

'She feels she can't ask Dad because it would be against everything he stands for. She sees having a medical student for a daughter as her next best option.'

'What a nightmare.'

'She sees it as a simple request to her daughter. I get her some pills; she takes them, and there's an end to her pain, her suffering and her indignity. We kiss, say goodbye and it's all over. Done and dusted. Only, of course, it isn't quite like that for the rest of us . . .'

'What did you say?'

'I told her not to be so silly. She should hang in there. She could still beat this thing if she put her mind to it. The papers are always full of stories of people beating the odds. The medical profession is proved wrong on an almost daily basis. But of course, that was all rubbish. I was bullshitting my own mother. I know damned well that things are only going to get worse for her, and there's a doctor's surgery in the house for God's sake. Getting the drugs wouldn't be a problem. I was just desperate to get out of a situation I didn't want to be in. In the end, I just put up the shutters and refused to talk any more about it.'

'Did she accept that?'

Caroline shook her head and her eyes became moist. 'She pleaded with me to change my mind. Can you imagine what it's like to have your own mother plead with you to end her suffering?'

Gavin grimaced and shook his head.

'But you know the worst thing?' continued Caroline. 'It wasn't feelings of pity or compassion that overwhelmed me. It was anger. I was angry that she'd put me in that position. She was my mother and I was furious she was doing that to me. I stormed out of the house and came back to Edinburgh and now . . . I am so ashamed of myself. I am so consumed by guilt that I just want to curl up and die.'

The tears were flowing freely down Caroline's face now as she looked to Gavin. 'Well, Gavin . . . what should I do?'

'You know I can't tell you that.'

'Not good enough. You're big on truth and telling it like it is. I need your take on this.'

'It was you who pointed out that people don't always want to hear the truth.'

'This time I need to hear it,' countered Caroline.

Gavin's reluctance made him consider for a long time before he said, 'You can't afford to become involved in ending your mother's life. It would be illegal and you'd probably get caught. You'd be charged with murder, or more likely manslaughter, and possibly go to jail. There would be lots of sympathy and understanding for you, but it wouldn't translate into permission to break the law. Either way, there would be no place for you in medicine any more. Your career would be over before it started.'

'And Mum's wishes?'

'They don't come into it.'

'Ouch.'

'Sorry.'

'Now tell me the *right* thing to do, Gavin. Not the legal thing or the sensible thing but the *right* thing.'

'I can't do that.'

'You can tell me what you *think* the right thing to do is?'

'That can get messy when it's different from the legal, or even the moral, thing.'

'Stop fencing. Tell me what you think.'

Gavin took a hesitant breath. 'The right thing to do is to help your mother end her suffering. She can't be cured, and the medics are only interested in keeping her alive as long as possible to make their survival rate figures look better. Success is measured by how long they keep you alive, not how good your quality of life is. There are no boxes to be filled in for pain and indignity. They don't figure in the notes.'

'Thanks, Gav.'

'But you can't. The stakes are too high.'

Caroline nodded.

'Your father should do it.'

Caroline recoiled at the sting in the tail, and made a face to emphasise just how out of the question Gavin's suggestion was. 'You don't know my father,' she exclaimed.

'No, but I know the situation. If anyone should help your mother it should be him.'

'My father gets ill at the thought of parking on a double yellow line,' exclaimed Caroline. 'His whole life has been governed by rules and regulations, manners and convention. The idea that he should help my mother commit suicide is just . . .' Words failed her.

'Maybe he needs you to spell it out for him.'

'How?'

'Shock him out of his comfort zone. He obviously believes that he is doing all he can to help the woman he loves so dearly. Tell him that feeling bad about everything doesn't do a damn thing to help her. Point out to him that he has the means to stop your mother's suffering if he'd just start thinking for himself instead of having the BMA and Church of England do it for him.'

'I couldn't do that to him.'

'Desperate times, desperate measures.'

Caroline shook her head as she thought it through and came to the same conclusion. 'I just couldn't.'

'Then you'll both watch your mother go through hell until the *Good Lord* or whoever relents and lets her go. Still, a couple of choruses of "The Lord's My Shepherd" and a few words of comfort from the vicar should make everything all right. Flowers on the grave every first Sunday of the month and a picture on the piano . . .'

'You bastard!'

'Sorry.'

'No, I asked you to tell me what you thought,' said Caroline, enunciating each word carefully 'And that's exactly what you did. I thank you for that. And, if it's any comfort, I still love you.'

Gavin's shoulders relaxed.

'But just who the hell are you to talk?'

'I'm sorry?'

'Come on, Gavin, you're in cancer research. You've come up with a way of treating tumours, and not once have we discussed this in relation to my mother. Why not?'

Gavin sat back in his chair and appeared to look in all directions for inspiration. 'Because I work with test tubes. It's a world away from real people. A few lab experiments have worked out okay and things are looking promising but . . .'

'Do I hear the sound of furious back-pedalling, Gavin?'

'Okay, I do think it has a chance of working if anyone ever gets round to giving it its chance, but even then there will be hurdles to jump before it's tried out on people.'

'But you have the wherewithal to try it?'

'I've got the drugs, if that's what you mean . . .'

'So your objections are . . . legal? You don't have the necessary paperwork, permissions, approvals, etc?'

'I suppose . . . but there's more to it than that. There's what you have to prove before you get the paperwork.'

Caroline chose to ignore the proviso. 'How about moral objections? It's wrong to experiment on people?'

Gavin shrugged, clearly unhappy with the way the conversation had turned.

'So if you can't do the legal thing and you can't do the moral thing, what does that leave us with . . . the *right* thing . . . does it not?'

'Carrie . . .'

'I just thought I'd tell you what *I* thought, Gav, since you were so obliging when I asked. I think it all boils down to me finding it strange that we're sitting here discussing who should kill my mother, when you might well have the means of saving her.'

'Wow,' said Gavin under his breath. 'Where did all that come from?'

'Come on, you're not telling me the idea never crossed your mind?' said Caroline, looking incredulous. 'We both know that we've been avoiding having this conversation, ever since you got that great result in the lab, right?'

'I suppose,' conceded Gavin. 'When you first told me your mother had cancer I remember thinking how great it would be if I came up with a cure for her . . . how impressed you'd be. You'd fall in love with me and we'd live happily ever after. And then again when I saw the tumour cells dying in the lab – but these were just fairy-tale thoughts, like standing on the terrace at a Liverpool game when the manager comes up to you through the crowd and says, "Gav, we're a bit short of strikers." It's just a dream. It's just not the way things happen . . .'

'She's got cancer; you have a possible cure. I think you should try it.'

Gavin shook his head. 'It would be wrong. I don't even know if it works on all kinds of tumours. There could be a cross-reaction between the two drugs in human beings. There are all sorts of reasons . . .'

'And none of them valid for a woman who is in pain and dying. Paperwork is for people who are guarding their own arses . . . if I might quote you.'

'But if every –'

'We are not talking about *every* here. We are talking about my mother.'

Gavin rubbed his temples.

'Think about it, Gav. That's all I ask. Give it some serious thought?'

Gavin nodded.

'Another beer? Crisps?'

Gavin shook his head.

'You're not going to go all quiet on me, are you?'

'No, this is exactly the kind of moment when we should go on speaking to each other.'

'So tell me what you're thinking.'

'I suppose I'm thinking that if I got caught doing something like this, there are a lot of people in the department who'd have a field day. Smart-arse Donnelly isn't content with doing all the science on his own; he's now started treating the patients. They'd laugh all the way to the courtroom.'

'I'll treat Mum,' said Caroline. 'You just give me the drugs and tell me what to do.'

'It could destroy us both.'

'On the other hand, it might just work.'

TWENTY-TWO

Gavin didn't sleep much. He tossed and turned as he struggled to make sense of his predicament and tried to see a way out. The thing he hadn't told Caroline was that if he were to hand over what Valdevan he had, there would be none left to carry out the final confirmatory experiments. He hadn't said this because he felt sure that she would have seen it as just another excuse. True, the planned experiments were only repeats of what he'd done before, and the paper might still be accepted without the insurance they offered, but equally well, it might not – it would all depend on which referees it was sent out to for comments. Happily, it was unlikely that it would be sent to anyone in the same department, or even the same university, but word going out on the grapevine might still make things difficult if old pals were to make phone calls and old favours were to be called in. This was why Frank Simmons wanted the data to be watertight before they submitted for publication.

Although he felt bad about it, it wasn't as if he had any doubts about what had to be done: the interests of the many had to be put before those of an individual, even if that individual happened to be Caroline's mother. This was what his head was telling him, but his heart was telling him something else. Caroline loved her mother and he loved Caroline. Doing the right thing would mean hurting one of them deeply and denying the other a possible chance of life. There was also the possibility that it might already be too late for her mother – but this was just another doubt that rolled in on the tide of angst that denied him any relief from mounting stress.

He wished there was someone he could confide in, but there wasn't. Anyone capable of understanding the factors involved was already an interested party, and therefore had an axe to grind. Frank would see publication of the science as paramount. Carrie would cling to any chance at all of helping her mother. He, of course, would like to see both these things happen. Grumman Schalk, on the other hand, were determined to consign Valdevan to history and wanted the science to disappear – as did the university, who were siding with Grumman for financial reasons. If either of these parties were to catch wind of any plan to use the drug therapeutically, they would almost certainly call in the police. Alternative agendas? He couldn't move for them.

He didn't fall asleep until what passed for daylight in Edinburgh on a morning in February appeared in the sky, and assured him that the demons of the night had gone. He dozed until eleven before taking a lukewarm shower and making himself some coffee and toast. His flatmates were out at work so he had the kitchen to himself as he planned the day ahead. There was now no need for him to stay away from the department. Tom Baxter's confession had absolved him from any blame over what had happened to Mary. He and Frank had to talk, and the sooner the better.

Frank wasn't in the lab when Gavin arrived and there was no sign of him having been there: no jacket hanging behind the door in his office and no battered briefcase sitting at the side of his desk. Gavin's nerves stopped him hanging around waiting. He went down to the cell culture suite to see if relations had improved now that the staff knew that he wasn't to blame for the fire.

He found Trish in contrite mood. 'I'm so sorry, Gavin. We never dreamt that anything like that could happen, in the university of all places. Everyone was so sure it had to have been an accident, then when we heard that Tom Baxter had set the whole thing up deliberately . . . he must have been off his head. Makes you wonder who you're working beside these days . . .'

'The sooner we start picking up the pieces and getting back to normal the better,' said Gavin.

'Do you think you can? I mean, apart from you, Frank's group has virtually gone . . . his lab's a complete mess . . .'

'We've got to try,' said Gavin. 'If you believe in what you're doing you have to get on with it. Looking backwards never got anyone anywhere.'

Trish shrugged uncertainly.

'I'm going to see if someone will give me lab space to set up a few experiments. I was wondering where I was in the queue for cell cultures right now?'

Trish looked as if she was walking on eggshells. 'Honestly, Gavin, I'd love to be able to tell you that we'll get right on to it, but a problem has come up. We had a circular round from Professor Sutcliffe. He says that all requests made under Frank Simmons' grant numbers should be suspended for the time being . . .'

'What for?' exclaimed Gavin. 'There's loads of money in the accounts. Frank's one of the best-funded scientists in the department.'

'I'm sure you're right . . .' Trish looked uncomfortable. 'But I don't see how we can ignore it. Maybe you should speak to the prof?'

Gavin knocked on Liz's door and entered. She looked as if she had been expecting him. 'He's on the phone at the moment. I'll ask if he'll see you when he's finished.'

Gavin nodded, and turned his attention to the painting on the wall while Liz got back to her typing. He was on the third tilt of his head in a search for a meaningful angle when Liz said, 'That's him finished.' She pressed the intercom button and said, 'Gavin Donnelly wonders if he might have a word?'

'Give me a couple of minutes.'

Liz made a face and Gavin turned his attention back to the picture on the wall. Five minutes later, Sutcliffe opened the door of his office and said, 'Come in, Gavin. I'm glad you dropped by. I wasn't sure if you'd be in today.'

'I've just been down in the cell culture suite. They tell me Frank's grants have been suspended?'

'Frank and I had a long conversation last night,' said Sutcliffe, ignoring what Gavin had said. 'There was a meeting up at Old College. Understandably, he's very upset over what happened to Mary and Tom, and the faculty wanted to do anything they could to help. Frank will be taking some time off to rest and recover. He's been granted six months' leave of absence, effective immediately. I understand he and Jenny plan to visit relatives in Australia.'

'Australia?' exclaimed Gavin. 'Six months?'

'What with his lab being out of action and everything else that's gone on, it seems like the right time. That is why I took the step of suspending the use of his grants this morning. Everything is going into suspended animation, as it were.'

Gavin sat, wide-eyed and speechless.

'And you, of course, are wondering where this leaves you . . .'

I have to finish off the experiments for the paper we're about to submit,' said Gavin, feeling totally disorientated. 'I need more cell cultures . . .'

'There's no question of you carrying out unsupervised research,' said Sutcliffe, pausing to let the words sink in. 'Frank, of course, expressed concern for your immediate future, and I have made preliminary enquiries about the possibility of an alternative supervisor for you. Jack Martin – very kindly I thought in the circumstances – would be agreeable to taking you on . . . but on the clear understanding that you would work on one of his projects. It wouldn't be too late to change; you've only been here six months, and I'm sure the first-year review committee would take that into consideration when the time came for your first-year assessment.'

'I need to finish off the Valdevan work,' said Gavin. 'It won't take long and it won't be expensive.'

'I'm afraid that is out of the question.'

The words hit Gavin like a death sentence. The curtain had fallen, and he hadn't even heard the fat lady sing. It was over. Game, set and match to Sutcliffe. The anger and impotence he felt made him get up from his chair and leave the room without saying another word.

'Let me know your decision,' said Sutcliffe pleasantly to his back.

'All right?' asked Liz as he passed.

'Bastard,' murmured Gavin.

He had to speak to Frank, was his one thought as he hurried along the corridor to the lab. What the hell was he playing at? Two technicians from the computing support group were coming out of the lab as he arrived. 'Problems?' he asked.

'No, everything's fine,' said one.

Gavin sat down on Simmons' chair in his office and called his home number. Jenny answered.

'Jenny? It's Gavin Donnelly. I need to speak to Frank.'

'I'm sorry, Gavin. Frank needs a few days away from everything to do with the lab. I really don't want anyone bothering him.'

'It's important.'

'So is his health.'

'Yes, sorry, of course. Maybe I could come and see him in a couple of days' time? There's quite a lot we have to sort out.'

'I'm sure.'

⁓

Gavin's head was spinning. What on earth was Frank thinking of, going away for six months when they were so close to finishing the Valdevan work? He desperately needed something to cling to, and right now, anything would do. He tried building a raft with positives. He had the drugs safely at home in the flat; he had a copy of Frank's first draft of the paper, and he had all his notes containing the raw data. He saw that it would be more convenient to have electronic versions of both, so they could be transferred more easily, so he turned on Frank's computer to make copies from the hard drive to disk. But as he did so, his blood ran cold, and he suddenly realised why the computer technicians had been in the lab. He had the confirmation in front of him. The hard drive on Frank Simmons' computer had been wiped clean. The master copy of the paper had been deleted. He rushed out into the lab to check the other computers. All the hard drives had been wiped.

For the very first time in dealing with opposition to his work, Gavin felt fear enter the equation. Anger and frustration were no longer his leading emotions. The opposition were winning, and he felt powerless to do anything. At that particular moment, there was no record anywhere in the department of the work he'd done on Valdevan, and when he turned down Jack Martin's offer of an alternative PhD project – as they must know he would – Sutcliffe would have the MRC cancel his grant, resulting in there being no record of him either. Gavin Donnelly would be a soon-to-be-forgotten name who had once spent six months in the department before giving up and leaving. You had to respect opposition like that.

It was less than an hour since he'd given Trish a lecture about not looking back. Now he found himself having to heed his own advice. He had to move on. It was no longer going to be possible for him to finish the repeat experimental work: the paper would have to go off and take its chances with what data they had. The first thing to do would be to type the text into his laptop from the hard copy he had, and then update all the data. When that was done, he would need Frank to write a covering letter. It was essential that the paper be submitted with a statement giving the origin of the work as Edinburgh University and signed by a senior member of the academic staff. If he tried to submit on his own, Sutcliffe would disown both him and the research. With that clear in his head, the top of the agenda now was Valdevan. What was bad news for experimental work was good news for Caroline's mother.

Gavin locked the lab door from the inside before opening his rucksack and moving quickly round the lab, collecting bits and pieces he might need: sterilising filters, syringes of assorted capacity and needles to fit, a few bottles of sterile distilled water and a couple of sterile beakers. He returned to Frank Simmons' office to check the second-year medical students' lecture schedule for that day, and found that Caroline would finish at 4 p.m. He was waiting for her when she emerged from the lecture theatre.

The other students seemed chatty and animated, but Caroline, when she appeared, seemed alone and preoccupied. She smiled wanly when she saw Gavin and kissed him on the cheek. 'I wasn't at all sure if I'd see you today.'

'Let's get some coffee.'

They made their way round to the student union.

'Frank's going to Australia,' said Gavin as they sat down with their coffee.

'What?' said Caroline.

'For six months.'

Caroline looked incredulous. 'Why?'

'I haven't been able to ask him that. Apparently, he's been taking what happened pretty badly.'

'Understandable, I suppose – but Australia for six months? What's going to happen to you and your research?'

'We'll have to send off what data we have and hope for the best,' said Gavin. 'Jenny says I'll be able to talk to Frank in a couple of days or so, and I need him to write a covering letter. As for me, Sutcliffe's given me the choice of a change to Jack Martin's group with a change of project, or . . . out on my ear.'

'That's outrageous. What's Frank playing at? He can't let this happen.'

'That's what I keep thinking,' said Gavin. 'But every time I pinch myself, I find I'm awake.'

'There has to be more to this than we're seeing,' said Caroline. 'There just has to be.'

'I've been thinking about what you said about treating your mother . . .'

'Forget it. It was a crazy idea,' said Caroline.

'Your mother is probably too far gone to be helped.'

Caroline nodded.

'If I use up the Valdevan on her, there will be none left to complete the experiments, if and when lab space should ever become available.'

Another nod.

'There probably isn't enough to treat your mother anyway.'

'Gavin, you don't have to explain . . .'

'But we're going to give it a try if you're up for it.'

Caroline's mouth fell open. 'You're serious?'

'The sooner we get started the better,' said Gavin. 'But where will your father fit into all this?'

'I can't possibly tell him. I'll have to give Mum the drug when he's not around.'

'Will you tell her what you're doing?'

'I think I have to. It's important that we have her permission . . .'

In case things go wrong, thought Gavin, filling in the blank. But even with that proviso, he could imagine a hostile barrister mouthing the words: *You preyed on the hopes of a desperate woman in order to carry out a wholly unlicensed experiment . . .*

'Getting her to agree won't be a problem,' said Caroline. 'But . . .'

'But what?'

'The minute I tell her about this, her whole demeanour is going to change. No matter how much I warn her that it might not work – probably won't work – she is going to cling to it like a life-jacket, because it's the only hope she's got, and that's what people do in her situation. She'll want to tell Dad. She'll want him to share that hope.'

'Presumably he'll go apeshit if he finds out?'

'Absolutely.'

'Your mother wasn't going to tell him about her assisted suicide request.'

'She could hide despair from him. I'm not so sure about hope.'

'Sounds like we're falling at the first fence.'

'I could strike a bargain with her . . . I could tell her that if your idea fails . . . I'll give her the help she wants, providing she doesn't say anything to Dad about Valdevan.'

'The stakes are getting really high.'

'For all of us. When do we start? How do we do this?'

Gavin confessed that it was going to be guesswork all the way, but he could calculate the dose of Valdevan if he knew Caroline's mother's body weight. Caroline was able to tell him exactly, adding, 'She was weighed at the hospital last Thursday.'

'Then the only big unknown is the growth rate of the tumour,' said Gavin. 'Tumours grow at vastly different rates. Cell doubling time can vary from about twenty-five days to over a thousand, with an average of about a hundred. I'm assuming that, because she's gone downhill so fast, your mother's is at the fast end – bad for the patient but good for us – the faster the better. The sooner the cells take up the drug the sooner they'll develop membrane damage and become susceptible to polymyxin. We're only going to get one chance, so I think we have to give her as long as possible on the Valdevan and then give her the polymyxin. We've got enough Valdevan for fourteen days, maybe a bit longer.'

'Whatever you say.'

'When do you plan on going home?'

'I'll tell the university I'm going to have to drop out of my course for a few weeks and hope they'll understand. All things being equal, I could go down tomorrow morning.'

'I'll prepare what you need tonight and write out instructions. I'll meet you at the station in the morning?'

'I don't want to be alone tonight.'

———

Caroline returned to the flat with Gavin and together they prepared a pack for Caroline to take with her in the morning. Luckily, Gavin had held on to the polystyrene box he'd brought the drugs home from the lab in, so it could be restocked with ice and would keep drugs cool until Caroline got home. They talked a bit about the injection schedule and possible side-effects to look out for but, as no lab monitoring would be possible, this would all be subjective.

They went out for a meal to Bar Napoli, an Italian restaurant known for its easy-going Mediterranean atmosphere, in the hope that it might afford them some escape from the growing strain they were under, but to no avail.

'I can't believe I'm going to do this,' said Caroline, playing with the food on her fork more than eating it.

'*We're* doing it,' corrected Gavin.

'I'm to blame. You're only doing it because of me.'

'It's not a question of blame. It's the right thing to do . . . when all's said and done.'

'What will you do while I'm away?'

'I'll write up the paper, adding in all the data I've gathered since Frank did the first draft, and then I'll talk to him and get him to do the covering letter.'

'It's not going to be easy, meeting him after what he's done. You won't lose your temper, will you?'

Gavin shook his head. 'Like you say, there's probably much more to it than we're seeing.'

TWENTY-THREE

Gavin had a pint of lager in the Abbotsford after seeing Caroline off at the station. It took the edge off the feeling that their lives would never be the same again, but despite the temptation to go on drinking, he stopped at one. It wasn't oblivion he needed to embrace right now, it was a sense of purpose. He decided to go home and start typing the paper into his laptop.

Before he could start, he had to decide on which journal the paper should be sent to, because this would determine the format of the text and tables. Frank had mentioned several possibilities at the outset but had not, as far as he knew, come to any firm decision. It didn't take Gavin long to decide to go for broke and write it up for *Nature* – one of the most prestigious scientific journals in the world. If Frank disagreed, the text and data would at least be in the computer. It would be easy enough to re-format it for another journal.

He had a couple of copies of *Nature* among his books and papers, so he looked up the 'Instructions to Authors' section in one of them.

Entering the text of the paper was straightforward, but when it came to inserting tables, his progress slowed to a crawl as he struggled to present data in the way the journal stipulated. He was still wrestling with the software when the first of his flatmates, Tim Anderson, arrived home and offered to help. 'Microsoft Excel is my middle name, Gav.'

Fifteen minutes later, Gavin was biting back the urge to point out to Tim that his first name should be 'Unable to Use', as skills learned in the world of life insurance did not translate well to Gavin's needs. 'Sorry, mate, I'm stumped.'

It took Gavin another hour back in his own room before things became clear, and the tables could be aligned in the stipulated way.

'How's it going?' asked his flatmate, when he went through to the kitchen to make himself a coffee.

'Sorted.'

Caroline phoned just after 8 p.m. 'Mum's had her first injection. I gave her it while Dad was doing evening surgery.'

'Does she know exactly what you're doing?'

'I told her everything,' said Caroline. 'She reacted just like I thought she would: her outlook changed in an instant. Now I understand how easy it is for charlatans to prey on the afflicted. I warned her that there was only the slimmest of chances it would work, and that it had never been tried on anyone before, but she saw the one thing missing from her life – hope – and snatched at it. She's been like a different woman.'

'Your dad will wonder what's going on.'

'She's promised to keep it secret. We came to an agreement.'

Gavin was pleased to hear Caroline sounding positive, even optimistic, but this was an unreal situation. He suspected that she hadn't looked ahead to what might happen if the treatment should fail. The plunge from hope into despair, and possibly bitterness, might well be even more dramatic. He tried broaching the subject.

'Believe me, I spelled it out to her. I went to enormous lengths to stress how experimental this was. Come on, let's not talk about failure on the very first day?'

Gavin agreed.

'What have you been up to?'

Gavin told her of his travails with Microsoft Excel.

'I'm convinced that half the workforce in this country spend their time trying to solve computer problems,' said Caroline.

'And the other half spend their time creating them.'

'When d'you think you'll have finished the paper?'

'Another two or three days, and then I'll arrange with Jenny to see Frank and get him to look it over it and do the letter.'

'Do you know how he is?'

'Jenny didn't want anyone from the lab calling.'

—

Gavin's flatmate took the finished paper to work with him on Thursday morning on a floppy disk, and returned in the evening with three laser-printed copies, courtesy of the insurance company's professional quality printers. Gavin called Frank's number and Jenny answered.

'Jenny, it's Gavin. How is he?

'Oh, he's a lot better, thanks, Gavin. 'A bit lacking in the *joie de vivre* department, but that's only to be expected. I've got him doing all the little jobs round the house he's been avoiding for ages. I guess it's him you want to speak to . . .'

'Hello, Gavin,' said Frank's voice.

'Hi, Frank, I was wondering if we might meet up and have a talk?'

'I was thinking much the same thing,' said Simmons. 'I don't think I want to sit with the ghosts in the lab right now, so why don't you come out here, say tomorrow about eleven?'

'Great, look forward to it.' Gavin put the phone down slowly, not quite sure what he was feeling. The situation seemed strangely surreal. Frank doing jobs round the house after all that had happened . . .

'Everything all right, Gav?' asked Tim.

'Sure. Come on; I'll buy you a beer.'

—

Gavin felt apprehensive as he got off the bus and walked towards Frank's house. He felt angry about Frank running off to Australia, but on the other hand he understood how he must be feeling after all that had happened. He liked Frank, and he thought that Frank had come to like him, but he knew their relationship hadn't developed to a point where they could put all their cards on the table and say exactly what they were feeling. He saw the visit as an exercise in damage limitation. He had his laptop in his rucksack and the three copies of the paper. If all went well and Frank didn't insist on the paper being submitted to some journal other than *Nature* – and he couldn't see why he should, because this was groundbreaking science – he could have everything in the post by that evening. That would be such a good feeling, and if the paper was accepted – which was a much bigger 'if' with the experiments not having been duplicated, but still very possible because of the importance of the subject matter – his worries about his doctorate and future career prospects could well be over. He would be out of reach of the Sutcliffes of this world.

Frank opened the door and invited him in, saying that Jenny was at work at the surgery. 'Coffee?'

'Thanks. How are you feeling?' asked Gavin, as he took off his jacket and hung it over the back of a kitchen chair.

'I'm not sure,' said Simmons, filling two mugs from a coffee flask. He plonked them down on the table and pushed sugar and milk towards Gavin. 'A bit numb, I suppose. One minute I have a lab and a research group, the next minute I don't. I've got nothing.'

Gavin gave a nod but did not speak.

'I keep seeing the look on Mary's parents' faces when they saw her lying there. As for Tom's parents and what they must be going through . . .'

'Maybe the least said the better,' said Gavin, with a hardness that Simmons picked up on. 'Of course, he meant it for you,' he said. 'It's all such a mess . . .'

'I hear you're off to Australia?'

Simmons nodded, becoming aware of Gavin's level gaze, and breaking off eye contact to concentrate on stirring his coffee. 'Jenny has relatives there. Give me a chance to recharge the batteries, that sort of thing.'

'Professor Sutcliffe wouldn't allow me to finish off the Valdevan experiments. He's offered me a change of project.'

Simmons looked down at the table surface. 'Look, Gavin, I'm sorry.'

Gavin felt anger rise up in him but he kept it in check. 'There's still a chance we can get the stuff published without the extra insurance of duplicate results,' he said, opening his rucksack and bringing out the paper. 'I've written it up for *Nature* but I could change it if you really wanted.' He pushed it towards Simmons, who said quietly, '*Nature's* fine . . . exactly where it should be.'

'Then all we need is a covering letter signed by you,' said Gavin, feeling relieved that a big hurdle had been crossed.

'Not possible,' said Simmons.

'I'm sorry?'

'In effect . . . I've relinquished my position in the department for the six-month period of my . . . sabbatical. My grants have been suspended, and so have all my other duties and responsibilities. I no longer have the authority to write such a letter.'

'You're kidding,' said Gavin.

''Fraid not.'

'So what happens to the Valdevan work?'

Simmons shrugged uncomfortably. 'Who knows? Maybe in six months, attitudes will have changed . . .'

'Yeah, right, Frank,' said Gavin angrily, as latent suspicion rose up inside him. 'Or should I say, *Professor* Simmons. Word gets around . . .'

'No, it was nothing like that,' insisted Simmons, as Gavin got up to repack his rucksack.

'Yeah, right.' Gavin slung his pack over his shoulder and made to leave.

'Wait, come back,' said Simmons as Gavin reached the door.

Gavin turned but remained standing defiantly at the door.

'You're not the only one who got mugged.'

Gavin relaxed his grip on the door handle.

'And not all muggers come from dark alleys,' said Simmons.

'What's that supposed to mean?'

'The night Tom died I was summoned to Old College and given a choice,' said Simmons. 'I could either do what I've ended up doing, and temporarily relinquish my position, take a six-month break on full pay, and then return to my job to rebuild my career or . . . they would instigate disciplinary proceedings against me and suspend me from my position pending an investigation. Either way, I was out of the department.'

'Disciplinary proceedings for what?' asked Gavin.

'What I said at the meeting. Apparently it is a serious matter to subject a senior member of the university to sustained verbal abuse.'

'Christ,' said Gavin. 'Where did they dig that one up from?'

'No prizes for guessing what the outcome of such an investigation would be . . . they wouldn't exactly be short of witnesses: the whole department heard. I have a wife, two children and a mortgage. What do you think you would have done in the circumstances?'

Gavin gave a resigned nod. The bottom had just fallen out of his world, and he felt hollow inside. He found it impossible to sustain any one emotion for any length of time. Anger quickly changed to understanding, understanding to pity, pity to suspicion, and back to anger again. 'Enjoy Australia, Frank,' he said, as he turned and left.

Simmons, still sitting at the table, held his head in his hands. Was there to be no end to this nightmare? He was just trying to do what was right and yet . . . it all felt so bloody wrong. After a few moments he had the feeling he wasn't alone, and looked up to see Jenny standing there.

'I came in the back door. I heard what you said.'

Simmons tried to decipher her expression, but found it uncomfortably neutral.

Caroline was pleased with the way things had been going. She had explained the rationale behind the dual drug therapy to her mother, and made sure that she appreciated that she would not notice any change in her condition until the second drug came into play after the fourteenth day of Valdevan. This meant that everything was on hold for two weeks, but happily this included her mother's new-found optimism, which Caroline was hoping her father would ascribe to another remission. It was all to come unstuck, however, on the thirteenth day, when Dr John James came into the bedroom and found Caroline giving her mother an injection.

'Amazing, only two patients at evening surgery,' he began. 'Must be something good on the telly . . . What are you doing?'

Caroline felt the blood drain from her face.

'She's giving me some vitamins,' said her mother, her voice sounding strained and tight.

'Vitamins? What on earth for?' John James strode across the room and looked at the box of vials at Caroline's side. He snatched up one. 'Valdevan!' he exclaimed. 'What the hell do you think you're doing, giving your mother this?'

Caroline had never seen her father so angry. 'We have to talk, Dad.'

'She's helping me,' pleaded her mother, becoming upset.

Although furious, John James could see the effect arguing was going to have on his wife, and fought to control himself. 'We seem to be at cross-purposes here,' he said. 'Caroline's right, my dear; she and I have to talk.'

Caroline and her father went through to his consulting room, where his anger reignited and he hissed, 'What the hell do you think you're doing, giving your mother that stuff? A useless drug, taken off the market years ago. Do you realise what upsetting the delicate balance of her chemotherapy could do to her?'

'Mum's dying, Dad. No *delicate balance of her chemotherapy* is going to change that, and you're jumping to conclusions. I'm not doing what you think I'm doing.'

'I demand an explanation.'

Caroline gave her father a brief synopsis of Gavin's research and admitted that she had persuaded him to let her try it out on her mother. 'The results in the lab were spectacular, Dad, really amazing.'

'So good you are using your own mother as a guinea pig!'

'There's a real chance it will work, and that has to be better than no chance at all, don't you think?'

'If there was any chance this nonsense would work it would be all over the medical journals. This is just cruel, heartless rubbish that has given your mother false hope. How could you?'

'You don't understand, Dad. Believe me, you don't understand the half of it,' pleaded Caroline.

'I've a good mind to report you and this damned boyfriend of yours to the relevant authorities, and let you both take the consequences. Who is his head of department?'

'Mum asked me to help her . . .'

'Don't pretend your mother forced you into this.'

'You don't understand. She asked me to help her die.'

There was a silence in the room that both of them found almost unbearable.

'I don't believe you,' said John James hoarsely.

'She asked me to help her because she felt she couldn't ask you . . .' said Caroline flatly, knowing the hurt she was causing, but feeling that she had to fight back. 'She knew you wouldn't

244

consider it because it *isn't allowed*.' She paused to let the words and the cruel inflection she'd put on them sink in. 'I thought that persuading Gavin to try out the new therapy would be a better option because . . . I couldn't face doing what she wanted me to, and when all's said and done . . . Mum has nothing to lose, has she?'

John James' anger disappeared, and tears started to run down his cheeks. Caroline wanted to put her arms round him but found she couldn't.

'What stage are you at?' croaked James.

'We're about to start the second drug tomorrow. She's already had fourteen days on Valdevan . . .'

'I didn't realise your mother felt like that. She never said anything to me . . . nothing at all.'

'Mum knows you love her and would always do your best for her, Dad. There's no question about that. I just hope that you might come to realise that the same applies to me . . .'

Both Caroline and her father were in tears as they embraced each other.

'Well, where do we go from here?' asked Caroline, wiping her eyes and giving a final sniff as a sign that she was back in control.

'We go back and tell your mother how much we both love her, and that you will be carrying on with the new therapy. To do anything else at this stage would be unthinkable.' John James seemed to take a few moments to consider before saying, 'Damn this bloody awful disease. Damn it to hell.'

'Let's tell Mum.'

John James paused as they reached the door. 'This Gavin of yours, he sounds like a remarkable chap.'

'I think so.'

'The university must be very proud. You must tell me all about him.'

'Later, Dad.'

Caroline heard the sharp intake of breath when she told Gavin that her dad had found out what they were doing. 'But it's all right. We had a long heart-to-heart and it's all right, really it is.'

'If you say so,' said Gavin, finding this hard to believe, but keen to latch on to any good news that was going.

'I'm going to go ahead with the change of drug tomorrow as planned. She's due a scan at the hospital in four days time, on Friday. What should we do about that?'

'Let it go ahead.'

'Do you think there will be any change by then?'

'If it works, there should be a dramatic change. If it doesn't, then nothing.'

'No in-betweens?'

'No.'

'Sounds like Friday's going to be a pretty big day for all of us.'

'Yep.'

'You sound low. Did you sort things out with Frank?'

'Frank doesn't have the authority to endorse the paper. He's given up his position.'

'Why?' asked a stunned Caroline.

'Because the suits blackmailed him into it.'

'Gavin, I'm so sorry.'

'I'll think of something.'

On Friday, Caroline called Gavin as soon as she got back from the hospital. 'You're not going to believe this!' she practically screamed down the phone. 'There has been a thirty per cent reduction in the size of Mum's tumour. Thirty per cent!'

'Brilliant!'

'It works, Gavin, it works! The staff at the hospital were amazed.

They just couldn't think of an explanation, and I nearly couldn't keep a straight face. Coming home in the car was just like the old days when I was young and we were coming back from a day at the zoo or the beach; the three of us were laughing and talking.'

'I'm really glad, Carrie.'

'So what do we do, more of the same?'

'It's important she keeps taking the polymyxin. When is she due to go back to the hospital?'

'They want to do another scan next week, just to make sure it's not some kind of weird mistake.'

'Good. That should tell us what we need to know. The reduction should be greater, but maybe not as big as this week's.'

———

'Forty-eight per cent, Gavin! A forty-eight per cent reduction in the size of the tumour: almost half of it has been destroyed in two weeks! Can you believe it? Oh, my God, I wish we could tell someone.'

'But we can't,' said Gavin. 'They'd still hang us out to dry and attribute your mother's recovery to some kind of placebo effect.'

'So, we just keep on?'

'Same as before. I take it the hospital will be doing another scan next week?'

'You bet. They've never seen anything like it. One of the nurses said they were going to change the name of the place to Lourdes General.'

Gavin laughed, and Caroline said, 'It's been such a long time since I heard you laugh.'

'It's good to have reason to.'

'Dad can't wait to meet you.'

'Let's wait until your mum's better.'

'If you say so, but I'd sort of like to see you myself. Maybe I could come up for a couple of days?'

'That would be great.'

Caroline came up for the Tuesday and Wednesday, and returned home on the Thursday so that she could accompany her mother to the hospital on Friday morning. She called Gavin as arranged when they got back. He knew immediately by the tone of her voice that something was wrong.

'Gav, the tumour's stopped reducing in size. In fact, it's grown a bit. What's happening?'

'Oh, shit,' said Gavin, feeling lead fill his veins. 'Either the Valdevan didn't reach all of the tumour cells or some of them have recovered. Either way, the polymyxin isn't killing them any more.'

'So what do we do?'

'We give your mother more Valdevan . . .' said Gavin, but his voice had taken on the tone of a distant automaton.

'But there isn't enough,' said Caroline, before realising she was saying what Gavin already knew. Her voice betrayed the hopelessness she now felt. 'There's only enough left for a couple of days, not fourteen.'

'I'm so sorry, Carrie, we only had the one chance.'

'So Mum's going to die after all?'

'There was always that risk.'

'Oh, Gav . . . I'm sorry, I can't speak any more right now . . .'

The phone went dead, leaving Gavin looking at the wall. All the euphoria felt by Carrie's family and shared by him had gone . . . to be replaced by what? This didn't bear thinking about. Hero to zero didn't come close. He caught sight of the *Nature* paper sitting on his bedside table and, to compound his misery, admitted to himself for the first time that it was never going to see the light of day.

Gavin couldn't remember ever feeling this bad before. He couldn't find one single thing to feel good about, or offer anything resembling hope. His life had become an endless desert of unhappiness with nothing appearing on any horizon . . . until it occurred to him that Grumman Schalk might not actually know about the university machinations to neutralise Frank Simmons. After all, it wasn't something they'd brag about openly.

Gavin rummaged through his notebooks until he found something with a Grumman Schalk letterhead on it. Ironically, it was a copy of the covering letter that had come with the first consignment of Valdevan and had the words 'not for therapeutic use' in it. He took the phone number from the heading and called Max Ehrman.

'Who?' exclaimed Ehrman, as if he couldn't believe his ears.

'Gavin Donnelly, in Edinburgh.'

'What can I do for you?' came the guarded response.

'You can send me some Valdevan.'

Ehrman let out a snort of disbelief, but let a moment pass before saying, 'I seem to remember making it quite clear that there would be no more Valdevan for a line of research the company feels uncomfortable with. That still stands.'

'I'm offering you a deal.'

'I don't know what you mean.'

'Hear me out. It's my guess that you guys are trying every trick in the book to come up with a new product that simulates the sequential action of Valdevan and polymyxin – one that you can patent?'

Silence.

'But unless you get really lucky, that's going to take time,' continued Gavin. 'When our paper creates the stir you know it must, your efforts will have been wasted and public opinion will force Valdevan back into production by anyone who cares to make it, now that your patent's expired. Whatever way you look at it, you're going to take a mega-buck hit.'

'You've got quite a sense of your own importance.'

'The deal is . . . you give me a supply of Valdevan and I'll pull the paper.'

'You're a postgrad student, for God's sake. You don't make that sort of call.'

'I do in this case. No one in the department wants it published – and you know why.'

Gavin took Ehrman's silence as a positive. He took a deep breath before planting the lie. 'Frank Simmons has had a nervous breakdown and won't be back at work for a long time, but he signed the authorisation before he fell ill. That just leaves me. The paper's sitting in front of me as we speak, all ready to go off. Now, do I pop it in the post, or do you give me what I want?'

'What are you up to, Donnelly? What's this about?'

'It's straightforward.'

'You're treating someone, aren't you? That's it. You're trying out your crazy idea on someone and you've run out.'

'That needn't concern you. You give me the Valdevan, I pull the paper. That's the deal. What d'you say?'

'And if your highly illegal experiment should work – not that I think it will, mind you – you'll splash it all over the papers.'

'Don't be ridiculous. Who'd print a story like that? Student cures cancer? Jesus.'

'It must be someone close to you, right?'

'Like I say, that doesn't concern you, so what's it going to be? A few grams of Valdevan or a mega-buck hit for GS?'

'In the unlikely event of my agreeing to this, where would you want it sent?'

Gavin swallowed and dared to allow himself a small, inward sigh of relief. 'Send it directly to me at this address.' He read it out. 'There's no need to involve the university. I need therapeutic grade Valdevan in injection vials.'

'So you *are* treating someone. You know, Gavin, for such a bright guy . . .'

'I need it in two days.'

Gavin put the phone down and spent a long time just looking

at the wall in front of him. He'd played the only cards he had left, and he was bluffing. He wondered if Ehrman would check with the university about Frank. Even if he did, being told that Frank was off work might sustain the lie he'd told. He had two days to tough it out. He called Caroline. 'There's a chance I can get some more Valdevan,'

'How?'

'It's a long story, but there's a chance Grumman will change their minds. It should be here in a couple of days if it's coming, but there's no guarantee.'

'Then I won't say anything to Mum or Dad.'

'That would be safest. Your mum must be at rock bottom right now?'

'You could say. I think Dad's started blaming me again for giving her false hope.'

'Shit, I'm so sorry.'

'Gavin . . . are you all right?' asked Caroline. 'I mean, you sound a bit distant?'

'I'm just tired.'

'I'll bet. I wish I could hold you. I miss you, but I don't think I can come back right now.'

'I miss you too. I'll call you the minute the stuff arrives.'

—

Two days later, Gavin was woken by the sound of mail coming through the letterbox. His flatmates were all out at work and he had a hangover, but his first clear thought was that the postman should have rung the bell. The package from Grumman Schalk should have been too big for the letterbox, and it should have needed a signature for coming express delivery. Alarm bells were ringing inside his head as he got out of bed and padded across the hall in bare feet to pick up the untidy bundle. There was only one letter addressed to him, but it did have the Grumman Schalk logo on it.

He took it to the kitchen table and slumped down, staring at the white envelope for a full thirty seconds before summoning up the courage to open it.

Dear Gavin,

Further to our telephone conversation, I and my colleagues have decided after much consideration to decline your request for further supplies of Valdevan. Although your research findings in recent months have proved interesting, we still feel that they do not comprise any sound basis for encouraging false hope in cancer sufferers, and certainly do not warrant any kind of therapeutic experimentation. We have conveyed our feelings to your university. They in turn have assured us that all relevant scientific journals have been warned that any material submitted by you will not carry university approval.

We feel sad that we cannot come to an understanding to work together for the common good of cancer patients. With this in mind, we are prepared to offer you sponsorship to continue your studies, with a view to designing a more acceptable form of treatment, based on your research findings and matters discussed in our recent telephone conversation. We understand that this would be acceptable to your university and such studies would count towards your PhD and, hopefully, to subsequent employment by us. We urge you to consider this offer, which we feel could lead to a happy outcome for all of us.

Yours sincerely,

Max Ehrman

'Tossers,' growled Gavin, scrunching up the letter and throwing it across the room. 'Devious, fucking tossers.' He got up and walked over to the window to stare out at the rain, while gripping the edge of the kitchen sink until his knuckles showed white. The implications of the letter came at him from all angles. Carrie's mother would now die and, although the suggestion to treat her had been hers, Carrie would always see the extra dimension to her mother's death as being down to him. Her father was already seeing it that way. The suggestion of 'therapeutic experimentation' had been made to the university, and it wouldn't take Inspector Morse to figure out what had been going on, should they decide to call in the police. The bottom line was very clear as he continued to look at the rain through the tears that were running down his face. You either play the game our way or you don't play at all . . .

—

When Gavin didn't call about a new supply of Valdevan, Caroline called him, but failed to get an answer. He didn't respond to either the flat phone or his mobile, and a call to the university revealed that he had not been seen in the department. This was to go on for three days before she became so anxious that she packed a bag and told her father she was going up to Edinburgh to find out what was wrong. Her first port of call was the flat in Dundas Street, where Tim Anderson told her that Gavin had not been home 'for a couple of days'. He invited her in and offered her coffee when she told him who she was, and said, 'I thought maybe he had gone south to your place. I understand your mother's not well.'

'No. I haven't managed to contact him since Tuesday.'

'He seems to have been a bit low lately,' said Anderson.

'Could I see his room?' asked Caroline.

'Sure, on you go.'

Caroline swallowed as she entered Gavin's room. Maybe it was what Tim had said, but she was filled with foreboding. Something was dreadfully wrong. Gavin didn't have much in the way of clothes but most of them seemed to be there, except perhaps for his beloved green jersey, and his denim jacket, which wasn't hanging on the back of the door. He certainly hadn't packed up all his belongings and gone off somewhere. His laptop was lying on the floor beside the bed, with what she saw when she picked them up were three copies of the Valdevan paper. She froze when she saw the white envelope that had been lying underneath. It had her name on it. She opened it with trembling fingers.

Dearest Carrie,

Grumman Schalk refused to play ball. No more Valdevan I'm afraid.

I'm so sorry for all the heartbreak I've brought into your life and the lives of others. I just hope that you will find it in your heart one day to forgive me and, if you should ever find yourself alone on the road to forever, you'll find me waiting there.

All my love,

Gavin.

Caroline's sobbing attracted Tim, who knocked gently on the half-open door. 'I couldn't help but hear . . .'
Caroline handed him the tear-stained letter. 'Oh, God, what's he done?' she sobbed.

Tim accompanied Caroline to the police station, where they reported Gavin missing and showed the desk sergeant the letter so that they would be taken seriously.
'And you are?'
'His girlfriend.'
'His flatmate.'
Caroline and Tim were invited to take a seat, and gazed unseeingly

at the information posters on the walls while they waited. They were eventually asked into another room, where a plain-clothes officer invited them to sit in front of a table. Caroline could see by the expression on his face that he might have bad news to impart, although he began by taking what he called 'a few details'.

'Have you any idea what Gavin might have been wearing when he disappeared?'

Tim shrugged but Caroline said, 'I think maybe his green jumper, probably jeans and a denim jacket.'

This seemed to be what the officer was looking for. He put down his pen and said, 'I'm so sorry, but the body of a young man was taken from the sea at North Berwick this morning. His clothes match your description.'

Caroline shook her head, as if unable or unwilling to accept what she was hearing. Tim put a tentative arm round her shoulders.

'I wonder . . . would you be willing to . . ?'

Tim nodded.

———

No one spoke on the rain-swept drive over to the City Mortuary, not even when they got inside. The officer disappeared for a few moments before coming back and gesturing for Caroline and Tim to follow him. They were shown into a room that both of them felt they had seen a million times before on TV and in films. One of the fridge doors was opened and a body tray slid out on to the rails of a waiting trolley. The sheet covering the body was pulled back and the attendant stepped back in practised fashion. The officer nodded to them.

Caroline approached the trolley first, and found herself looking down into Gavin's cold, pallid face. His eyes were closed. She nodded for the benefit of the officer, and closed her eyes for a moment, as if summoning up strength before bending to kiss Gavin's forehead. 'Oh, Gav,' she sobbed. 'You stupid . . . stupid . . .'

Caroline returned to the flat in Dundas Street, but only to pick up Gavin's laptop and the copies of the Valdevan paper. Tim suggested that she stay the night, saying that she shouldn't be alone, but she declined, knowing that she couldn't bear to be anywhere near the little room where she and Gavin had first made love. She took a taxi over to Pollock Halls, where two classmates helped her through a very long night.

The report of Gavin's death made it to the papers next day.

> Yesterday morning, the body of Gavin Donnelly, a postgraduate student at Edinburgh University Medical School, was taken from the sea at North Berwick in East Lothian. Police believe that he had taken his own life. He was the second student from the same department to have done so in recent months following a fire in which another student was badly injured. The head of the lab in which all three worked is currently believed to be on leave and was unavailable for comment. The head of department, Professor Graham Sutcliffe, described the loss as tragic, saying that Gavin had been a particularly brilliant student who would be sorely missed.

Caroline felt a deep anger inside her as she read the report over and over again. 'Two-faced, mealy-mouthed bastard,' she growled. Gradually, her attention moved from Sutcliffe to Frank Simmons, who was 'on leave'. She turned to Moira, one of the girls who had supported her through the night. 'I have a favour to ask,' she said.

'Anything, Carrie.'

'You have a car. I have a delivery to make.'

Moira stopped outside the Simmonses' house and Carrie got out, carrying Gavin's laptop and the Valdevan paper. 'I won't be long,' she said.

'Take as long as you need.'

Jenny opened the door. 'Yes?'

'I'm Caroline, Gavin's girlfriend.'

'Oh, my God. We've just read it in the papers. Oh, my dear, what can I say? Come in, please. I don't know if you know Frank?'

'Yes, from my classes.'

Jenny led the way into the kitchen, where Frank Simmons was sitting, arms crossed on the table, with the *Scotsman* open in front of him.

'It's Gavin's girlfriend, Caroline,' said Jenny softly.

Simmons got to his feet slowly, as if in a trance. He was wondering what fate was about to throw at him now. He gestured with one hand to the paper. 'Caroline, I wish I could think of something sensible to say . . . but I can't. This is absolutely bloody awful. I'm so sorry.'

Jenny ushered Caroline into a chair opposite Simmons, and they both sat down while Jenny made fresh coffee. Although Caroline could see that Simmons was genuinely upset, she also sensed that he was wondering why she was there. 'I thought you should have these,' she said, pushing the three copies of the Valdevan paper across the table, and immediately invoking in Simmons memories of Gavin recently doing the same thing.

'Thanks,' said Simmons, looking down at the title page, but really wondering what he was going to find in Caroline's eyes when he looked up. When he did, there was no anger there, only sadness, and something he suspected might be resolve.

Caroline put Gavin's laptop on the table and said, 'The paper's also on the hard drive. You can return the laptop to me when you've done whatever you plan to do with it . . . if anything . . . and I'll return it to his folks.'

The *if anything* hung in the air like an accusation.

'Thank you,' said Simmons.

Jenny brought over coffee, but Caroline got to her feet saying, 'Not for me, thanks, there's someone waiting outside. I just thought I'd bring these over and tell you, Frank.'

'Tell me what?' asked Simmons in trepidation.

'Gavin didn't blame you.'

Jenny showed Caroline out, and returned to the kitchen to find Simmons sitting staring at the closed laptop. 'Are you all right?'

'No,' said Simmons quietly, continuing to stare at the laptop.

'Frank?'

Simmons suddenly smashed his fist down on the table and looked up at Jenny. 'I am most definitely not all right. We are not going to Australia. We're not going anywhere. We are staying here. I've got too much to do.'

In the silence that followed, it dawned on Simmons that there had been no reaction from Jenny. 'Well?' he prompted.

'It would seem that I've just got my husband back,' said Jenny. 'And about time too, if I may say so.'

Simmons shook his head. 'I NEVER EVER AGAIN want to feel the way that girl has just made me feel.'

Jenny stood behind him and put her hands on his shoulders. 'You did what you did for the noblest of reasons, Frank . . . as always . . . and your children and I thank you for it. But maybe this time . . . the safe option was not the one to go for?'

Simmons squeezed her hand.

'Anything I can do to help?'

'I need the names of every scientific or medical correspondent on every national newspaper in the UK. Someone is going to listen.'

━━━

Only a small group of people outside immediate family attended the funeral of Gavin Donnelly in Liverpool. When the flowers were removed at the end of the ceremony, attendants were puzzled to find, lying under them, a can of Stella Artois lager and a packet of bacon-flavoured crisps. A short note said,

> I won't play the game either, Gav, I promise.
> Love always,
> Carrie. xxx.

Author's Note

Although a work of fiction, *Hypocrites' Isle* is based on something that happened to me when I was a researcher in microbial genetics. I was working on the genes determining cell shape in the bacterium *E. coli*, when I stumbled across the reason why an old antibiotic had failed in practice when, in the research lab, it had appeared to have great promise, and had been given an expensive launch by its manufacturer some twenty years before. I also discovered how it could be used to great effect if it were to be combined in a particular way with other drugs. My hope was that this new technique could be used to clear up a persistent, recurrent, urinary tract infection called pyelonephritis. This condition is nearly always caused by *E. coli*, and affects a great many people across the world, mainly women. Although not fatal, it often becomes chronic, and many women suffer from recurring infections throughout their lives.

I was naïve in thinking that the drug company would be delighted. They didn't want to know. I was later to discover that the antibiotic in question was out of patent, and the company no longer had the exclusive right to make it. Apart from that, it would have been difficult for them to relaunch a product that had already failed, and sales of their more recently developed drugs would have suffered. A more cynical view put to me at the time was that chronic conditions are big cash cows for the pharmaceutical industry, much more so than any condition they can clear up.

Not happy with the commercial view of things, I approached the university body which acted as an interface between academia and business. They were very excited at first, but became less enthusiastic when they learned that the new treatment did not involve any new compounds: they wanted something they could patent to 'protect the university's interests'. They thought that it might be possible to patent the intellectual property of the idea, and this was confirmed by lawyers, but in the end they pulled out, arguing that *E. coli* was a relatively 'soft' pathogen and there were plenty of other drugs available to treat it. I approached my employer at the time, the Medical Research Council, who had a similar body. They informed me that, as I had already told the pharmaceutical company about my findings, it would actually be impossible for them to patent the idea, so they had no further interest.

At no time did anyone think that just curing the disease was a good idea: everyone I approached was primarily concerned with whether or not they could make money. My assertion that I just wanted the idea to be put into practice cast me in the role of an ivory tower academic, who didn't understand 'the real world'.